HE IS THE PRINCIPAL

HE IS THE PRINCIPAL

SCHOOL OF HARDER KNOCKS™
BOOK TWO

MICHAEL ANDERLE

LMBPN Publishing
2375 E. Tropicana Avenue, Suite 8-305
Las Vegas, Nevada 89119 USA

Version 1.00 December 2024
eBook ISBN: 979-8-89354-457-2
Print ISBN: 979-8-89354-458-9

THE HE IS THE PRINCIPAL TEAM

Thanks to the Beta Readers
John Ashmore, Kelly O'Donnell, Charles Tillman

Thanks to my JIT Readers!
Christopher Gilliard
Daryl McDaniel
Diane L. Smith
Dave Hicks
Sean Kesterson
Deb Mader
Jeff Goode
Wendy L Bonell
Dorothy Lloyd
Rachel Beckford
Jackey Hankard-Brodie
Jan Hunnicutt
Angel LaVey

If I missed anyone, please let me know!

Editor
Lynne Stiegler

This book is dedicated to Micky Cocker.
The truest of friends and the glue that bound us all together.

CHAPTER ONE

Kirian panted to draw in the oxygen his burning muscles needed to continue building his lead on the eleven thousand pounds of hangry reptilian predator whose singular focus was on making crunchy snacks out of him and the triplets.

The team's shit-talk about whether the creature snapping its gargantuan teeth at them could be classified as a dinosaur had become irrelevant the moment they'd stumbled into her nest. They were now trapped in the narrow jungle canyon with hunger personified on their heels.

Meddox let rip with his shoulder cannon, dislodging the loose rockfall from the precipice above the trees. He missed, but the distraction gave Kirian the time he needed to avoid joining the remains of the unfortunate creatures lodged between the not-a-dinosaur's teeth. He launched into a low slide, taking advantage of the slick mud to escape certain death—and disqualification from the tournament.

Someone screamed nearby. The cry cut off almost as soon as

it began, heralding the untimely exit of one of the other four teams in the semifinal round. He hoped it wasn't Xander and Ari. Less competition was good, but taking first and second place would be the cherry on top of the summer break for the group of friends.

Rolling to his feet with the assistance of his armor's powered joints, Kirian resumed running for his life. "Thanks for the save," he wheezed as he caught up with Meddox. "Dying in a gust of rancid dinosaur breath is *not* how I want to be immortalized in the highlight reel."

Meddox's reply was lost in a fetid roar that flattened the undergrowth and sent purple foliage showering from the canopy. Kirian spotted a low fissure in the canyon wall around five hundred feet from their position.

The gap in the rock looked considerably smaller than the deceptively easy path out of the canyon that had gotten them into this situation, but, given its narrow width, they had a better chance of surviving the round if they encountered another surprise. All they had to do was make it to the fissure in one piece, which was easier said than done.

"How far are we from the extraction zone?" Nerril asked as they banked toward the hole.

"It's not going to matter if we don't do something drastic," Lutian managed through his panting. "Ideas, anyone?"

Adrenaline—biology's gift to the soon-to-be-eaten—coursed through Kirian's body. More importantly, since he didn't want to end up as an hors d'oeuvre, it fired his synapses. Three Noel-nis and one human had more brainpower than any predator. The question was, could their evolutionary advantage counter their pursuer's weight advantage?

Kirian spied a streak of green among the riot of purple and blue undergrowth and abandoned the plan to hide in the fissure and wait out their pursuer's murderous rage. "Got the sucker! Follow me!"

The team bore left to gain the ground they needed to stay alive for a few moments longer. The creature roared its annoyance, and trees shrieked as they were smashed to splinters by the predator's abrupt trajectory change.

A few moments was all they needed. Kirian and Meddox skirted the right side of the clearing. Lutian and Nerril went left, and they all reconvened on the far side, hoping to make it to the rotten log pile where they were going to make their final stand. As one, they unleashed everything they had at the monster. If their Hail Mary failed, it was the end of their championship hopes.

The overgrown lizard screeched, shrugging off the bullets peppering its near-impenetrable hide. Maddened by pain and its killer instinct, it failed to register the telltale bubbles on the swampy surface ahead of it. Murky, stagnant water sprayed as it plunged into the clearing.

Kirian doubted himself when the not-a-dinosaur made it four steps into the clearing. His yell of defiance harmonized with his team's screams. This was it. Game over.

He held steady, though, determined to go out fighting. The predator hit the center of the clearing and roared in surprise when its foot refused to come free. All four players heaved a sigh of relief as the reptile's struggles dragged it in deeper.

"How'd you know there was quicksand there?" Meddox yelled over the noise the reptile made as it tried to break free.

"Would you believe me if I said I learned how to spot it from a book?" Kirian batted away the handful of dirt Meddox threw at him in response. "No lie. I'll send you guys the link when we get out of here."

Out of respect for its ferocity, they climbed the log fall to watch the terrible lizard meet its sucking death. "Anyone else feeling sorry for it?" Nerril asked. Everyone agreed that they did.

Lutian got to his feet and saluted the reptile. "To the greatest chase we'll ever have."

"The greatest," Kirian, Meddox, and Nerril echoed with feeling.

As the reptile's final throes gave way to soupy gurgles, the team's thoughts returned to why they were in the wilds of the Southern Continent. Meddox stated, "We need to get back on the marked route and hope we didn't miss any checkpoints."

Kirian groaned at his HUD's refusal to connect. He took his helmet off and grunted when he saw the shattered remains of the comm chip, "I'm shit out of luck."

"Hey, you got that monster off our asses," Lutian consoled him. "We can complete the mission without your HUD. From inside the stomach of a gigantic reptile, not so much."

The triplets scratched a rough approximation of the HUD map in the dirt and spent the next few minutes debating which route would get them to the evacuation zone, the EZ, ahead of the other teams.

Meddox commented as they set off, "The other teams probably had run-ins with the local wildlife too. We might be the only ones left."

Kirian thought two other teams had a chance at the final round of Dreamland's tournament. He shouldered his rifle and took the lead, cutting a straight path toward the EZ. His mind was on Baba Yaga's arrival at the Institute later that day.

High Tortuga, Northern Continent, City of Thon, Undisclosed Location, Institute of Education-Focused Extrajudicial Foundational Studies

One month had passed since Baba Yaga had appointed Lerr'ek headmaster of the Institute. Barely enough time to get construction in the former laboratory underway and develop a challenging curriculum for the exceptional students his Mistress expected him to identify and recruit.

If Kirian was the benchmark, Lerr'ek would need assistance.

The young human had proven himself to be relentless and indefatigable over the last cycle. He'd pushed himself as hard academically as he had in physical therapy and combat training.

Lerr'ek wiped the nervous sweat from his forehead as Baba Yaga's Pod landed. He hoped his progress in all other areas would deflect her displeasure at his failure to expand the student body.

He knew Baba Yaga was the Etheric Empress, but he had to swallow the overwhelming fear that washed over him as the dark-cloaked figure from nightmare stepped from the Pod. "You're early." He winced when his voice cracked.

"You're cute," Baba Yaga growled. "And you smell of bad news. Spit it out before we start the walkaround."

Lerr'ek cleared his throat. "I wouldn't say it's bad news, Mistress. Construction is ahead of schedule, and ADAM has been instrumental in building a curriculum that will train the students to the level you require."

Baba Yaga tapped one high-heeled boot on the permacrete while pinning him with a stare so cold it would kill a lesser being. "But?"

Lerr'ek sighed. "Finding students has eluded me thus far. Scouring school records hasn't gotten me anywhere. I identified several youths who looked good on paper, but none of them meet the criteria we laid out."

"Hmmm." Baba Yaga's expression softened. "We will revisit that subject after the tour."

Lerr'ek released the breath he hadn't realized he was holding. "Thank you for your understanding. I guess we should get started."

Baba Yaga strode past him with a predatory smile that revealed serrated teeth. "Who said anything about understanding?"

Lerr'ek groaned as he followed her inside. "You're going to decide how pissed you are about the student issue based on how satisfied you are with the remodel, aren't you?"

Baba Yaga's answering laugh grated on Lerr'ek's bones. The sensation reminded him of ore running through the wash plant at the rare metals refinery from which ADAM purchased the materials for the Institute's comms and network wiring.

Two things prevented him from begging for mercy. The first was the high-spec finishes in the completed areas of the building. The second was that his logical brain, although it was not running the show right now, knew his Mistress was giving him shit because it amused her. She had invested too much in this project to give up so soon. They all had.

His logical brain was proven correct when they reached the foyer. Baba Yaga stopped in her tracks to take in the drastically altered space. She shook her head, shed her disguise, and smiled.

Lerr'ek smiled back.

She swept a hand to encompass the clean lines and tasteful décor that had replaced the dead space the building's previous owners had wasted on an unused seating area. "I love what you've done with the place."

The trickle of the fountain halfway between the entrance and the small reception area that formed a curved barrier around Lerr'ek's office door was the only sound while he fought to regain his ability to speak. "I…um…"

"Snap out of it, Lerr'ek." Bethany Anne clapped her hands. "We'll start with the ops center. Then I want to see the training facilities."

The elevator pinged, saving the headmaster. Kirian stepped out and grinned when he saw them. "Bethany Anne, you're early!" He walked toward them with barely a hint that his body was supported by the exoskeleton he wore at the Institute.

"So everyone keeps saying." Bethany Anne eyed Kirian's posture. "That exoskeleton is working out for you, huh?"

"Like you wouldn't believe." Kirian demonstrated a hop, a skip, and a jump. He let his crutches dangle from his elbows and gave her jazz hands and a cheerful, "Ta-daaa! Cool, right? I wrote the people at R2D2 to say thanks. The frame supports me without doing all the work, so I still use the crutches, but I'm getting stronger every day."

Grateful for the reprieve his only student had given him, Lerr'ek asked, "Would you like to join us on the walkaround, Kirian?"

"And watch you explain what we've been spending Bethany Anne's credits on?" Kirian's eyes twinkled with mischief. "Sure. Should be fun."

"Great. Lead the way, kid." Lerr'ek gave Kirian the side-eye behind Bethany Anne's back as they rode the elevator down to the first sub-level.

Kirian responded with a "Who, me?" look and a wry smile. Lerr'ek rolled his eyes, sending up a silent plea to deities he didn't believe in that Kirian's playful nature would counter his nervousness about not living up to Bethany Anne's trust in him.

I hope you don't think our young friend will distract me from the reason I'm here, Bethany Anne told Lerr'ek.

I wouldn't dare assume I could be that lucky, he replied.

Hmmm. You're worried that you are not up to the responsibility I gave you.

If you got that from my thoughts, you don't need me to tell you this is way beyond my comfort zone. Doing business is easy. You fail, and the loss is on you. I fail in this, and Kirian's future and the futures of the other students are on the line.

Bethany Anne looked him in the eye. *You're taking this seriously, as you should. Good. Keep that fear front and center and use it.*

"If you two are done discussing me, the elevator stopped a full minute ago," Kirian cut in, easing past them to the open doors.

"Welcome to the ops center," Lerr'ek told Bethany Anne as they stepped out onto the mezzanine. "As you can see, we are set up for minimal staffing. Most of the surveillance operations will be run by ADAM 2.0—"

"That's not going to work," Bethany Anne interrupted.

Lerr'ek shrugged. "That was what he went by after ADAM created him. He became Xavier when he agreed to sound different for my benefit."

A familiar voice came from the overhead speakers. "I haven't fully altered my personality matrix yet, Bethany Anne," ADAM 2.0-slash-Xavier explained.

Bethany Anne pressed her lips together. "Okay. That will fly for now, but you need to settle into your individuality sooner rather than later. Talk me through the setup here, please."

Lerr'ek nodded. "Our ultimate objective is to monitor the city for situations that will serve as appropriate live training exercises for the students. Anything beyond that level is passed on to Stephen."

"There have been twenty-seven such incidents since the net went live," Xavier supplied. "Twenty-three were categorized as being beyond the scope of the student body's capability."

"And the other four?" Bethany Anne raised an eyebrow at Kirian, who was spinning in a chair at one of the five desks in the pit.

"White-collar crimes."

He observed Bethany Anne's reactions as Xavier walked her through the surveillance net they had cast across Thon a cycle ago. She asked questions about their access to public and private communications networks, how they were protecting the net from the multitude of hackers in and around the city, and their projections for expanding the net to cover the whole of the Northern Continent.

"Infiltrating the undercity was our first priority," Lerr'ek interjected. "R2D2 will ship us drones bi-weekly for the next several months. This time next year, we will have coverage of every major city on the continent and be well on our way to wrapping the smaller population centers into the net."

"I've been helping with security in my downtime," Kirian

added. "Not that I get a lot of it, mind you. Prof and Dr. Ericson have kept me busy with assignments and combat training disguised as physical therapy."

Lerr'ek smiled. "The kid's been invaluable. I wish I had ten more like him." He winced the moment the words left his mouth, but it was too late.

"I'll settle for five," Bethany Anne told him. "Kirian, you have more to offer. I want you to work on this problem with Lerr'ek. It's your school, too."

Kirian grinned. "I have an idea of where we can find one. We might have to get creative to get him here, but no one will regret it."

"Creative we can manage," Lerr'ek assured Bethany Anne as well as himself. "Maybe I've been approaching this from the wrong direction. I've been thinking like a headmaster instead of a business person."

"This is a military school as well as an education facility. There's nothing preventing us from running side ops after a few classes graduate." She tilted her head, amusement softening the seriousness in her eyes. "ADAM, the original and best, suggests you call the effort Operation First Class."

Xavier laughed. "Then I need an *X-Men*-themed name."

Lerr'ek did a quick search of the human entertainment database on his wrist-holo since the name of the franchise was vaguely familiar. "You could stay with Xavier," he suggested after flicking through the character list.

"Wait," Kirian countered. "If we're going with an *X-Men* theme, the only choice is Cerebro."

"A most satisfactory suggestion, Kirian," Cerebro agreed, his voice changing to a crisp British accent with a hint of Scots.

"The computer Professor X uses to locate mutants," Kirian explained when Lerr'ek's face crumpled in confusion.

Lerr'ek was startled when Bethany Anne put her hand on his shoulder. "You have something much more challenging than mutants to locate, Lerr'ek. One new student by the end of the cycle, and one each cycle until you have the assets for a fully operational unit."

"What's the purpose of this unit?" Kirian asked.

Bethany Anne lifted a shoulder. "Whatever I need it to be."

CHAPTER TWO

<u>High Tortuga, Northern Continent, City of Thon</u>

Kirian had Bethany Anne's directive on his mind for the remainder of the day. He skated through the assignments in his learning portal without absorbing the material and begged off his PT session in favor of meeting his mom for an early dinner at a diner they both liked in the commercial district.

Janet ruffled his hair and eyed him the way only moms can. "What has you so preoccupied that you are barely touching your food? Is the school pushing you too hard?"

"No, Mom," Kirian answered quickly. "I love it there. I'm finally getting the education I need." He took a bite of his bistok burger and chewed it thoroughly, giving himself time to gather the right words. "Don't get me wrong. The Grier Free School did its best, but it was the best for the student body as a whole. I wasn't pushed there. Not really."

"You had advanced classes." Janet pointed a perfectly salted fry at him. "I know you had to do most of them with an EI tutor..." Understanding dawned on her face, and her mouth formed an O. "That's your point, isn't it? You have real tutors and other kids as smart as you at the Institute."

Kirian cringed internally, still uncomfortable with the need to dance around the truth with his mother. "I've been thinking about Tor still slogging along with the EI tutors while I'm out there living my best life."

Janet shrugged. "He could apply to the Institute. From what you've told me, he's a smart cookie."

"It's not that simple. His home situation? There's something going on that he hasn't shared with me, but I know the last thing he wants is to draw attention to himself."

Janet's easy demeanor vanished, and her eyes flashed with the fire Kirian recognized from the times she had advocated for him at the Free School. "Is his family mistreating him?" she asked bluntly.

Kirian shook his head, thinking about Gralen and Charr'est, who *were* experiencing abuse from family and community. "His family doesn't seem to be around much. Well, at all. I've never met them, and we've been friends for a while."

Concern replaced Janet's fiery expression. "Neglect is abuse too, Kirian. I ought to—"

"Please, don't. He's just starting to trust me. I don't want to scare him off coming in all heavy-handed. I hope he'll agree to let me speak to Professor Lerr'ek on his behalf. The Institute would benefit from having him as a student, and Tor needs the stability he'll get from enrolling there."

Janet nodded with a look in her eye that Kirian couldn't place. "You remind me so much of your father. Always looking out for others. You will come to me if you need help with this, right?"

Kirian reached across the table and squeezed her hand. "Mom, I will always ask for your help if I need it."

Janet squeezed back. "You need me less and less these days. That's hard, although I'm proud of you and happy for you."

"I'm just happy that your life doesn't revolve around working to pay for my healthcare anymore. Speaking of, how did your first class at the arts center go?"

Janet grinned, tapped her wrist-holo, and transferred a file to him. "See for yourself."

High Tortuga, Northern Continent, City of Thon, Undisclosed Location, Institute of Education-Focused Extrajudicial Foundational Studies

Having a late supper in the staff dining room had become a tradition since Kirian arrived at the Institute. Tonight was Kirian's turn to cook, and he had made good use of the prototype food printing unit R2D2 had sent with their latest batch of drones.

Stephen speared a pappardelle noodle and dipped it in the rich wild boar ragu in his dish. "It never ceases to amaze me that a machine can prepare pasta exactly the way it tasted when I was in Tuscany. All credit to Team BMW, although I suspect Tina's determination to outcook William had a lot to do with the advances in this technology."

Jennifer raised her glass of Brunello. "I'll toast to that. This is an excellent supper, Kirian."

Kirian grinned, happy that his idea to make Stephen feel at home had worked. "I asked Bethany Anne for inspiration before she left. We have lemon pannacotta for dessert."

Lerr'ek took a sip of his wine and made a face. "Why do humans like this tart beverage?"

"Because it tastes delicious to those of us with refined palates." Stephen chuckled. "Stick to Coke. Leave the wine for those of us who appreciate it."

"Not *my* Coke, Prof," Kirian interjected, pushing to his feet. "There are regular Cokes in the kitchen. I'll go get you one."

"Sugar and caffeine are sugar and caffeine," Lerr'ek called after him, waving away everyone's teasing.

"I see BA gives you the good stuff." Jennifer nodded at the

Coke bottle Kirian brought for himself. "You still need to watch your sugar intake, kiddo."

"I'm pretty sure you'll help me burn off the extra calories in training, Doc." Kirian laughed and sipped the extra-sweet Mexican Coke Bethany Anne had delivered, along with the other food supplies it was difficult to source outside the Empire. "Let me enjoy this, please."

The idle table conversation turned to the reason for Bethany Anne's visit.

"Was our Empress satisfied with what she saw today?" Stephen inquired.

Kirian busied his mouth with a forkful of pasta to avoid answering.

"Everything but the lack of a student body." Lerr'ek sighed. "It has become apparent that recruitment is not my strong suit. Kirian is now assigned to assist me in locating mutants… I mean, students."

Jennifer rolled her eyes at Lerr'ek and graced Kirian with a warm smile. "I bet you already have some ideas."

"It's like you know me," Kirian quipped. He placed the Coke on the table. "You've met Tor."

Understanding dawned on Jennifer's face. "I see."

"What?" Lerr'ek asked.

"This is the friend who helped you teach those bullies a lesson?" Stephen nodded. "I approve of anyone who has the inge-nuity or good luck to circumvent ADAM.'"

"Bright kid, skittish as all hell," Jennifer told him. "You think he meets the enrollment requirements, Kirian?"

Kirian nodded. "'Skittish' is an understatement, but yeah. His skills complement mine in ways I'm still amazed by. He can build anything, given the resources."

"Does the boy suffer from the same lack of stimulation in his schooling that you did before you transferred here?" Stephen asked.

"Tor is smarter than me. He finds ways to keep himself entertained." Kirian wouldn't give up his friend's secrets. "The issue is, if Prof and the doc show up like they did at my house, he'd nope out so fast you'd think he was enhanced. Whatever is going on in his family, he's not opening up about it."

Inspiration struck him. Tor wasn't the only one who had skills that would be useful on a multi-purpose team. Whether their reputations would preclude them from being admitted to the Institute was up to Lerr'ek, but Kirian knew the headmaster's past was not squeaky clean. "I have two more names as well."

Lerr'ek all but pounced on him. "Gimmee!"

"Gralen and Charr'est." Kirian shook Lerr'ek's hand off his arm. "Gralen is a fighter, and Charr'est is a mechanic."

Jennifer set her glass on the table, frowning in confusion. "Aren't those two of the three kids who were making your life hell?"

Kirian sighed. He'd managed to keep the details of his research for the lesson he and his friends had taught their tormentors from the adults. What they didn't know couldn't get him grounded, right?

But now he had no choice if he wanted the nominations to be taken seriously. By the time Kirian had finished relating the full story, supper was long over. He wanted to get out of his exoskeleton and into bed with a couple of pain patches to ease the aches from overusing his body that day. However, sleep looked like it was a ways off.

"You haven't nominated the ringleader," Lerr'ek pressed.

"Dex?" Kirian wearily shook his head. "Definitely not. He's on a path to destruction."

"What makes the other two different?" Lerr'ek's question held no malice, just curiosity. "Shrillexians especially aren't known for anything besides violence."

"Careful, Prof," Kirian retorted. "Your prejudice might be why you're having trouble finding new students."

Lerr'ek's hands balled into fists, and his shoulders tensed. Then he sighed and forced his body to relax. "You might be right, kid. Okay, so, what makes that Gralen kid so special?"

"His dedication," Kirian told them without hesitation. "He has a gift for financial math that got him into the Free School. He's the only Shrillexian student there." He got to his feet. "I need to get out of this suit before I end up needing bed rest tomorrow."

Jennifer looked him over. "Go take care of yourself. This can wait."

When Kirian was gone, Lerr'ek shared his concerns with Stephen and Jennifer. "What kind of person invites their enemies to live and work alongside them?"

"An exceptional one," Jennifer answered.

"What she said," Stephen agreed. "I cannot imagine our young friend suggested we enroll these boys lightly. My question is how much of his motivation comes from the pity their challenging lives stirs in him."

"You already vetted these kids?" Lerr'ek guessed.

Stephen nodded. Jennifer reached for the wine to refill their glasses. "I had them checked out when Kirian first told me he and his friends were getting bullied."

Lerr'ek laughed. "Why, so you could take them out?" Jennifer said nothing, which said everything. He sucked in a breath. "Stars! That's cold, Jennifer."

Her eyes flashed yellow, and her chin snapped up. "You didn't know Kirian before we started his nanocyte therapy. He was more pain patch than human. All skin and bones. He didn't know he was in the final stage of the disease that was eating him alive, but he knew suffering, and he still had the wellbeing of others front and center."

She drew a calming breath when Stephen took her hand. "My

point is, that boy stole my heart from the moment I met him and there wasn't much I wasn't prepared to do to make life easier on him."

Lerr'ek chuckled. "He has that effect on me, too. So, what do we do about his suggestion?"

"You could hear me out," Kirian announced as he wheeled his chair into the room.

Stephen leaned back and offered Kirian a reassuring smile. "Of course we'll listen to what you have to say."

"If Bethany Anne wanted you on this, it's because she believes you have something to offer," Jennifer told him.

Lerr'ek got to his feet and moved a chair to make room for Kirian at the table. "We'll discuss Tor tomorrow."

"The day *after* tomorrow." Jennifer shot a stern look at Lerr'ek. "Kirian needs a rest day, which means no Institute-related activity."

"My bad." Lerr'ek held up his hands in a conciliatory gesture before returning his attention to Kirian. "I'm interested in your motivation for suggesting we offer two boys who, by your own account, made your life and your friends' lives miserable."

Kirian had expected an inquisition and had taken his time stripping off and storing his suit to figure out what he would say. "Those two followed Dex because he represented strength to them. His entitlement and brutality stand out in the Free School, and it was familiar to them both. Gralen because he is Shrillexian too, and Charr'est because his father is who Dex will grow into."

"What I'm hearing is that they are both followers." Lerr'ek didn't hide his distaste. "They did Dex's dirty work for him and didn't question his directives."

Kirian would concede part of that point. However, it was also on the list of reasons he was making a good suggestion. "I believe they would respond to being shown a better path, Prof. You did. Isn't Bethany Anne all about giving people a chance?"

Stephen chuckled and clapped. "Touché, Kirian. He's got you there, Lerr'ek."

Jennifer mirrored Stephen's amusement. "Enough rope to either pull themselves out of the hole they're in or hang themselves."

"I'm serious," Kirian insisted. "Gralen gets his ass handed to him in fights because he takes the Empire's serum."

"What fights?" Jennifer asked.

"You know, the Shrillexian fight ring in the undercity." Kirian missed the edge in her voice in his desire to get the support he was looking for. "I think they're looking for the strongest and best fighters to send off-world. You know that the majority of Shrillexian males sign up with mercenary companies when they come of age."

He was relieved when the adults confirmed that they knew. "Well, I'm pretty sure the fights decide which companies they get to work for. Gralen mentioned something about wanting to do well so he could get hired by a better company, and I know they're not teaching combat skills at the Free School."

Stephen and Jennifer shared a look that made Kirian change the subject. "That's not important right now. When we researched Gralen, we found out he doesn't just study hard. He also helps the families who don't have a male around."

The glazed look in Stephen's eyes could only mean he was reading Kirian's memories. With a sinking feeling, he recounted Gralen's visits to the homes of widows and females whose part-ners had deployed. He ended with Gralen's devotion to his mother and sister and what they'd learned about his goals for supporting his family as soon as he graduated.

He finished, "As for Charr'est, his life sucks all around. Still, he had the courage to question Dex. I'm almost certain he threw the tournament, and he'd started holding back when Dex stepped up his attacks on me. I think he could be redirected to make good choices and maybe stand up to his father."

"How do you see them, including Tor, fitting into your team?" Stephen's amusement returned at the surprise Kirian couldn't hide.

"*My* team?"

"Yes, Kirian," Lerr'ek confirmed. "The first team will be your command."

Kirian nodded, absorbing the information. "If it's my team, I want people who will support each other so no role relies on one person. Tor isn't a fighter, but he can support me with tech and Charr'est with mechanics. Gralen fights, and he can support me with tactical and ops. Charr'est can support Gralen and Tor, and we could all stand to get our combat skills to a level that will reduce the risk of any of us getting hurt on an assignment."

"Last question." Lerr'ek laced his hands on the table and met Kirian's calm stare. "Why these three and not the friends you grew up with?"

"The requirements, sir," Kirian answered with finality. "I don't know what Tor's deal is, but he qualifies on merit alone. Charr'est and Gralen? Well, their attributes speak for themselves. This Institute's purpose is to give people a hand up, not a handout. I care about my friends, but they're not what Baba Yaga is looking for."

Stephen clapped. "That is the perfect answer."

"I'd be happy to offer all three candidates a place at the Institute," Lerr'ek told Kirian. "However, I will need to get Baba Yaga's approval before moving forward."

"Because of their circumstances?" Kirian hazarded.

Lerr'ek nodded. "The information you've given us is actionable."

"Bethany...no, *Baba Yaga* will shit kittens when she finds out there's a Shrillexian fight club funneling children into mercenary companies," Jennifer added.

Kirian was about to ask how the Institute was any different but stopped himself. He had nominated Gralen because he knew life at the Institute would give him a reprieve from nightly no-holds-barred fights and allow him to pursue his education while taking care of his community.

He pulled himself from his thoughts and paid attention to the adults, who were discussing who got to play messenger when Bethany Anne was next on High Tortuga. Being fully aware of what the Empress was capable of when she was Baba Yaga didn't bother him.

Kirian cut in. "I'll tell her. If this is my team, I'll take responsibility for it from the start."

CHAPTER THREE

<u>High Tortuga, Northern Continent, City of Thon, Undisclosed Location</u>

Bethany Anne awoke from a dream of Michael's final moments, heartsore from the separation that had been her reality for far too long.

In her dreams, the only man she would ever love was torn away from her over and over. However, until recently, she'd felt that a trace of him remained in the Etheric, which had been enough to sustain the hope she'd refused to relinquish. She laid her forearm across her eyes and fought back the tears that threatened to form in the absence of the thin thread she'd held on to for all these years.

Filled with restless energy she would have to make someone else's problem before it became one for her, she threw the covers back and got up to grab her robe. After a moment's deliberation, she snagged a Coke from the fridge before reaching out to Jennifer.

Hey, you made it early, Jennifer greeted in a bright voice.

The General preferred standing in for me to the diplomatic incident that would have gone down if I'd had to spend another day

with the Ta'lah trade delegation. Empressing is a royal pain in the ass. Bethany Anne drank some Coke and almost groaned in relief when the sugar and caffeine hit her system. *I had a shitty night that's going to become a shitty day unless I do something about it. I'm calling a girls' day out.*

I'm sorry you had a bad night, Jennifer responded. *Want to talk about it?*

Nope. Hashing it over is as useful as sitting in a rocking chair. Gives you something to do but doesn't get you anywhere. I want some action. Your choice. Retail damage or physical damage?

Depends on whether I'll be the one taking the physical damage. I didn't have training in mind. Kirian is off for the next day or two, so I can come spend some time with you.

Very funny. I wasn't thinking about training if that's what you're hesitant about. I'm sure it wouldn't take more than kicking a couple of rocks to find a squirming mess that needs to be cleaned up.

Jennifer paused. *Hmmm, hold that thought. We're going shopping.*

Works for me. I'll pick you up in an hour.

After a quick shower, Bethany Anne got ready for a day in public. She took a black, mid-sleeved hooded cloak from her closet and tossed it on the bed, along with a knee-length dark gray pencil skirt and a deep teal blouse with a high neckline.

While she swept her hair into a messy bun, she checked in with her onboard companions. *You two are suspiciously quiet this morning.*

ADAM responded first. >>There's a lot of correspondence from the Empire today.<<

Anything that needs my attention?

>>Nothing you can do anything about from here.<<

Then it can wait. I need a me day off.

We made lunch reservations for you and Jennifer while you were showering, TOM told her. The restaurant is in a spa, but we did not book any treatments since we weren't sure if you would appreciate them being chosen for you.

Bethany Anne smiled. *That was thoughtful. Thank you.*

TOM cornered ADAM. **When are you planning to tell Bethany Anne that one of those communications concerns Michael?**

>>When I have confirmation that the message Lance received was truly from Akio. You've seen how her dreams are affecting her. Why give her hope without knowing for sure if she's going to get her heart broken all over again?<<

TOM sighed. **You're right. Okay. We'll sit on it for now.**

Several hours later, Bethany Anne and Jennifer perused the menu at the restaurant, their feet immersed in a sea of shopping bags beneath the table.

Bethany Anne ordered a medium-rare bistok steak salad, and Jennifer ordered a grilled fowl native to High Tortuga with roasted vegetables.

As the android waiter walked off. Bethany Anne picked up her water glass and fixed Jennifer with a questioning look. "I held off on searching inside your brain, but manners only go so far, so spill."

Jennifer scrunched her nose. "It's that obvious, huh?"

"Come the fuck on," Bethany Anne told her. "This is me you're talking to. What's going on?"

"I'd love to tell you." Jennifer sighed. "But you're not going to like it, and—"

Bethany Anne's lip curled as she cut in. "Just tell me. I'm not going to be mad if we get to round today out with some action *without* me having to scuff my favorite boots to find it."

Jennifer raised an eyebrow at the Louboutin-clad foot Bethany Anne stuck out. "You're not going to let me get away with switching the subject to shoe envy?" She lifted a shoulder after Bethany Anne shook her head.

"Kirian is a responsible kid, and he wanted to be the one to tell you. I wasn't keeping it from you, but since you asked, we have three potential candidates for the Institute. All three have issues that need to be resolved before they enroll."

Bethany Anne tilted her head in curiosity. "What kinds of issues?"

As Jennifer gave her the rundown on the potential students, Bethany Anne's temper rose. "These children have been on our radar, and nothing has been done to protect them?"

"Peripherally." Jennifer eyed the trio of haughty Torcellans making a hasty exit from the table closest to theirs. "This is a harsh planet, Bethany Anne. Life is hard for everyone without wealth to cushion their existence.

"On the surface, the Zhyn male's life looks good. His family lives above ground, and he's in a good school. Same with Tor. He does well in school and keeps his head down. The Shrillexian should have thrown up flags, but Shrillexian culture is different outside the Empire."

"Different enough that no one bats an eye at them running a fucking fight club and forcing their children to compete for employability?" Bethany Anne waved the approaching waiter off. "The adults are old enough to make their own stupid choices. Indoctrinating the next generation is crossing the line. The only fight club on this planet is one *I* allow."

"You're not going to take cultural expectations into account?" Jennifer asked. "I mean, I kind of get why they do what they do, even if I don't agree with it. The only way out of the undercity for most of them is with a mercenary company."

Bethany Anne waved a hand, dismissing the explanation. "It stops being cultural when the children are brought up without the option to question their parents' expectations or make a different choice."

Jennifer shrugged. "That I agree with. I just don't see where they've had much else in the way of options. It has to be stopped, but how do we achieve that without tearing their society apart?"

"By giving them better options after we put an end to the fights." The tattoo of Bethany Anne's nails on the polished wood of the table filled the silence that ensued. "What those options will be, I don't know…yet. Have Kirian dig into his friend's situation. I'll approve Tor for enrollment in the Institute, but I want to know why his family is seemingly absent from his life and why he's hellbent on keeping it a secret."

"Not a problem," Jennifer assured her. "What about the Zhyn kid, Charr'est?"

Bethany Anne pressed her lips together. "We have an abusive prick of a male to smack down. Then we'll see if the boy is Institute material."

High Tortuga, Northern Continent, City of Thon, Brasak Sector

Kirian found being back in his chair frustrating after he'd been getting around on his own two feet. However, as far as the rest of the world knew, he required the chair, so he was wheeling in power mode through the residential area where Tor lived to get to his house.

Knowing about his newest friend's obsession with all things Etheric Empire, he'd wanted to give him the good news in person since Jennifer had already spoken with Bethany Anne and passed along the Empress' approval for Tor's admission to the Institute.

Tor hadn't responded to his messages, and Kirian's attempts to call hadn't gone through. Worry for his friend had dissipated the joy he'd felt at the prospect of making Tor's conspiracy theorist dreams come true. He'd set off in as much of a hurry as he could without his exoskeleton to ease the journey.

Had he been thinking rationally, he would have gone to

Professor Lerr'ek or the doc and asked for a ride in a roamer. Then it occurred to him that he hadn't informed anyone where he was going.

A quick message to Cerebro from his wrist-holo—what he wouldn't give for a neural implant!—solved that issue. Then he arrived at Tor's house.

Kirian hadn't been there since he and Tor worked on the bully trap, but he didn't remember the place standing out among the gently rundown homes in the neighborhood. Now, the yard had grown wild, and the locked shutters and mail piled on the porch spoke of abandonment.

Stomach sinking, Kirian opened a line to Cerebro. "Hey, you can pilot the roamers, right?"

"I can indeed. Would you like me to send one for you?"

"Yes, please." He gave the empty house a last forlorn look before turning his chair around. "It doesn't look like anyone has been here for a while."

After he returned to the Institute and exchanged the chair for his exoskeleton, Kirian headed to the ops center.

"Cerebro, let's test the net. I need to know the last time Tor was home." He strode to the main console with a purpose that belied his fears for Tor and pulled the net's interface up on the main wallscreen.

"We only have one full cycle of above-ground drone coverage," Cerebro reminded him.

Kirian snapped, "Then pull from Baba Yaga's satellite surveillance. Don't tell me that's not what that sat is doing up there. We need to find Tor."

"I wouldn't dream of it," Cerebro responded.

The AI's chagrined tone stopped Kirian in mid-keyboard smash. He ran a hand over his face as guilt heated his cheeks.

"Sorry, Cerebro. I'm scared for my friend, but that's no excuse for the way I just spoke to you."

"Apology accepted," Cerebro told nim. "Tor left his home in the dead of night eight days ago."

Kirian wasn't sure whether he was relieved or if the information made him even more scared for Tor's safety than he had been. "Can you tell where he went and if his family is doing anything to find him?"

"I was able to track him to the undercity tram station at the east boundary of Brasak Sector. He lost himself in the crowd there, however."

"Yeah, he's good at blending in. What about his family?" Kirian pressed, minding his tone after his earlier outburst. "I'm not finding anything more recent than last year from them on the holonet."

"Hmm…" Cerebro paused for three seconds that felt like an eternity to Kirian. "The police don't have a missing person report."

"Maybe they don't trust the police," Kirian hazarded, although his worry was getting stronger by the minute. "They might be looking for him themselves. Has there been any other activity around the house? Other Noel-nis, maybe?"

"No," Cerebro answered. "I searched all available surveillance, including from Baba Yaga's satellite. I did find something curious. There has been no activity at the family home for the last eight cycles besides your friend's comings and goings."

Kirian frowned. "Nothing?"

"Only deliveries," Cerebro confirmed. "Tracing those payments back, I was bounced around the dark net. The trail led through several shell accounts obscuring the account belonging to Tor's father."

"Sounds needlessly complicated," Kirian murmured. "Why go to all this effort, Tor?"

"The evidence points to Tor's family disappearing eight cycles ago. He has been fending for himself this whole time."

Kirian couldn't imagine life without his mom and Gramps taking care of him. What had Tor been through? A neglectful family was one thing, but abandonment? "Can you activate Tor's wrist-holo? Not being able to get through to him was what set my panic off. Maybe you can do something I can't so I can speak to him."

"I can do anything ADAM can." This time, Cerebro was silent for almost a minute. When he spoke again, the AI's voice held frustration. "It appears that Tor's wrist-holo is no longer functional."

"What do you mean, no longer functional? Was it switched off, or was it destroyed?"

"Destroyed. If it was switched off, I could have reactivated it. However, I cannot find a trace of it on the system. On *any* system."

That was not good. The slight relief that Kirian had felt upon learning that Tor had left his house of his own accord dissipated. Kirian was back to fearing for his friend's life. "I don't know what to do next," he admitted.

"Did you check his holonet history?" Cerebro inquired. "You are more familiar with any aliases he uses and the areas of the net he frequents. Perhaps his last activity online could give us a clue as to what triggered his flight or where he was headed."

Kirian started typing. "I have a better idea. I'm going to respect his decision to go off-grid and trust that he'll reach out when he feels safe."

"Then what are you posting in…Sally's Hole? Really, Kirian? That site isn't for teenagers."

"Shows what *you* know," Kirian quipped as he left a bread-crumb trail for Tor to follow when he surfaced. "The Hole is a front for hackers. No one thinks to look beyond the services being offered, and the site's owners didn't put any trackers in the UI."

"I don't think that UI hosts anything beyond the horrifically inept messaging function. Did toddlers code it?"

Kirian laughed. "It sucks, but it does what we need it to do as long as we don't post any character combinations that trigger the censor."

Cerebro chuckled. "From what I see, half the users are males who have never seen a female in the flesh, and half are people misusing the site for sales."

"The Venn diagram of those two groups is almost a circle." When Kirian reread his message, he was satisfied that Tor would realize it was for him, so he clicked the send button. "Okay, I'm done. I just need to copy this to—"

Lerr'ek's voice came from the overhead speaker. "Kirian, wrap up what you're doing and meet me in my office, please."

CHAPTER FOUR

<u>**High Tortuga, Northern Continent, City of Thon, Undisclosed Location, Institute of Education-Focused Extrajudicial Foundational Studies**</u>

Lerr'ek sighed and waved to freeze the holoscreen embedded in his desk. His attempts to reach Charr'est's family had borne no fruit. Either the parents had no interest in the advancements their son was being offered, or the father refused to allow the young male an opportunity to outshine him.

Unfortunately, Lerr'ek was not a psychologist. Fortunately, he had someone who was.

"Cerebro, I'm hitting dead end after dead end. Maybe it was naïve of me to think the Zhyn family would be the easiest to deal with. Baba Yaga might punch me if I tell her that I gave up because no one picked up the call."

"I suggest you use the resources available to you. Kirian has shown that he is willing and able to take responsibility for those he requested for his team, so utilize that."

Lerr'ek nodded. "Where is Kirian right now?"

"He is in the ops center, thinking outside the box to locate Tor."

Lerr'ek thumbed the intercom button on his desk and spoke into the microphone embedded beside the holoscreen. "Kirian, wrap up what you're doing and meet me in my office, please."

He returned to answering his mail and came across an unexpected message. By the time Kirian arrived, the seed of a plan had taken root. He motioned for Kirian to take a seat in the guest chair across the desk from him.

"What's up, Prof?" Kirian asked.

"The candidates," Lerr'ek told him. "One is missing, one is being used by his people for entertainment, and one was denied admittance by his parents."

"Tor will show up." Kirian's expression did not match the certainty in his voice. "I've done everything I can to make sure he reaches out when he surfaces. In the meantime, Cerebro is searching for him."

"Be that as it may, my focus has to be on the other boys until he shows. That brings me to the reason I called you here. While I was waiting for you, I found an email from one Professor Gloomin in my inbox."

"What did he want?" Kirian's brow creased. "Credits for my classes were transferred to the Institute, right?"

"Apparently not." Lerr'ek forwarded the message to Kirian's wrist-holo. "He says he will only approve the transfer of your history credit if you take the midterm you missed when you were out sick."

Kirian laughed. "Good old Gloomy. How does this figure into your plans? Am I going in undercover?"

"As yourself, yes." Lerr'ek was amused by Kirian's enthusiasm. "I will accompany you on the pretext of forming a relationship between the school and the Institute."

Concern stifled Kirian's excitement. "How long do I have to prepare for the midterm?"

"Three days. Plenty of time to treat this like any other assignment and prepare for it accordingly."

"I won't let you down, Prof." Kirian got to his feet and headed for the door. He paused with his hand outstretched. "I only see one problem."

"What's that?" Lerr'ek inquired, sensing the snark his only student was about to deliver.

Kirian grinned. "No one will believe you're a teacher."

Lerr'ek chuckled. "O ye of little faith. Wait and see before you decide I can't pull this off. Cerebro will be there during the midterm. You need to pass it, but don't stress the outcome."

Surprising him yet again, Kirian refused the AI's assistance. "I remember most of the material, and I enjoy history. I have three rest days scheduled. I'll get with the guys tomorrow and cram before the tournament."

Lerr'ek nodded. "If you want to go the hard route, I won't stop you."

High Tortuga, Northern Continent, City of Thon, Brasak Sector, Entertainment District

Kirian didn't have to pretend he was in pain as he moved from his chair to the edge seat of their usual booth in the diner on the first floor of Dreamland. His training the previous day had pushed him to his limit and then some.

Luckily, he had three days off from the brutal regimen-slash-training program Bethany Anne had put him on. He had a meeting with Stephen and ADAM after the tournament that afternoon to discuss his and Tor's sim being adapted as a horror POV for the arcade. He had hoped Tor would attend too, but there had been no word from him.

First came an early breakfast and the emergency study session his friends had arranged after Kirian had told the triplets about the surprise midterm.

"How does a failed midterm count as an emergency?" Ari

wrinkled his nose and yawned. "You know old Gloomy is just being his usual anal self, right?"

Kirian raised his hands in defense, looking at Meddox and Lutian for support. He found none. "My place in the Institute is dependent on my grades. It doesn't matter why Gloomy is on a power trip. It only matters that I don't fail the midterm. Are you guys here to help me cram or to bitch about how early it is?"

"We didn't say we wouldn't help," Meddox grumbled. "But let's eat first."

"We've got you, Kirian," Fern assured him, slipping into the booth beside Ari. "Move over, you big lugs." She shoved the boys. "Tianel will be here any—"

She half-stood and waved over Kirian's shoulder. "She's here."

Everyone turned to greet the final member of their friend group, and a desert sprang up in Kirian's mouth when he saw Tianel walking toward the booth in a pale purple sundress with her long silver hair unbound.

He almost forgot he wasn't supposed to reveal the improvement in his condition and had to check himself when he started to rise to greet her. Fortunately...or not, he was so flustered that he stumbled as he turned and pitched forward into Meddox.

Meddox caught him easily, eyeing Kirian with confusion when he encountered the taut muscle beneath the loose long T-shirt he wore. "You good, buddy?"

Kirian nodded, still tongue-tied, and slid back into his seat, leaning on the table for support. Tianel returned his shy smile as she gracefully slipped into the space Fern had made for her on the opposite side of the table.

"So, what are we studying?" Xander asked, snapping Kirian out of his daydream about walking hand-in-hand along a tree-lined riverbank with the pretty Torcellan.

Nerril groaned. "The economics of the Empire, and the course material sucks. Whoever wrote it was on a massive downer."

"Maybe it was old Gloomy." Lutian pushed the table's menu pad over to his brothers, who started arguing about whose turn it was to order.

Kirian ignored them and focused on setting up the portable holoprojector containing the notes he'd compiled the night before in the center of the table. "It's dry, but the subject is pretty interesting. I never considered how only part of the Etheric Empire's expansion was due to military intervention."

Tianel laughed. "If you listen to the anti-Empire media, the Empress built the Empire on the blood and bones of every species she encountered. That narrative suited the Leath. The reality is that much of the expansion was built on diplomacy and trade."

"What do you know about diplomacy and trade?" Nerril inquired with interest.

"My mother is the minister for domestic trade back home," Tianel answered with a tinge of some emotion Kirian couldn't identify. "She needs to be informed about our exports as well as domestic products to do her job."

Nerril wrinkled his muzzle. "Does that mean you're going to take over as minister when she retires? You're an only child, right?"

"I wish I wasn't," Tianel admitted. "I like it here."

Kirian swallowed the lump in his throat. "You're leaving?"

Tianel nodded, looking down at her lap. "I start college in a few weeks. Mother and I are leaving for Torcellan at the end of the next cycle."

Fern put a comforting hand on her cousin's arm. "We've had a great time with you here."

Tianel shook off her sadness and smiled. "I'm glad I got to be friends with you all. This has been the best year of my life."

Her smile landed on Kirian, and his heart almost shattered. Tianel shrugged and waved her hand at the projector. "Shall we begin?"

Kirian jumped when Meddox's elbow hit his ribs.

"Dude, we're a klick from the infil point," Meddox yelled over the roar of the ancient helicopter's blades. "Get your head in the game!"

Kirian winced. He couldn't keep thinking about Tianel's coming departure from High Tortuga. "Sorry, man. I'm with it. I promise."

The final level of the sim stripped away all modern conveniences, forcing the teams to rely on the archaic technology and weapons the pre-event tutorial had briefed them on to complete their objective.

The helicopter spat them out within walking distance of the heavily fortified compound in which fourteen kidnapped scientists were being forced to build a planet-killing bomb. If they didn't reach the hostages before the bomb detonated, they failed. If more than fifty percent of the team died, they failed. If the maniacal dictator who'd had the scientists kidnapped escaped, they failed.

After the infodump in the tutorial, each member of the final two teams received two heal tokens, one Bowie knife, and one M4 carbine. Allowing two box magazines per player was one of the few concessions by the game developers, ADAM and Stephen.

They also had modern comm buds that allowed them limited access to Weston and Saima, and three random item tokens. Those could be used at any time, but there was no guarantee the item that spawned would be useful.

"Wait up," Kirian called before the triplets departed for the fortress. "We have to be smart about this. Can we agree to use an EI assist? I want to know if our spawn items vanish after a set amount of time."

"Why?" Lutian asked. Then comprehension dawned in the

bright eyes peering from between the top of the scarf covering his muzzle and the rim of his metal helmet. "Oh, right. Yeah, I'm good with that."

"Me too," Meddox agreed.

"Me three," Nerril chimed in.

Kirian tapped his comm bud three times to call one of the EIs who ran the sim.

"The spawned items will remain for the duration of the event." Saima had a gentle Pakistani-accented voice.

"Thank you, Saima," the boys chorused.

"Who's going to do the honors?" Kirian asked.

Nerril stepped forward. "I'll do it." He took the three random item tokens and tossed them on the ground one at a time. They exploded into opaque gray smoke plumes that wavered in the breeze but did not blow away.

The boys watched and waited. After a long moment, the smoke plumes contracted and transformed into their mystery items.

The first plume was replaced by a three-pronged hook with a carabiner at the non-business end to attach to a rope. The second produced an olive green case with an unreadable M-number stamped on the side. The third plume gave them...a wooden spoon.

The triplets made a beeline for the case and the grappling hook, ignoring the wooden spoon. Kirian picked up the simple eating utensil and examined it. There was nothing special about the spoon save for the hinge that allowed it to be folded.

He folded the spoon and tucked it into one of the pouches on his utility belt, then knelt to see what the triplets were so excited about.

"This is better than grenades," Meddox argued.

Nerril scoffed. "Do you know how to use this without blowing your tail off?"

Kirian peered at the plastique nestled in among everything needed to set and detonate it. "I do."

"For real?" Meddox closed the case.

Kirian nodded. "I'm learning all kinds of cool stuff at the Institute."

"They teach you how to use explosives?" Lutian exhaled loudly. "That's pretty cool, dude."

"In a holo, right?" Nerril asked, concern creasing his features.

Kirian snagged the grappling hook and set off toward the fortress. "Well, yeah. They don't want students blowing themselves up in training."

He realized he'd said too much, having been caught up in the comfort of being in the final with his best friends. Kirian tapped his comm three times and asked Saima to flag his comment for ADAM's attention so the audio got scrubbed.

He changed the subject to improvements they expected to see in the new arcade sims. As Lutian and Nerril debated whether they'd want the realistic experience of being injured during a game, Meddox fell into step beside Kirian and spoke in a quiet voice that didn't carry.

"You didn't need my help when you stumbled at breakfast, and now you're an explosives expert. What are you learning at that Institute, Kirian? Should I be worried?"

>>**I am running interference on your team's audio,**<< ADAM told him. >>**You can speak freely.**<<

"What about the need to keep everything secret?" Kirian asked under his breath, knowing the AI would hear.

>>**We knew this moment would come sooner or later, and Bethany Anne knows trustworthy friends when she sees them. Put their fears to rest.**<<

"Kirian?" Meddox prompted.

He'd been on the other side of this situation plenty of times since he'd fallen feet-first into Bethany Anne's world. "Sorry. I wanted to tell you guys everything, but it all happened so fast, and, well, it's nowhere near done yet."

"You're not making sense, Kirian." Lutian turned his attention to Meddox. "What do you mean, he didn't need your help?"

"Our dude somehow went from wasted muscles to being secretly ripped under those baggy clothes he wears."

"Is that true?" Nerril asked.

"I'm too skinny to be ripped." Kirian protested. He had taken point and was using his Bowie knife to make a path through their verdant surroundings.

"But you're seriously buff," Meddox stated. "That's not the only thing you've been keeping from us, is it? We didn't say anything because we thought you acting weird was because of everything that happened with Dex. Start talking, Kirian. What have you been hiding from us?"

Kirian gritted his teeth. It was now or never. If he told them the full truth, they'd probably look at him differently, but brushing them off would sound the death knell for their lifelong friendship. The thought of losing the triplets made the decision for him. "When Baba Yaga put an end to our revenge on Dex, she offered me a deal."

At the mention of the Witch, the brothers' bickering stopped. "That's why you're not sick," Maddox stated. "You sold your soul to Baba Yaga, and she healed you."

Kirian laughed. "You've watched too many B-holos, bud."

"So, the Witch *didn't* force you to drink blood and swear a secret pact of loyalty in exchange for..." Lutian dissolved into laughter. "Sorry, bro," he managed. "Too easy. Kirian is right. You love trashy horror holos too much. We're not living in the plot of one."

"Hey!" Nerril complained. "Have some sensitivity!" He clapped Kirian on the back. "Congrats on getting some relief for the time you have left."

"I didn't have to enter a blood pact, but I'm not dying now,"

Kirian told them. "Not as fast as I was, anyway. You've all been to PT with me. Doc Ericson's treatments are working, and she says my prognosis is good. I'm going to see my fifties or sixties."

The triplets were stunned into silence. Then they dogpiled Kirian, cheering. Their celebration was cut short by discordant shouts from up ahead.

"There goes our advantage." Kirian couldn't be mad at his best friends for their joyous reaction. They'd all grown up with the specter of his condition hanging over them. The reprieve belonged to Meddox, Lutian, and Nerril as much as it did to him.

Kirian motioned to a break in the thick foliage. "This way. We'll circle around them."

CHAPTER FIVE

They emerged from their game Pods ninety minutes later, their moods only slightly dampened by their loss.

"We need to celebrate," Nerril insisted, slinging an arm around Kirian's shoulders. "All of us."

"Yeah, *before* Tianel goes back to Torcellan," Lutian agreed.

Everyone laughed when Kirian blushed beet-red at the mention of his hopeless crush. "We can set something for my next rest day. I'm sorry we can't do anything right now. I have to get upstairs for a meeting with the arcade owner. There's a chance that I could get some income from writing sims for Dreamland."

He accepted their teasing and wishes for good luck, then said his goodbyes and headed for the staff elevators.

There was no wait when Kirian wheeled himself into the service corridor by the admissions booth. The elevator doors slid open, and ADAM greeted him from a small speaker in the recess above the key card slot.

"Stephen is waiting for you in his office. Sorry you and the triplets didn't win the tournament."

Kirian grinned as he directed his chair into the elevator.

"Thanks, ADAM. Don't sweat the tournament. We're good. Better than we have been since everything in my life changed."

"It's normal for you to experience upheaval in your social life in this situation," ADAM assured him. "The gradual reversal of your terminal illness due to Jennifer's therapy regime doesn't have to be hidden."

A pang of guilt fluttered in Kirian's stomach. Or maybe he was hungry? He was always starving these days. "No one thinks I'm ungrateful, right?"

ADAM laughed. "No, Kirian. Everyone is more than pleased by how you've handled the changes. Keeping secrets isn't easy, and no one wants to see your friendships unnecessarily deteriorate because of them."

"I was lucky to have my family and the friends I've made." Kirian savored the warm feeling in his chest when he thought about his loved ones. "If the cost of being here for my mom was losing my friends, I would have paid it gladly. Knowing I don't have to give them up makes my new lease on life that much sweeter."

His stomach let out a rumble, so he was indeed hungry. "Does Stephen have snacks?"

"He does," ADAM confirmed as the elevator door opened. "However, Jennifer requested that a meal be delivered for you."

"It arrived five minutes ago," Jennifer interjected as Kirian powered his chair into the leafy atrium of the penthouse that served as Stephen's office.

Kirian submitted to the doc checking his vitals before they made their way to the huge goldwood table in the center of the main room. Despite seating fourteen in a pinch, the table did not dominate the space. The floor-to-ceiling windows' blinds were open, adding the sparkle of the city's lights to the tasteful cream décor that was broken here and there by potted ferns and the graceful local vines that draped the support columns.

The vines were in bloom, but their sweet fragrance was overlaid by the spicy and savory aromas coming from the cartons of food that covered the end of the table where Stephen and Professor Lerr'ek were sitting, deep in conversation.

Stephen stood to greet Jennifer, then pulled out a chair for Kirian. "Join us for dinner, my young friend," he invited.

Kirian smiled. "I'm going to stay in my chair if that's okay. The haptics in the gaming Pods are still a little rough, so I took a few knocks while we were getting our behinds handed to us this afternoon."

"Are you in pain?" Jennifer asked. She turned her attention to Stephen when Kirian nodded. "Start eating without me. I need to get Kirian some patches since he told me he was out earlier today."

The adults continued their discussion on the viability of feeding the best gamers from the tournaments into the Institute's pilot program when Lerr'ek was ready to expand in that direction. Kirian didn't say much beyond thanking Stephen for passing him a full plate and was deep in a delicious bistok and hot pepper noodle dish that made his eyeballs sweat when Doc Ericson returned with the pain patches. He stopped eating as she placed two on the nerve clusters at the base of his spine.

"Better?" she asked a minute later.

Kirian nodded and picked up his two-pronged eating utensil. "Much. Thank you, Doc." He waved the utensil. "This would have been a much better item for today's sim. I lost a vital second snapping that spoon in two. The big bad saw it coming and threw me into the wall before I could stick the halves of the spoon into his eyes."

"Bloodthirsty little bugger, aren't we?" Stephen chuckled. "Good."

"That's…*good*?" Kirian dipped a dumpling in a savory sauce. "Okay, then."

"Why snap the spoon?" the prof asked. "You only needed to pierce one eyeball to penetrate the brain?"

Kirian sometimes forgot that Lerr'ek had not always been in education. Then he said something like that, and all the frayed tweed and elbow patches in the Empire couldn't hide that the male's calm and measured exterior concealed a cold-blooded murderer.

He considered. "Only if the spoon wasn't too flimsy. Then it would have snapped, and he would still have had one eye to see out of. Not that it mattered. We all died horribly, and the bomb went off, killing everyone else. Not going to lie. That was my least favorite sim so far in the new batch."

"That, young man, is why we are here tonight and not at the Institute." Stephen waved his chopsticks as he spoke. "Today's sim was a recreation of a personal experience. The others are extrapolations of training sims used by students of the Etheric Academy—"

"Which is why it's a great idea to admit the best players to the Institute," Lerr'ek interjected.

"I don't disagree, but this is an entertainment company." Stephen smiled at Kirian. "The imagination you and Tor showed in creating your Were sim got me thinking that your creativity is what Dreamland needs to stay ahead after our competition gains the technology that gave us the edge."

Kirian was lost. "I thought we were here to talk about commercializing the Were sim."

"That will have to wait until Tor returns," Stephen told him.

Kirian nodded. "That was what I was going to say. I couldn't have built the sim without him, so it wouldn't be right if I kept the profits."

"ADAM will be your partner for any new sims," Stephen informed him.

"ADAM could do this alone," Kirian pointed out. "Why involve me?"

"Because we wish to invest in your future." Stephen smiled. "I'm sure you have considered the potential income from sims, but did you also consider that you will want to build a life outside of the team you're going to build?"

"I…" Kirian had never needed to look beyond his teenage years, let alone into the intimidating concept of adulthood. "I guess I need a plan, and using and furthering the skills I already have is as good as any. Okay, I'll do it."

High Tortuga, Northern Continent, City of Thon, Undisclosed Location, Institute of Education-Focused Extrajudicial Foundational Studies

Waking up in his bed at the Institute was beginning to feel as normal as being at home. Kirian wondered if the atmosphere of "home away from home" would remain after other students arrived.

He dressed in a loose T-shirt, an oversized hoodie, and baggy jeans to hide his exosuit. If he was cornered by the boys he hoped to recruit, he would need the support to avoid another incident like the one in the quad. He still felt stiff and sore from the overzealous sim haptics, so his chair was a relief this morning.

Kirian made his way to the atrium. Professor Lerr'ek awaited him by the elevator that led to the surface. Kirian eyed him, unable to keep from laughing at the male's obvious discomfort in the ill-fitting brown suit he wore.

"What's so funny?" Lerr'ek grumbled, hooking a finger into the stiff shirt collar that was attempting to contain the thick muscles in his neck.

Kirian waved a finger to encompass the suit. "That. I know you have better suits."

"Suits that are too expensive for a public educator."

Kirian snorted. "So, you dressed like you raided a thrift store bargain bin in the dark?"

"That chair does not exempt you from respecting your elders,"

Lerr'ek reminded him. "Any more sass and I will run your next PT session instead of Jennifer."

Kirian laughed harder. "Can I be there when you tell her that? I need to improve my offense, and watching her kick your tush from here to Tulimer Heights would be *very* educational."

Lerr'ek growled. "Kirian…"

Kirian held a hand up. "I'm sorry, Prof. It's just…you look like ten pounds of hamburger stuffed into an eight-pound corduroy bag. I can't believe you were serious about the elbow patches!"

The proud Zhyn's shoulders slumped, and he sighed.

Kirian patted the prof's arm as he powered his chair into the elevator. "Now you look crushed enough to be a public educator. Hold onto that. I was just helping you with your cover. The suit is not that bad."

Lerr'ek rolled his eyes. "I sincerely hope you don't expect me to thank you."

"Wouldn't dream of it, sir." Kirian grinned.

Cerebro landed the roamer in the parking lot at the Free School, and Lerr'ek handed Kirian a comm bud and chip.

"We will be separated while you are taking your exam," the professor explained. "This chip goes behind your ear and allows you to speak sub-vocally. I might need your help when I'm talking to those kids."

Kirian pressed the chip into place and inserted the tiny bud into his ear canal. "Are you nervous?"

"I don't have much experience with kids. I don't think they will be as easy to be around as you've been."

Kirian's grin returned. "Was that a compliment?"

Lerr'ek opened the roamer's door and got out. "Don't let it go to your head. Come on. You're going to be late."

CHAPTER SIX

<u>Etheric Empire, Yollin System, QBBS Meredith Reynolds</u>

Bethany Anne or Baba Yaga? Was there a distinction anymore beyond the physical differences? If she took the time to examine her various personas, she would have to admit that Baba Yaga was her rage personified, and the Empress was the aberration.

She had fought her nature to become this calm, measured, and diplomatic. On the outside, at least.

Outwardly, she listened attentively to the delegates from some shit-pot planet make their case for whatever it was they wanted. Internally, she wanted to backtrack Akio's message to Earth and bitch slap Michael into the next century for abandoning her all these years.

Bethany Anne, you are scaring our guests.

Barnabas' mental reminder snapped Bethany Anne out of her thoughts. She realized that everyone in the throne room was struggling not to flee from the heavy blanket of anger suppressing them.

TOM?

On it.

He cut her emotions off, and Bethany Anne got to her feet. "My apologies. Please excuse me. I'm not feeling well."

She stepped into the Etheric without waiting for a response and unleashed a scream of frustration that started in the pit of her stomach and traveled for miles.

The mists churned in response to her floodgates bursting, but Bethany Anne paid no attention to the swirling particles of Etheric energy. The message from Akio filled her mind, broke her heart, and tore her soul in two.

Michael was alive.

Being vindicated for her insistence that he hadn't really died saving everyone in Colorado should have been a relief. However, the grief she'd carried for so long had become such an intrinsic part of her that the news that he had returned transmuted the pain into anger.

Anger was *good*. It was clean and sharp, and despite what everyone else said, it had a purpose for her. It had no space for frustration or restriction, made no excuses, and allowed no bistok-shit rules to dissuade it.

Suppressing her anger for so long had led to the split that had created Baba Yaga.

Those wounds were still raw. A rage she hadn't felt so strongly since she'd understood that her mother wasn't coming back washed over and through her, and she screamed again, unleashing her fury in bursts of fire and lightning that would have destroyed the *Meredith Reynolds* if she hadn't had the foresight to remove herself to the one place where she couldn't do any real damage.

Michael was alive, and he was on Earth.

Bethany Anne shut down TOM's attempt to soothe her.

Let me feel, *fuckdammit!* Touch my endocrine system without my permission, and I'll tear my own spine out to remove you from my body.

Bethany A—

NO!

Her screamed denial caused thunder to roll around her, but she didn't care. The formerly inert mist crackled as Bethany Anne increased the energy she pulled, creating a feedback loop that resonated harder with every barrage of fire and lightning she released. She raged for hours, the unlimited Etheric energy fueling her relentless purge of every emotion she'd kept suppressed since the day her love was taken from her.

Michael was alive, he was on Earth, and she had no way to get to him.

She snatched a bolt of lightning and redirected it into the roiling mist that was forming walls around her as she drew on the Etheric.

The Empire had not filled the empty space where her heart should have been. She had cut pieces of herself out and suppressed others to do right by everyone she was responsible for. Although her family, friends, and allies had helped her build that Empire, without Michael by her side, it was a vast and empty place.

Logically, his supposed death had been another factor in her drive to leave Earth and take the fight to the Kurtherians. However, Bethany Anne had set logic aside the moment she succumbed to her rage and became Baba Yaga.

She was done with Empressing. Done with pandering to asshole politicians for the sake of the many. Done with everything that didn't help her work around the destruction of the Sol Gate that had cut her off from the only thing she wanted in this whole universe.

Michael was alive, he was on Earth, and she had no way to get to him...

Yet.

. . .

High Tortuga, Northern Continent, City of Thon, Brasak Sector

Kirian felt like the atmosphere in the Free School corridors was lighter now. Maybe it was the absence of Dex and his reign of terror. More likely, it had to do with him no longer attending the school.

Either way, the nerves that had racked him on the ride over had vanished when he'd left the professor in the capable hands of Ms. Bzant and made his way to the room Professor Gloomin had arranged for him to take the midterm. He hadn't realized so many of the students knew who he was or that they would be so pleased to see him.

"You are almost late, Mr. Larsen," Kirian's former history teacher greeted him when he arrived.

"Sorry, sir," Kirian apologized as he wheeled into the room. "Everyone I passed on the way wanted to say hi."

Professor Gloomin pressed his lips together. "Socialize on your own time, Mr. Larsen. I trust you are prepared?"

Kirian dropped his wrist-holo and datapad on the teacher's desk. "As ready as I can be."

Professor Gloomin's stern expression relaxed. "Pick a desk so we can begin."

The test took Kirian all of twenty minutes to complete. Professor Lerr'ek and Vice Principal Junie had begun their introductory conversation. He took his time returning to reception, listening to Lerr'ek's smooth pitch on the comm bud.

"Forgive me," Vice Principal Junie interrupted, "but 'extrajudicial' makes your Institute sound like a training facility for would-be hackers and mercenaries."

"You misunderstand our mission," Professor Lerr'ek assured her. "The Institute's purpose is to identify exceptional young people whose circumstances are likely to lead them to lives where their potential is either wasted or used for criminal purposes. We give them a chance to do something good instead."

"How does Kirian Larsen fit into that mission?" Vice Principal Junie asked, the doubt in her voice clear over the comm. "We both know he doesn't have much time left."

"Kirian is the exception to the exception," Professor Lerr'ek told her. "He found us. His medical status combined with his tenacity and intelligence earned him a place at the Institute and a reprieve from the early death he would otherwise have suffered."

"Don't be ridiculous. Such technology is the province of the Etheric Empire, and no one gets access to it without the Empress' permission."

"Not the Empress," Professor Lerr'ek told her. "Her representative."

The vice principal gasped. Professor Lerr'ek was silent. Kirian snickered.

"It…it cannot be," she stuttered.

"This planet will be cleansed of corruption from top to bottom, per the Mistress' wishes," Professor Lerr'ek stated without inflection. "At all levels of society."

"Social engineering?" Vice Principal Junie inquired with interest.

She wasn't the only one who was interested. Kirian parked himself in a corner of the reception area where Ms. Bzant wouldn't see him through the potted plants and listened intently.

"Of a sort," Professor Lerr'ek confirmed. "You might be aware that the criminal population of the major cities has seen…shall we say, a reduction in number. Other measures are being taken that I am not at liberty to discuss with you. My role is to run the Mistress' investment in the upcoming generation, the Institute."

That was the second time Kirian had heard one of the adults talk in terms of investment when they discussed the future of High Tortuga's young people. He hadn't thought much about it when Stephen used the word, putting it down to the old vampire's sometimes old-fashioned way of speaking.

Hearing it from the professor made him think of a question

on the midterm he'd just taken that had sparked a series of connections in his mind that explained Bethany Anne's intentions for the planet. "A populace subjugated by military can either buckle and lose hope or fight their oppressors," he murmured.

"Kirian, what are you doing behind those plants?" Ms. Bzant asked loudly, snapping him out of his thoughts.

He maneuvered his chair out of the corner. "I was listening on my earphones while waiting for Professor Lerr'ek and Vice Principal Junie to get done with their meeting," he explained. "Don't mind me, Ms. Bzant. I know how busy you are."

"Nonsense," the homely Noel-ni told him with a warm smile. "I always had time for you. That hasn't changed just because you go to a different school. How are you, dear?"

"I'm doing great, thank you." Kirian grinned, then decided to give her a moment of brightness in another boring day of filing paperwork and fending off parents, students, and teachers. "Want to see something cool?"

Ms. Bzant tilted her head. "I don't know. Do I?"

"Watch this." Kirian eased to his feet and carefully walked toward the reception desk. "I've been working hard in therapy."

"Oh, my!" Ms. Bzant cooed. "You *have* been! I'm so pleased for you."

The door to the vice principal's office opened before she could ask any questions. Vice Principal Junie looked surprised to see Kirian on his feet.

"I told you he had been given a reprieve," the professor remarked wryly. "Kirian, would you like me to take your chair while we tour the school?"

Kirian's grin widened. "Sure, sir. Let me get my crutches."

Lunch period was in full swing as the vice principal led them through corridors packed to the seams with hungry teenagers.

Lerr'ek had never seen so many young people in one place. He was grateful that his enhancement hadn't included an upgrade to his senses.

The air in the cafeteria was thick with hormonal sweat barely covered by copious applications of body sprays and perfumes. Added to that, the discordant clamor of hundreds of voices would have driven him insane if he hadn't known that the assault on his ears and nose was temporary.

"How did I survive this when I was a kid?" he murmured to himself.

Kirian didn't seem to be affected. He soaked up the attention offered by his former schoolmates. Possibly he was immune due to his age and familiarity with the environment. If so, the kid must be bored out of his mind at the Institute, where he only had a few adults to interact with.

Vice Principal Junie failed to notice Lerr'ek's distraction. "The third student you inquired about took a leave of absence with his family. I will pass along your interest in recruiting Tor when he returns. Stars know the boy is criminally under-stimulated here. We try to accommodate his academic needs, but students like Kirian and Tor are so far ahead of their peers that it's not easy."

Kirian caught Lerr'ek's eye and gave him a pointed stare. The professor shook his head minutely and smiled at the vice principal. "A partnership could benefit both schools, Ms. Junie. As I mentioned earlier, the Institute has partnered with the Etheric Academy to ensure that our students have the finest curriculum available. I'm sure you could use the course materials as well."

"I don't know what the Free School could offer in return for such valuable resources," Vice Principal Junie admitted.

Lerr'ek spread his hands, smiling. "The most valuable resource of all, Ms. Junie: students. Young minds to help shape the future of this planet for the better."

"Young minds like Gralen's and Charr'est's?" Vice Principal

Junie blushed. "Forgive me. I don't mean to disparage any of my students, but those two don't have the best track records."

"Nevertheless, they both have qualities beyond being easily led by bullies." Lerr'ek's gaze remained on Kirian, who was showing off his improved mobility. "I would say what happened to Dex was a shame, but I would be lying."

"I can't pretend the students were unhappy to see him leave," Vice Principal Junie stated noncommittally. "You believe those two could make more of themselves?"

"I don't know, but Kirian nominated them both. Frankly, that young man gets whatever he asks for from my boss. You know his family history, yes?"

Vice Principal Junie swallowed hard. "I know enough. His father was in the military. They came from the Empire after his death."

"The Empire owes them." Lerr'ek glanced at her. "Kirian has proven beyond a doubt that he is worthy of the opportunities he has been granted. If he says that Gralen and Charr'est are worthy as well, I will do my part to make it happen."

CHAPTER SEVEN

Kirian stretched out on the back seat of the roamer to take off the joint supports. The bright spots of pain from showing off in the cafeteria were secondary to the icy-cold anger rolling off Professor Lerr'ek in waves so thick Kirian could have cut them with a knife.

"Prof, you okay?" Since Lerr'ek's knuckles were white on the steering yoke, Kirian knew the answer.

"Do you know how hard it is to bruise a Shrillexian?"

The words came out in a low growl that again reminded Kirian that the Zhyn was a killer in teacher's clothing.

"I noticed that Gralen was walking a bit cautiously when Vice Principal Junie asked him and Charr'est to join you at the faculty table. What did you talk about with them? It looked...awkward."

Professor Lerr'ek sighed gustily. "Cerebro, take over, please." He released his grip on the steering yoke and turned around to face Kirian. "'Awkward' is one way of describing the conversation. Gralen wasn't the only one hiding bruises. They both assumed they were in some kind of trouble. It took me and Ms. Junie a while to convince them otherwise."

"Charr'est was hurt?"

"He favored his right side. He did recognize my name when the vice principal introduced me. Problem is, he told me he has no interest in switching schools."

"He doesn't want to leave the Free School?" Kirian frowned. "Maybe your pitch needs work."

"My pitch was fine, thank you. The boy lied because he is afraid of something."

"His father, I bet." Kirian couldn't hide his disdain. "He doesn't want anything good to happen for his son. What parent wants to hold their child back in life? I don't get it."

Lerr'ek's lip curled in disgust. "I do. He's weak, and he can't stand to see his kid make more of himself than he ever could. Nothing would make me happier than beating that male to a bloody pulp in front of his son to show the kid there's nothing to fear."

Kirian's eyes widened. "You could do that?"

Professor Lerr'ek shook his head. "Not without destroying any chance we have of getting the boy out of there, but there are more ways to skin an alict. This is going to require finesse. You know as well as I do that Bethany Anne won't stand for it, and if she takes matters into her own hands..."

Kirian nodded. As long as there was hope, he could live with karma having to wait her turn. "What about Gralen?"

"He said he would love to take the opportunity, but he would need permission from someone called Joryan before he could accept."

"I heard that name when we were spying. He runs the fights, and he's not going to let Gralen go easily. He's too valuable to him. There are too many moving parts, Prof. We need help."

"I reached out to Bethany Anne before we left the school, and she will be on-world tomorrow evening. Take the rest of today and go spend time with your friends."

Kirian checked his wrist-holo and saw he had several messages waiting in the group chat, including the location of their meeting for the celebration his friends had pulled together.

"The plans changed. We're camping at Ocie Falls tonight. Can I take one of the roamers? I'll need my chair, and taking public transport out of the city with it sucks."

Lerr'ek laughed at his pleading expression. "Sure, kid. I'll help you load up, too. But be back in time for the war council tomorrow."

"'War council?'" Kirian echoed. "We're not at war."

Lerr'ek laughed. "You'll see how Bethany Anne takes the news."

High Tortuga, Northern Continent, Ocie National Park, Ocie Falls

The gang was in the midst of settling into their campsite when Kirian arrived in the roamer. He had showered and slapped pain patches on the achy places before departing.

He left his crutches in the passenger seat and climbed out to cheers from his friends.

"Told you!" Nerril crowed when Kirian walked around the back of the roamer unaided. "Xander, you owe me ten credits."

Kirian's eyes widened when he saw the amount of supplies Professor Lerr'ek had crammed into the storage compartment. "Quit busting everyone's balls and give me a hand with all of this," he called.

Fern and Tianel returned to building the fire. The triplets and Ari and Xander helped Kirian unload his tent and supplies.

"You know we're only here for one night, right?" Ari heaved a large cooler filled with Cokes out. "There's enough food and drinks here for twice as many people."

Meddox bumped him out of the way. "Human food?"

"Yup." Kirian tossed a package of hotdog buns at his friend. "These should be better than Garlem's mycelium dogs."

"I like Garlem's dogs," Meddox reminded him.

"That's because you have no taste," Kirian shot back, waving the genuine Empire hotdogs he'd fished out from behind the buns. "We also have bistok taco meat, prepped veggies, chips, dips, fixings for s'mores—"

"What's a s'more?" Tianel asked.

Kirian grinned. "You never ate a s'more?"

She shook her head and wiped her hands on her pants. "I never left Torcellan before I came here. I haven't had much contact with human culture."

"Same," Fern added. "What's in them?"

"Let me get my tent situated, and I'll show you," Kirian promised.

"You're in for a treat," Lutian told the girls. "The best part of backyard camping when we were kids was Janet's s'mores. She makes them with chocolate fudge cookies and huge marshmallows instead of a separate piece of chocolate."

"I've tasted chocolate." Tianel blushed. "Mother brings some back whenever she has a conference on the *Meredith Reynolds*. It's magical! She says we can't eat a lot because it's a narcotic."

"So are caffeine, capsaicin, sugar, and several other ingredients in human food," Kirian added. "Nothing that's dangerous for any of you in moderation."

"That's because humans know how to do food," Meddox enthused as he passed out Cokes.

Kirian's heart leapt as his friends dissolved into a discussion of who got to choose the music. He pulled the cord on his tent, and the sides sprang into place. It was a few minutes' work to get his air mattress and sleeping bag set up. Then he sat between Lutian and Tianel and built s'mores for everyone as the sun set over the conifer forest.

As the sparks from the fire floated into the gloaming, Tianel's hand brushed his, and their eyes met.

"I've never seen anything as beautiful as the firelight dancing in your eyes," Kirian blurted without thinking.

Before he could apologize, she leaned over and cupped his face with her hand. "You say the sweetest things, Kirian," she murmured, then got up to go dance with Fern.

Kirian stayed on the log, determined to remember this night for the rest of his life. Much later, he crawled into his sleeping bag, exhausted but too wired to fall asleep.

Amused by one of the triplets' snoring, he lay back and added his photos and video clips to those being dropped into the group chat by everyone who was still awake. He had paused on a clip of Tianel whirling to the beat with her hands above her head, her silver-blonde hair flying out around her, when he received a message from an unknown sender.

Curious about who could bypass his security settings and hopeful that the someone in question was Tor, Kirian opened the message and read the single line of text.

I know you've been trying to reach me. I'm okay. I'll be in touch when it's safe.

High Tortuga, Northern Continent, City of Thon, Dreamland Arcade, Stephen's Penthouse

Bethany Anne reviewed the information that Lerr'ek had compiled for her on the potential students, then set the datapad on the conference table. "I'm impressed with your initiative in creating partnerships with the Free School and Dreamland."

"That will help us source engineers, logisticians, mechanics, and pilots," Lerr'ek told her. "You see where I'm going with the fighting force?"

Bethany Anne inclined her head. "Something needs to be done about the Shrillexian fight ring. I have no problem with

Shrillexians beating the shit out of each other as a matter of honor. That's a cultural thing. I *won't* stand for that Joryan asshole taking that proud tradition and twisting it to scalp thirty percent of the income the people he sends to the mercenary companies make."

"It's about *profit?*" Kirian asked, shocked.

Bethany Anne's heart ached for the boy's innocence. However, although she hated to wipe the rose tint off the lenses through which he viewed the world, she wouldn't sugarcoat the truth. "Honey, in my experience, when people like him do shit like that, it usually is."

"Sometimes it's about vengeance or a straight-up power trip," Lerr'ek countered. "But this one looks like it's all about profit."

"But it's been going on for years!" Kirian exclaimed. "Bethany Anne, Prof, please tell me we're going to do something about it!"

"We're going to do what we can to help all three. That's why we're here: to figure out how to get them out of the situations they're in." Bethany Anne tapped her nails on the pale wood, the familiar rhythm settling her racing mind. "We can't do anything for Tor until we find him or he shows up, though."

"I'm on that." Kirian told them about the message he'd received the night before. "I'll have Cerebro help me bypass the proxy and track the IP of the device he used to send the message. That should tell us where he's laying low."

"Helping Gralen will take a little more time," Lerr'ek reasoned.

"Agreed," Bethany Anne told them. "Stephen and I will investigate Joryan's reach before I take action, though. The last thing we want is another opportunist stepping into the gap I create when I take him out."

"Which leaves Charr'est." Lerr'ek paused. "That one is mine. It irks me that a Zhyn kid is suffering at the hands of his parents. It's not how we raise our kids."

Kirian looked curious. "How *do* you raise your kids?"

"Not much differently than you were raised. Children are our most valuable resource."

"Zhyn culture is comparable to human culture," Stephen explained. "It was before the Zhyn Empire was folded into the Etheric Empire."

"I think his father is the problem," Kirian told him. "When we were spying, it seemed like his mom was afraid of his father too."

Lerr'ek shook his head. "The mother bears some of the responsibility for remaining in the family home. Stephen is correct that Zhyn culture is similar to human culture, and when it comes to marriage, there's no stigma associated with ending an unsuccessful union. The boy needs to be rescued from both parents."

"Wait," Bethany Anne told him. "Domestic abuse isn't a cut-and-dried situation. You don't know what the mother has been subjected to or what the male has done to maintain control over the family unit."

"She might not be complicit, but she's allowed her kid to suffer," Lerr'ek stated flatly. "I don't need to know anything else."

Bethany Anne shook her head. "You can't go in there guns blazing."

"I might have a solution," Stephen offered. "My work with restructuring the city government included establishing laws to combat the issue of orphaned children being inducted into undercity gangs. We can legally remove the boy from what is clearly an unsafe family environment."

Lerr'ek nodded vigorously. "I suggest we involve the school. Ms. Junie can corroborate that Charr'est has seemed injured on multiple occasions. We discussed it after the boys went back to their classes. She had assumed he was getting the injuries from fighting and was dismayed that the school had missed the signs of abuse when I informed her about his home situation."

Bethany Anne ceased her tapping. "Then we have our assignments. I will be on-world for a few days while the BYPS satellite launches take place. We will meet again to discuss our progress before I return to the *Meredith Reynolds*. In the meantime, good luck with the less challenging student intakes you will be overseeing, Lerr'ek."

High Tortuga, Northern Continent, City of Thon, Brasak Sector

Lerr'ek pointed out the house attached to the auto shop. "It's that one. How do you want to play this?"

"Just like we planned," Stephen told him as he released the camera drone all public employees used when interacting with the people they served.

Kirian controlled this one from the ops center at the Institute. No one else would know that its purpose was to give him and Cerebro eyes on the situation.

Stephen knocked on the door and waited. A few moments later, a female Zhyn answered. Lerr'ek noted that her makeup did a good job of concealing the bruises on her face and held back his anger.

"How can I help you?" she asked.

Stephen flashed the ID card hanging from the lanyard around his neck. "My name is Stephen, and I am from the Child Welfare Commission. We're here about your son."

"Who is it?" a gruff male called from inside the house.

"Government people." Her voice quavered as she responded. "They're here about Charr."

The male who came to the door was strong in the way people who worked physical jobs were, but his gut protruded, stretching his coverall across his midsection.

"Go back in, Yari," he told his wife, then turned his attention to Stephen and Lerr'ek. "What do you want with my son? Is he in trouble again?"

"He's not in any trouble," Stephen assured him. "Mister..."

"Carrash," the male ground out. "If the boy isn't in trouble, why are you at my door?"

He leaned against the frame as he spoke, accentuating his indolent attitude. Lerr'ek fought to remain silent and let Stephen handle the situation. Outwardly, the human displayed none of the anger Lerr'ek knew was boiling beneath the surface.

Stephen's voice held the steel hidden by his affable demeanor. "We had a report from Charr'est's school. They recorded several instances of your son showing up with minor injuries. I have to investigate and ensure your child is not at risk."

Carrash straightened to fill the doorway, his bored expression darkening with aggression. "You know how boys are. He gets into fights, is all."

Stephen inclined his head, but his expression made it clear that he didn't buy the excuse. "Be that as it may, I need to hear it from your son. May we come in?"

"No," Carrash spat. "You can go back to whatever office you came from and tell your bosses we're just fine. We don't need the government sticking their noses in where my family is concerned."

Lerr'ek didn't have a chance to lose his temper with the sorry excuse for a male. Stephen's hand was suddenly on Carrash's throat, his neatly manicured nails now tiny curved knives that drew pinpricks of blood from the Zhyn's skin.

"You have no choice, shit-for-brains." Stephen all but snarled the words, his eyes flashing red. "Baba Yaga sent me, and she is aware of every way in which you have failed the wife and child you swore to protect."

As fast as he had grabbed Carrash, Stephen released him. "You can deal with me, or I can inform the Mistress that you want to forgo the legal route and deal with her instead."

Carrash rubbed his throat and stepped aside without a word to give them access.

"Wise choice," Stephen stated calmly as he walked into the house ahead of Lerr'ek. "You have a chance of surviving me."

CHAPTER EIGHT

Yari emerged from the kitchen and invited them in to sit at the table before calling Charr'est to join them at Stephen's request.

"I just have a few questions for you," Stephen began. "You're not in any trouble, I promise."

"Then why are you here?" Charr'est's gaze remained on Lerr'ek as he spoke.

"As you are aware, we invited you to enroll at the Institute of Education-Focused Extrajudicial Foundational Studies," Lerr'ek told him.

Carrash slammed a hand on the table, causing his wife and son to flinch. "I already told you. My son doesn't need your fancy school. Quit giving him ideas above his station, or we're going to have a problem."

Stephen waved off Lerr'ek's response. "We *already* have a problem. One way or another, your reign of terror in this house is over."

"What's that supposed to mean?" Carrash demanded.

"You will find out in due time. I'd like you to leave so we can speak to your wife and son without you here to interrupt what they have to say."

"I'm not going anywhere," Carrash snapped. "Anything you have to say to them, you can say in front of me or not at all."

"So be it." Stephen nodded at the camera drone. "You had your chance to resolve this painlessly. Your choice to refuse that route is noted."

Carrash surged to his feet, his response dying in his mouth when Baba Yaga appeared in the kitchen.

Yari screamed. Charr'est yelped. Carrash stumbled back into the counter as Baba Yaga reached for him. It was over in less than a second. Baba Yaga pushed Carrash, and he vanished from the room. She turned to everyone else and, without a word, took the seat Carrash had vacated.

"As I was saying," Stephen continued as if nothing had happened. "I have some questions. Charr'est, Yari, do you want to be free of Carrash?"

"Is he..." Yari's gaze darted to Baba Yaga, then to Stephen. "Did she just kill him?"

"I did not," Baba Yaga confirmed, her grating voice soft. "He will be safe until I choose to bring him back. *If* I choose to bring him back."

"Leave him there," Charr'est blurted. "He deserves to panic."

"Charr!" Yari exclaimed. "He'll come back!"

"No, Mom," Charr'est argued. "Let him stay there. That way, he won't hurt us anymore. I'll quit school and run the shop. You can get a job. We'll be better off."

All eyes were on Yari. She slowly nodded. "Okay. It will be hard, but we can do this. Unless..." She looked at Baba Yaga. "Can he come back?"

"Not unless I bring him back," Baba Yaga told her. "Do you want that?"

Yari shook her head. "I would have left years ago if I wasn't afraid of what he'd do to me and Charr. What will become of him?"

"He'll get Justice," Baba Yaga answered. She rose from the table. "Stephen, do you have the item I asked for?"

"Printed out, as you requested." He extracted a sheet of paper clipped to the back of his datapad.

"Thank you, Stephen." She turned her terrifying smile on Lerr'ek. "I'll leave the rest of this to you. I hope you get your student."

"Thank you, Mistress," Lerr'ek told her before she vanished again.

Stephen got to his feet. "My part here is done now that we are sure young Charr'est is safe." He smiled at the mother and son. "I advise you to take the opportunity that is about to be offered. It was good to meet you both. I'll see myself out."

Lerr'ek faced Yari and Charr'est across the kitchen table. "I happen to know that you have potential as a mechanical engineer, Charr'est. You could be building starships by the time you graduate."

"How much is this going to cost me per semester?" Yari inquired. "I want this for my son if that's what he wants. No more being held back, Charr. You get to live whatever dreams you can build for yourself in this life."

Charr'est shook his head. "Not if it means you have to work yourself to death for me."

"I think we have a misunderstanding," Lerr'ek told them both. "Students' living and schooling costs are covered as part of the scholarship Charr'est has been nominated for."

"He was nominated?" Yari asked. "By whom?"

"Kirian Larsen." Lerr'ek gave Charr'est a moment to absorb the news and kept his attention on Yari. "I know you managed the day-to-day running of the auto shop while Carrash worked on the clients' vehicles. You won't struggle to find employees. I'm willing to help with the interview process and any paperwork you have to file to get the business put entirely in your names."

Yari recoiled in suspicion. "Why would you do that for us? We're strangers."

"Why would Kirian nominate me after everything I've done to him?" Charr'est added.

"You would have to ask him that," Lerr'ek told Charr'est. "As for why I'm doing all of this, you just met my boss. Her boss… well, let's just say that Baba Yaga wants better for this planet, and she has a *particular* way of taking care of her people. The choice is yours. She won't be mad if you decide to go your own way."

"Forgive me, but people don't get something for nothing," Yari countered. "You must have a personal stake in this."

Lerr'ek felt protective toward this family that had been broken by the person who was supposed to protect them. "You're right. I have the personal stake anyone who sees someone in need should have. You are not the only family whose child is being offered a scholarship, but I also want you to see a male who wants nothing in return be there for you in your time of need."

Charr'est pushed his chair back and got to his feet. "If I quit school now, I won't ever amount to anything. I won't let Dad win. I want to learn so I can take over the shop when the time comes. I'll go."

Yari turned in her chair and grasped her son's hand. "Is this what you want? Really, Charr?"

Charr'est nodded. "You heard what Professor Lerr'ek said. I could be building starships in a few years. Who knows how far I can take the family business with that knowledge?"

"Then I'll sign whatever they need me to," Yari told him.

Lerr'ek clapped. "Then the only thing left for you to do is pack, Charr'est."

Yari spoke in a quiet voice once her son had left the room. "Your boss… She's going to make me a widow, isn't she?"

Lerr'ek nodded. "If she hasn't already."

. . .

<u>High Tortuga, Northern Continent, City of Thon, Undisclosed Location, Institute of Education-Focused Extrajudicial Foundational Studies</u>

Kirian met the roamer, wanting some space after a long day of classes and preparing for the open house the Institute would be holding in a few weeks for potential students nominated by Dreamland and the Free School.

"Thank you for your help today, Kirian," Lerr'ek greeted. He eyed the light wheelchair Kirian used at the Institute when he'd had a full day. "Would you mind showing Charr'est to his room while I wrap up here?"

Kirian wondered if he'd looked as lost on his arrival as Charr'est did right now. "You want to go straight to your room, or do you want to hang for a while? I have time to give you the tour."

"Thanks, kid." Lerr'ek patted both males on the shoulder. "I figure you two have some talking to do. If it gets physical, no breaking my building. We clear?"

Kirian laughed. "Crystal, sir. It won't be a problem, right, Charr'est?"

"No?" Charr'est ventured. He seemed to be screwing up his courage to ask something.

"You good?" Kirian asked.

"Why are you doing this for me?" Charr'est blurted.

"That's my cue." Lerr'ek left.

Kirian whipped his chair around, balancing on the back wheels. "Where do you want to start? Classrooms? Dining hall? We'll save the training wing for tomorrow. I have PT in ninety minutes, and the AR suites deserve at least three hours to get comfortable—"

"Seriously, why?" Charr'est interjected. "After everything I've done to you. Why would you nominate me for a place here?"

"Because I needed someone on my team who can build what I ask for, and you fit that description." Kirian lowered the chair and allowed the passion that bubbled beneath his laid-back exterior to shine through. "Look, we've all known each other since we were little kids. I know what you can do with the right tools and training, and I know you have something to prove."

Charr'est bristled. "What do you mean, I have something to prove?"

"You need to prove to yourself that you're worth the chance you now have. I'm not going to let what you did with Dex slide, but neither will I hold it against you. We have a new start and an opportunity to help shape our world for the better. I'm willing to do whatever it takes to make the most of it, including letting go of the past for the sake of the future. Are you?"

Charr'est stood straighter and offered Kirian his hand. "Call me Charr."

Kirian's wrist-holo pinged before he could respond. He read the message and winced. "My PT session got moved up. Come sit in, and we'll hit the kitchens after Doc is done putting me through my paces. Unless you want some space?"

"I'm good," Charr'est assured him. "Doctor Ericson is the physical trainer, right?"

"Yeah, and she doubles as the Institute's primary physician. We'll go via the dorms so you can drop off your gear."

They made a quick detour so Charr'est could drop off his bags, and Kirian switched to his combat chair.

Their entrance echoed in the empty gym. Kirian brought the modded wheelchair to a stop and transferred to the reclining chair in which he was given the nanocyte solution during every session.

"Sit anywhere," he told Charr'est. "This first part will be pretty boring, so you can ask questions if you have any."

"Is the rumor true that Baba Yaga killed Dex and his family?" Charr'est asked. "They just vanished."

Kirian couldn't help the laugh that escaped. "They were assholes, but they didn't deserve to die."

"They took Dex to the Empire. No one died," Doc Ericson informed them as she walked into the gym.

Charr'est paused before asking, "Where are the other students?"

Twenty minutes and a half-dozen questions later, Kirian's eyes were alight with anticipation as he waited for Doc Ericson to unhook him from the IV. He slid into the combat wheelchair and ran his fingers over the sleek arms before slipping the three-point harness over his head.

Marveling at the precision engineering BMW had put into its creation, Kirian couldn't help his surge of excitement. The chair was made from the same ultralight polymer as his exosuit and fully integrated with the HUD in the hood that paired with the suit for seamless maneuvering. The fusion of technology and artistry had been tailored to his needs.

He couldn't wait to test it.

"I'm looking forward to the end of the question, 'Is it ready yet?'" Doc Ericson teased. She had become more than Kirian's physical therapist. She was his friend and mentor on the long road to his rehabilitation. "Ready to kick some virtual ass today, Kirian?"

"You bet. I've been practicing in AR all week." Kirian grinned as he stuffed his head into the flexible hood.

Doc Ericson waited for him to clip the hood to the exosuit's collar plates. "They sent a couple more additions for your suit."

"What have we got, Doc?"

"This backplate. Lean forward, please." The doc held up a hexagon of blue metal and pressed it to the corresponding nexus of polymer plates between his shoulder blades.

As it had in the sim, Kirian's HUD offered the option to switch to armored mode. "And the sensor upgrade for the haptic feedback?"

"Contained in the nanocytes in your armor," Doc Ericson told him.

Kirian activated armored mode, and the six sides of the hexagon flipped out, disgorging a mass of rapidly reproducing nanocytes. They poured between the plates of his exosuit, leaving behind trails of dark blue metal that connected the polymer plates.

His exosuit transformed into a head-to-toe suit of armor. Kirian laughed with joy and some trepidation. As the nanocytes expanded, covering the precious polymer supports with a thin layer of translucent nanocarbon, the HUD offered him the option to enter training mode.

Charr'est paid rapt attention as Kirian's exosuit and chair glowed neon-blue and the holoprojectors around the mat took flight. The lights on the drones were currently red.

Letting the gentle current stimulating his muscles roll over and through him, Kirian wheeled into the center of the huge mat and cross-drew his batons from the undersides of the chair's armrests.

The lights on the drones turned green at Doc Ericson's command, and Kirian was pinned between a Shrillexian and a Zhyn. The doc caught Charr'est's concerned stare and grinned. "Whenever you're ready, Kirian."

"I'm good to—"

The Shrillexian burst into life, followed a second later by the Zhyn. Both males were close to fully mature, dwarfing the skinny human boy in the wheelchair. Neither expected his chair wheels to sprout blades of burning energy.

Kirian spun and angled the chair to take the Shrillexian out at the knee. He focused on using his body weight to stay balanced on one wheel while he brought his batons around to electrocute the Zhyn.

His second opponent down for now, Kirian returned his attention to the Shrillexian, who had struggled to his remaining foot to launch at Kirian.

Kirian dropped his batons into his lap and grabbed the chair, but he wasn't fast enough to evade the mass of bleeding fury. He surrendered to fate.

The Shrillexian plowed into him hard enough to bruise his ribs. Kirian allowed the momentum to take the chair down, tucking his feet into the Shrillexian's stomach as they fell. Mind and body in perfect sync, Kirian pushed hard with both feet at the apex of their arc, and his confidence soared. The limitations he'd lived with his whole life faded into the background.

"Nice form, Kirian!" Doc Ericson praised as he rolled to his feet. "Don't let your guard drop."

Kirian wound up at the waist and lashed out with his right foot.

Charr'est cheered as he executed a flawless strike. His holographic opponent vanished in a burst of pixels. "I need to know what that suit is doing for you!"

"Mostly zapping me as I move to stimulate my muscle growth." Kirian beamed with pride. "Thanks, Charr, but I couldn't have done any of this without Doc's guidance and the tech that assists me."

"Would you like to join us for the next set of exercises?" Doc Ericson asked. "It helps to have someone else holding the pads."

Kirian discovered that he enjoyed Charr'est's company when he was being himself. Their banter flowed effortlessly as they moved through the exercises. The nascent bond between them grew stronger as Doc Ericson talked them through each technique.

Kirian opened up, sharing stories of his past exploits and dreams for the future. Charr'est offered encouragement and ideas that supported Kirian's vision.

As the session drew to a close, Kirian's muscles buzzed with fatigue. Charr'est went to his room, and as Kirian lay back in the hyperbaric chamber, gratitude swelled within him. Doc Ericson departed, leaving Kirian alone with his thoughts. The Institute would become a community for like-minded individuals, a sanctuary for those who needed one, and a home away from home for everyone who ended up here.

Despite the challenges he faced, with the right people by his side, anything was possible. As he gazed at the holographic display above his head, he was hopeful about the future. Surrounded by friends and fueled by determination, Kirian was unstoppable.

CHAPTER NINE

<u>The Etheric</u>

Bethany Anne stalked through the Etheric, mist eddying around her ankles. A thin, broken line of darker gray hinted at a disturbance in the distance. Pinpricks of light flashed and illuminated the snaking false horizon. Bethany Anne realized she was looking at storm fronts light-years away from her location.

In the direction of the Empire.

Her mind went to using storms as defenses against Kurtherian attacks from the Etheric. Her second thought came straight from her heart. *A few tiny storms are not going to become an issue, right?*

>>You are aware of Newton's Laws.<<

Not the time, ADAM. You are not the only visitor this plane gets, TOM reminded her.

I affect the Etheric just by being here. Did I cause a permanent change?

Who knows? TOM answered truthfully. **No one has ever exerted control over the Etheric on the scale you have.**

>>That is because no one we know of has ever had the ability to manipulate Etheric energy on the scale BA can.<<

That's what has me concerned.

>>Without more data to extrapolate from, I can't say with certainty whether the storms are a natural phenomenon or if they were caused by a reaction to the massive volumes of energy you have been manipulating on your recent visits.<<

Maybe using the Etheric as a substitute scream pillow wasn't my best move, but there has to be some way I can process how I'm feeling without holding back. Her roving gaze landed on the dark spot she was looking for. *One problem at a time. Thankfully, this one is easily solved.*

Carrash had wandered into a huge bank of mist and was blundering about aimlessly, calling for help. Bethany Anne broke into a run, shot past the Zhyn, and ground to a halt. She released and reversed the energy in her trail like a whip crack, and Carrash dropped to his hands and knees.

Baba Yaga opened the folded sheet of paper she'd gotten from Stephen as Carrash stumbled to his feet. "Dislocations to the shoulder and jaw. Fractured orbital socket. Broken wrist. Broken ulna. Cracked ribs, cracked ribs again. Wouldn't you know, it's on here four more times."

Dehydrated and confused, Carrash stared dumbly at Baba Yaga. His eyes were wide with terror, and his body shook, stuck in freeze mode.

"Dislocated elbow. Broken wrist. Cracked and broken ribs. More bruises and other minor injuries than I care to list. Sprained ankles, dozens of broken fingers, toes, and another broken wrist."

Baba Yaga looked up. "For a male who claims to love his family, you did a piss-poor job of protecting them from harm. All those injuries are from the last six cycles. If I went farther back, I'd need a damn secretary to keep track of how many times you put your wife and son in the hospital. You hurt them just enough to get your kicks."

"I didn't mean to. I don't know my own strength sometimes."

She backhanded him, her measured strike fracturing the bone around his right eye and dislocating his jaw. "Please, go ahead with your excuses. I'd love for you to make this harder on yourself."

She picked him up one-handed by the clavicle, dislocating his shoulder. Carrash screamed when she grasped the wrist on the same side as the shoulder injury and *pulled*, separating his elbow joint and crushing the delicate bones in his wrist.

The returning mists muffled his sobbed apologies. He could be as sorry as he liked. It meant nothing to Baba Yaga. She methodically worked her way through the injuries recorded on hospital visits and by the faculty at the Free School.

When she had reached the end, Carrash's pleas for mercy had trickled into silence.

High Tortuga, Northern Continent, City of Thon, Undisclosed Location, Institute of Education-Focused Extrajudicial Foundational Studies

"This will be our last session this week," Jennifer told Kirian as she closed the hyperbaric chamber's door. "Stephen and I need to be at Bethany Anne's side for the big move. You'll only miss one session. I arranged for you and Charr'est to get some hand-to-hand training in its place."

"Cool!" Kirian grinned. "Guess I already gave away the element of surprise. Wait, you're going too?" He wasn't sure whether to be sad he was missing out on a trip to the Empire or glad to get a break from PT. "Moving an Annex Gate is a pretty cool reason to be there."

"Not happening." Doc Ericson grinned. "We'll be back in time for the open house. I promise. We need you here to keep Lerr'ek sane."

"I can't make any promises about his sanity," Kirian told her with a straight face. "The open house is getting closer, and he would be losing hair if he had any to lose."

"The Institute hired three new faculty and staff members this week," Doc Ericson reminded him.

"Which means onboarding for the new staff on top of everything else," Kirian grumbled in a passable imitation of his principal. "I hope one of those new people is an assistant."

"Better than an assistant, although Lerr'ek sorely needs one. An administrator from the Etheric Academy, Tel'ah Friday. She arrives tomorrow. The others will get here just before the Institute opens its doors."

Kirian imagined a homely battleax like Ms. Bzant with the decades of experience needed to help the professor build a school from the ground up. She had her work cut out for her.

Free for the rest of the day, Kirian decided to find Charr'est and make the most of their unlimited access to the AR suites before new students' arrival curtailed their gaming time.

Cerebro answered when Kirian called Charr'est from his dorm.

"Charr'est is currently taking an exam. His holo is on Do Not Disturb."

"How long until he's done?" Kirian's gaze skipped over the pile of clean laundry that needed to be put away in favor of the scaled-down yet functional—he hoped—Black Eagle model he'd been building at his desk.

"Two hours, thirteen minutes, and twenty...seven seconds," Cerebro informed him. "Charr'est's teachers were not as insistent as your history professor. They allowed him to take the exams here at the Institute."

Kirian resigned himself to the waiting and sat at his desk. "He might be losing his mind with stress, but the prof is doing an amazing job of balancing everything he has on his plate at the moment."

Lerr'ek hung up after speaking with the event manager he'd hired to take the open house off his to-do list. He poured himself some fruit juice and leaned back in his chair.

Work smarter, not harder. Getting the planner to source everything from decorations to catering, leasing a warehouse at the edge of the city to use as a drop-off point for the deliverable items, and hiring the transport and labor from an agency that would never know they'd met the Mistress of the Planet or where the personal bonuses for their work came from. All he had to do was show up to ensure the event went smoothly.

There were enough potential students for the flight program that the competition for the thirty places the Institute offered would be fierce. The academic program was the reason for the open house. The best way to showcase the Empire's teaching method was to give a practical demonstration.

Each potential student had been sent a datapad with a restricted version of the Institute's learning program as part of their prospectus pack. They could access three modules from several hundred listed in the directory after they completed the questionnaire to determine their learning patterns, interests, and general ability to adapt to the program.

His new hires had all passed the background checks, which the Mistress assured him had been done in person. Lerr'ek wasn't sure he wanted to know more than that. He had exchanged several messages with Ms. Friday, who looked to be the savior he needed to turn this from an empty building into a thriving center for driving change.

The Mistress had laid out her plan for the future of the planet, and his part was coming along after a slow start. A knock at the door cut his moment of self-congratulation short.

"Come in," he called. Lerr'ek couldn't place the name of the man wearing monk's robes who walked in.

"Barnabas," the newcomer reminded him.

"Sorry. It's been a crazy few days." Lerr'ek stood to shake Barnabas' hand the human way. "Welcome to High Tortuga."

He wasn't sure how to broach the question of the reason for the unexpected visit.

"Bethany Anne sends her apologies along with me." Barnabas' beatific smile hid a potential for violence beyond anything Lerr'ek could imagine. "I will assist with the cleanup of the planet. But first, you have some memories that need to be erased?"

"Not yet." Lerr'ek gestured at the seating area to the left of his desk. "Can I get you anything?"

Barnabas' nose twitched, and his gaze landed on the half-empty glass on Lerr'ek's desk. "I wouldn't mind tasting whatever you are drinking, thank you."

"It's just fruit juice." Lerr'ek poured Barnabas a glass and brought his over from the desk. He took the chair opposite Barnabas and placed both glasses on the table between them. "So, the Mistress sent you to assist with setting this planet straight?"

Barnabas shook his head. "I needed to step back from my duties and work through some anger issues. I will be acting in an…independent capacity."

Lerr'ek felt the blood rush from his face. "Here in Thon?"

Barnabas laughed, deep and throaty. "You don't need to worry. By all accounts, this city doesn't require a vigilante. No, I will go farther afield. Tethra, perhaps."

Lerr'ek grimaced. "Better you than me. There's nothing out that way besides mining operations and the people who work there."

Barnabas took in Lerr'ek's immaculately cut suit and nodded. "I imagine you would be out of your comfort zone in that environment."

Lerr'ek lifted his hands. "I am where I'm supposed to be."

"Mercenary-turned-school principal. How is that working out for you?"

Lerr'ek grinned. "Pretty well so far. I had a shaky start, but things seem to be coming together. The open house will validate the legitimate part of the Institute."

"Leaving you free to manage the not-so-legitimate part?" Barnabas chuckled. "Don't mind me. I've known Bethany Anne for a *very* long time. She wouldn't have invested as much as she has into this planet if she didn't have multiple schemes in her back pocket."

Lerr'ek chuckled. "So far, her schemes have done nothing but good for this planet. I have zero concerns except for how much it would hurt to break the Mistress' rule."

"A valid concern," Barnabas amiably agreed. "I once pissed Bethany Anne off twice in a few minutes."

"And you lived to tell the tale?" Lerr'ek let out a low whistle.

It was Barnabas' turn to chuckle. "It happened back before I realized why Michael had chosen her to be our Queen. I made the mistake of questioning her love for him and repeated the question when I regained consciousness."

"Tell me about Michael." Lerr'ek tried to imagine what caliber of male could survive being mated to the Witch, Bitch, Empress, and Avatar of Justice and Death.

"Michael is..." Barnabas tilted his head, expression shifting. "The Patriarch is honor-bound, inflexible, irascible, and inexorable. He is Bethany Anne's equal and opposite, and she now has a chance to reunite with him after over one hundred and fifty years."

Lerr'ek indulged his curiosity. "What, did they have a huge fight or something?"

"He sacrificed himself to save Bethany Anne's people." Barnabas waved off Lerr'ek's apology. "I see where you are coming from. My Queen and Michael *are* stubborn enough to spend a century and a half refusing to speak to one another after a quarrel. However, she spent that time grieving his absence. Most of us believed he was dead."

He leaned forward. "I am told that you see no difference between Bethany Anne and Baba Yaga. Why?"

"Because there isn't one." This wasn't the first time Lerr'ek had had this conversation with someone from the Mistress' life who had not met her splinter personality while Baba Yaga was driving the bus. "She has the same moral framework and core values. You are all allowing the unchecked violence to color your perception."

Barnabas raised an eyebrow and stared at Lerr'ek for a long moment before he burst into laughter. "'The unchecked violence.' That's what you call the trail of bodies and destruction Baba Yaga leaves in her wake?"

Lerr'ek lifted a shoulder. "Hey, it's rough out here. Plenty of people with bodies in their wake. How many of them only take out the trash? I'll admit that the Mistress is straight-up terrifying, but I'd rather have her at my back than anyone else I know, and I'll have hers if it costs me everything."

"How much has Bethany Anne told you about her plans?" Barnabas made a little noise of understanding. "Ah, I see."

"Do you have to read my mind?" Lerr'ek asked.

"It saves time." Barnabas drained his glass and got to his feet. "Thank you for your hospitality. I will return for the open house."

Lerr'ek walked him to the door. "I appreciate your help with keeping the Institute secure."

"You have enough on your plate keeping young Kirian safe. I have one just like him." Barnabas wrinkled his nose. "Well, not *just* like him. I doubt Kirian is as obsessed with his appearance as my ward."

"I've met Tabitha." Lerr'ek chuckled. "Kirian has his own quirks. Did you meet him on your way to my office?"

Barnabas smiled and shook his head, then opened the door.

Kirian was outside with his hand poised to knock. "Hello, young man."

Running footsteps coming from the exit elevator made everyone look. Charr'est skidded to a halt at the reception desk.

"Gralen is in trouble."

"Tor wants to meet up too," Kirian added.

"That is my cue to leave," Barnabas told Lerr'ek. "I'll see myself out with your AI's assistance."

Lerr'ek nodded, his focus on the young males. "Thank you for visiting, Barnabas. I hope we meet again soon. Kids, come on in."

CHAPTER TEN

Lerr'ek settled into the chair at his desk and swept a hand at the two guest chairs opposite. "Charr'est first. Gralen is in danger?"

"I think so," Charr'est told him. "He didn't show up at the arcade this afternoon. I holoed him just now, and he looks like he was beaten with a bag of socket wrenches."

"Do you know anything about his life at home?" Kirian asked.

Charr'est shook his head. "We've been hanging at the arcade since Dex left the planet."

The information assuaged Lerr'ek's immediate concerns. "We are already working to remedy the situation for Gralen's people as a whole. Kirian?"

"I got another message from Tor while I was waiting for Charr to finish his exams."

"You waited for me?" Charr'est asked.

Kirian shrugged. "Yeah. Can't play *Dynamo 2* by myself."

"You got early access to *Dynamo 2*?"

Lerr'ek chided, "Gentlemen. Stay on track, please."

"Oh, right." Kirian's face turned red. "I came to ask for an overnight pass. I figured I'd spend the night at home after meeting with Tor."

"When?" Lerr'ek asked.

"Day after tomorrow, sir," Kirian answered. "I won't miss my scheduled therapy session."

Lerr'ek pinged Kirian's holo with the updated schedule. "See that you don't. Also, I'd like your help with the open house. A lot of these kids are coming because you're the big-shot gamer they look up to."

"Capitalizing on my name, Prof?" Kirian's eyes twinkled. "I'm kidding. Mostly. I think it would be a good idea if I went to visit Gralen at home."

"You mean if *we* went," Charr'est interjected.

"We're a team." Kirian nodded. "My bad. We should both go. He'll probably talk to you more than he would to me."

"I don't like the idea of you two alone in the undercity," Lerr'ek told them. "We'll stick with the plan. No going there without backup."

The kids' immediate acquiescence told him Kirian had already found a loophole in his decree.

"By backup, I mean an enhanced adult such as me, Jennifer, Stephen, or the Mistress. Am I clear?" The disappointment on their faces was all the answer he needed. "Good. You can both go. Enjoy your game."

He gave it a moment after the boys had left before calling Cerebro. "I want to know where Kirian and Charr'est are at any given moment. If they leave the Institute outside of their scheduled times, tell me immediately."

"You don't trust them?" Cerebro asked.

"They're half grown and out to prove themselves. I don't trust them one bit."

Kirian sighed as he and Charr'est took the elevator down to the AR suites.

"You were pretty set on checking in with Gralen," Charr'est commented.

Kirian twitched a shoulder. "I don't like what he's caught up in."

"Who hurt him?"

"Could have been anyone." Kirian's face flushed with anger. "And who knows how long it will take to break up the fight ring."

He leaned on his crutches as he left the elevator. "Keep up, Charr," he called, picking up speed as his resolution to do what he thought was right solidified.

"Fight ring?" Charr'est echoed.

"The fight ring isn't the issue. It's the greedy asshole using Shrillexian culture to push adolescent males into mercenary companies too soon to line his pockets."

"Baba Yaga won't allow that to continue, right?"

"Right, except she wants the ringleader's associates as well. Who's looking out for Gralen and all the other boys in the meantime?"

Charr'est paused with his jacket halfway to the hook on the wall beside his AR Pod. "I didn't think of it that way."

Kirian balanced the crutches against the wall and stripped off his outer layer of clothing. "I understand that ending this means stamping out the demand as well as the supply, but Gralen and Tor have been on my mind since you got here. What kind of leader does nothing while his people are suffering?"

"You take that leader thing seriously." Charr'est pressed the button to open his Pod. "You believe in the team you're putting together."

"Hells yeah, I believe in what we're going to build!" Unsupported by his crutches, Kirian leaned on his open Pod. "Baba Yaga is only a monster to those who deserve a visit from one. She's going to change this planet for the better. You think we got an opportunity handed to us for no reason? We know how hard life is here, and we're going to be part of making life on High Tortuga good for everyone."

Charr'est said nothing for a full minute. Then he climbed into his Pod. "You know, spending time with you isn't helping me decide whether you're a mad genius or just plain mad."

Kirian snorted. "Thanks, I think?"

"I'm not done." Charr'est held his Pod door open. "I'll follow you either way, just like I'll do whatever Baba Yaga asks."

"I don't want followers. I nominated you because of your skills with engines. You learned a lot in a bad environment. I want to see what you do when you're not afraid to shine."

Charr'est shook his head. "I hope I can make up for what I did to Tor. You forgave me too easy, Kirian. That's why I'll follow you. Not because I owe you, but because I admire your passion for what our team's going to do."

"I appreciate it, dude, but we're all in this together. Or we will be soon. Now, are you ready to kick some cyborg ass?" Kirian grinned and lowered his voice. "I have a nefarious plan for getting out of here to come up with, and the day isn't getting any longer."

The next day, Kirian made a show of inviting Charr'est to join him on his regular visit to Madame Richelieu's orphanage.

Cerebro took a few seconds to generate a pass for Charr'est, leaving both boys hanging. Maybe it was because they knew they were at risk of having the plan fail, but it seemed like an eternity before Charr'est's wrist-holo pinged with his permission to use the exit elevator and roamers.

Kirian and Charr'est exited and packed Kirian's chair into a roamer. "Why do you need the chair?" Charr'est asked as they climbed into the vehicle.

"To conserve energy." Kirian thumbed the comm switch on the dash. "Orphanage, please, Cerebro."

"I know," the AI snarked. "I just created your passes."

"Well, excuse me for being polite," Kirian retorted good-naturedly. "I suppose I shouldn't bother asking you to be ready to take us back to the Institute three hours after we arrive."

"That information is actually helpful," Cerebro conceded. "Is there a reason for the extra hour?"

Kirian winced internally. "Um, no. No reason."

"As you wish," the Al intoned. "You usually spend two hours at the orphanage and the rest of the day at the arcade."

"The gang isn't meeting today." Kirian glanced at Charr'est. "We could hit the arcade after this if you like." The look he shot at Charr'est said to say yes.

"Sure, if you don't mind being seen with me outside the Institute."

Kirian rolled his eyes but gave Charr'est a surreptitious thumbs-up. "Guess we'll call when we're done at Dreamland," he told Cerebro.

***

Lerr'ek picked up Cerebro's call. "You were right. The boys are plotting," the Al informed him.

That hadn't taken long. Lerr'ek grinned. "Please inform Jennifer that she owes me fifty credits. Oh, and keep a drone on the boys. I want to know when they enter the undercity."

"So you can prevent them from endangering themselves?"

Lerr'ek shook his head. "That's not how the Mistress would handle this. No, I'll give them enough rope to either pull themselves out of whatever hole they end up in or hang themselves. What they choose is up to them."

Gralen was not at the arcade. Braving public transport, Kirian was grateful for his chair as they rode the tram to the edge of the sector where the access to the undercity was located.

They took the sloping ramp outside the tram station and headed into the graffitied subway. The last time Kirian had been down here, he'd been filled with the thrill of brushing up against danger. However, despite the training he'd had, venturing through the arch that marked the border between the over and under cities put him on maximum alert beneath the nonchalance he projected.

"Which way?" Charr'est asked when they reached the nexus of tunnels at the foot of the ramp. Kirian pulled up the route on his wrist-holo. "I made this back when I didn't know I would have adults helping. The place where the fights are held is around thirty minutes' walk from here."

Without either noticing the drone following them, they embarked upon their journey into the undercity. The strip lighting overhead washed everything out, their false luminescence failing to match the warmth of natural light. Kirian sent his chair forward before he lost his nerve and did a one-eighty to get away from the blank stares of the people around them.

The tunnels remained the same diameter. However, the stark differences in the art covering the walls created an illusion of expansion and contraction. Not an inch of bare permacrete remained. Bright scenes of nature, celebrations of community pride, and defiant declarations of the type made by oppressed people the universe over competed for space with hastily painted slogans, gang emblems, declarations in jagged letters, and bleak images depicting life underground.

The art comforted Kirian. *People* made art. He realized he'd given the undercity a status of otherness. This place wasn't unknown. It was dangerous, sure, but no more so than the part of the city he lived in now that Baba Yaga had the worst of the gangs under control.

Charr'est had remained quiet while Kirian was finding his courage. He turned his head and murmured to Kirian, "Are you sure you know where we're going? They don't seem to like us being down here."

"It's my chair," Kirian told him. "People with severe disabilities don't make it down here unless they have family to take care of them."

"How do you know that?" Charr'est asked.

"The kids at the orphanage. Most of them had never seen a wheelchair before meeting me." Kirian checked the map on his wrist-holo and indicated one of the cross tunnels ahead. "That's where we're going."

The next sub-level had none of the cheer of the upper tunnels. These were the sewers, the gas and power lines, and the maintenance tunnels. They twisted and turned, opening into huge, abandoned spaces.

Kirian's imagination went wild as to their purpose. "Smuggler hideouts. That's got to be it. Storage for contraband being smuggled off-world."

Just like the last four suggestions, Charr'est shook his head. "Fun, but it's not right."

"Then what?" Kirian asked.

"I saw this holovid when I was a kid about how the city was built. The upper tunnels were supposed to be shelters in the event of an emergency. We're on the maintenance level now. They had a dozen crews for each sector, and all of them lived underground for the duration of construction. The open spaces are their campsites."

Kirian sucked in a breath. "Okay, that's cooler than anything I came up with."

Charr'est chuckled. "I don't know. I liked your giant mole-bug theory."

"It could happen," Kirian protested. "You never know what's lurking just out of sight."

Kirian was proved right when they reached the end of the current tunnel and almost stumbled into the backs of many Shrillexians baying at the boys fighting in the center of the ring they had formed.

Kirian almost couldn't believe their luck until one of the adult males turned and spotted them.

"Hey, what are you doing down here?" he yelled, grabbing Charr'est by the arm.

"Let him go!" Kirian tried ramming the male's legs with his chair, but the tower of fully developed muscle wasn't affected.

They were drawing attention to themselves. More males turned to see what the commotion at the back was, and several called for Joryan, making it easy for Kirian to identify the male pushing toward them through the crowd. He was tall like the others. The main difference was the extra weight he carried around his midsection. The other males were all in fighting condition, as a Shrillexian should be. Kirian deduced that it had been a long time since the male had wondered where his next meal was coming from, unlike many of his followers.

Joryan looked them over, and his initial confusion was replaced by an expression of cruel amusement. "What are a couple of surface-dwelling kids doing down here? Didn't your mommies ever tell you it's dangerous in the undercity?"

That got a laugh from the crowd. Kirian had no choice but to acknowledge to himself that they were way out of their depth, but they were here now. It made no sense to turn tail and run when they were so close to finding Gralen.

"Well, boys?" Joryan mocked. "Alict got your tongues?"

"We came to find our friend." Kirian managed to keep his voice steady and maintain eye contact with Joryan.

"Oh, you have a *friend* here?" Joryan turned to the crowd, focusing his attention on the boys gathered at the far side of the makeshift fighting ring. "Anyone here want to claim these two as friends?"

Kirian spotted Gralen, who was looking at him and Charr'est like they'd sprouted an extra head apiece. Gralen shook his head minutely, so Kirian knew the other male would deny knowing them if asked.

Joryan continued, "See, boys, I think you are a pair of lookie-loo rich kids come to see what we live like down here in the slums. You know what we do to lookie-loos?"

Charr'est wilted beside Kirian, subdued by the huge Shrillexian's barely concealed aggression. Kirian swallowed his nerves and hoped his grin was enough to mollify Joryan. "You're going to let us hang out with you and watch the fight?"

Joryan's answering laugh shook his generous midriff like jelly. "Nice try, boy, but no. Randro, Halmish, show our guests to the cells."

Kirian didn't know whether the Shrillexian who plucked him from his chair like he weighed no more than a feather was Randro or Halmish. Whichever it was, he tasted like ass, which Kirian discovered as he fought tooth and nail to break the hold.

"The little shit *bit* me!" Randro-or-Halmish complained.

Kirian spat the male's blood on the sandy floor. "Put me down, or I'll keep biting, asshole."

Randro-or-Halmish cursed and flung Kirian over his shoulder in a fireman's carry, and fear gripped Kirian. Charr'est was out of sight, but Kirian could hear that he wasn't making it easy for his captor.

"You're making a huge mistake," Charr'est stated. "Baba Yaga will have your heads if you hurt us."

Kirian cringed at the sound of an open-handed slap and Charr'est's yell of protest.

"There's plenty more where that came from if you don't shut your yap and walk." Halmish-or-Randro grunted.

They were stripped of their wrist-holos and other belongings before being shoved into a small, windowless room. The single bulb overhead gave little light, but they could see that the only item in the room was a bucket in the corner, presumably to be used for their bathroom needs.

"Let's see the Witch-bitch get you out of *this*," one of the males taunted as he slammed the door.

Kirian wasn't completely helpless, thanks to his exosuit, but he had never been at the mercy of adults who were a threat to his safety. He huddled against the wall with his arms wrapped around his knees, shaking as his shock faded and the full extent of their situation hit him.

"No one knows where we are," he murmured to Charr'est.

"Hey, hold it together," Charr'est encouraged. "It won't take a genius to figure out we came down here."

Kirian wished he hadn't gotten them into this. "What do you think they're going to do with us?"

Charr'est's shrug was barely perceptible in the dim light. "I don't know, but they would have killed us already if they were going to." He laughed, the sound devoid of humor. "Maybe they're going to make us fight. All that training we do has to come in handy at some point, right?"

Kirian closed his eyes and rested his head on his arms. "We can't fight all of them. But we won't go down easy."

"What do you mean, you *lost* them?" Lerr'ek demanded.

"The Shrillexians spotted my drone and destroyed it," Cerebro clarified. "I was able to discern the direction they were taken before I lost the drone."

Lerr'ek considered going down there with a few "associates," then thought better of it. "Call Stephen."

Stephen answered almost immediately. "What's wrong?"

"Perceptive. Kirian and Charr'est went against my explicit instructions and were captured by Joryan and his enforcers."

"They *what*?"

Lerr'ek winced at the Mistress' harsh tone as she jumped into the conversation. "I'll tear anyone who lays a finger on those boys limb from limb," he vowed. "However, I would like to know I'm not in the undercity without sufficient backup."

"Stephen and Jennifer will leave the party and be with you by nightfall," Bethany Anne told him.

"Party, Mistress?" Lerr'ek inquired.

"We are celebrating the end of my reign." Bethany Anne still sounded pissed off. "I can't leave right now. I need to be here in case anyone decides I'm less scary now that I've demoted myself and tries to pull a fast one while the Empire becomes a Federation."

"They can try, my Queen," Stephen rumbled.

"I don't mind if they do. Better that the worms crawl out of the woodwork sooner rather than later. Besides, I'm still investigating the mercenary companies associated with Joryan. That shit-for-morals, toilet water-drinking fucksack is smart enough to have legitimate contracts with some of them, and I don't want him being alerted to my investigation until I'm ready to play judge, jury, and executioner on his whole operation."

Lerr'ek saw the wisdom in that. "Stephen, how long will it take you and Jennifer to get back here?"

"A few hours at most."

"Then I'll send a bunch of drones down there and make a full assessment of the situation. Nock and I will be ready to move the moment you arrive unless the kids are in immediate danger."

CHAPTER ELEVEN

<u>High Tortuga, Northern Continent, City of Thon, Undercity</u>

A noise outside the door woke Kirian from the light sleep he'd fallen into after hours of nothing happening.

Gralen's voice came from the other side of the thick metal. "What are you doing here? Together?"

"We came for you." Kirian's voice cracked. He was dehydrated, and his mouth and lips were filmy with his need for water.

"Yeah." Charr'est was doing a little better, but not much. "You might have a head filled with rocks, but you were pretty banged up the other day. I was worried about you when we found out you hadn't been at school."

"That doesn't explain why you're here together," Gralen pointed out.

"I took the offer from the Institute," Charr'est told him. "It was Kirian who nominated us both for the scholarship."

"What? Why?" Gralen didn't try to hide his surprise.

"Because I want you both on my team," Kirian croaked. "I'm guessing you haven't had access to the serum since you haven't been at school. I've never seen you so beat up before."

Gralen laughed bitterly. "No kidding. That Zhyn guy caused trouble I wasn't expecting. Wanting to switch schools is apparently getting ideas above my station."

"I feel that." Charr'est growled at the memory. "My father said the same thing and all but knocked the idea out of me."

"I thought you transferred?" Gralen asked in confusion.

"I did," Charr'est confirmed. "We had a visit from Baba Yaga. My pops isn't a problem anymore."

Gralen sighed. "I wish the Witch had visited here. I ship out next week. No more school for me."

The fear paralyzing Kirian vanished, replaced by burning anger. "That's not right. You're not old enough to contract with a mercenary company!"

"I will be next week." Gralen sighed. "Joryan says I've had enough time to get an education, and I have to do more for the community than play with numbers."

"That's rough, buddy," Charr'est commiserated. "You're as trapped as we are. You just avoided being locked up in here."

"Can you get us out of this room?" Kirian asked. "We'll get you to the Institute where it's safe."

"No can do," Gralen apologized. "I wish I could, but it's a biometric lock. Only Joryan or his overseers can open the door."

The small hope Kirian had allowed himself faded, plunging him back into despair.

"You can get word to our principal, right?" Charr'est asked. "That would be enough to save us from whatever Joryan has planned."

There was a long moment of silence from the other side of the door before Gralen spoke again. "I'll do my best. Trespassers are usually thrown in the ring with the stronger fighters. Joryan says it's good practice for the real thing."

Kirian had an idea what Gralen meant, but he had to ask. "The real thing?"

"Killing," Gralen clarified. "We're too valuable to waste. Strangers, though…"

Kirian swallowed hard, meeting Charr'est's identical stare of horror. "Gralen, how long do we have?"

"I don't know," Gralen answered in a dull voice. "I hear someone coming. I have to go before I get caught talking to you."

Too late. A familiar voice asked Gralen what he was doing.

"Joryan!" Gralen smoothly feigned embarrassment. "You caught me sizing up the fresh meat."

The adult male laughed. "Fresh meat, huh? You're eager for some experience at killing before you ship out? I always said you were a smart one, Gralen. You'll do your father and our people proud with the company who hired you."

"They'll be in the ring tonight?" Gralen asked.

"Well, I won't be wasting food on keeping them prisoner," Joryan replied snidely. "Come with me. I have a job for you. Do well, and I'll see that you get a shot at the Zhyn."

"What about the human?" Gralen asked.

Joryan made a sound of dismissal. "That weak creature is only useful as a punching bag for the youngers. You're better than that, son. A warrior in the making."

They heard the slap of a hand on Gralen's back, and Kirian saw a matching look of disgust and fear on Charr'est's face. A moment later, the hatch at the base of the door scraped, and a band of light shone across the floor. It was quickly blocked by a tray being shoved into their cell. The hatch slammed shut again, returning them to the murky light from the bulb overhead.

"Eat up, boys," Joryan called. "You'll need your strength for what's coming."

The Shrillexians' footsteps receded, leaving them in silence once more. Charr'est picked up the tray and placed it on the bare floor between them. Too hungry and thirsty to care what they had been given, they divided the bread and some kind of cheese and took turns drinking from the flask of water.

"I don't want to face Gralen," Charr'est admitted as he broke off a piece of bread. "I don't want to kill anyone, either."

Kirian closed his eyes, sickened by the thought of being pitted against children. "I get you, but unless Gralen can tell someone we're here, I don't think we'll have much choice."

"This isn't what I imagined when we decided to come down here." Charr'est stilled, horror dawning on him. "Oh, stars. If we don't get out of this, who will tell my mother what happened to me?"

Kirian lightly punched his arm. "Hey, don't think like that."

"How?" Charr'est asked. "If Baba Yaga was here, she could find us, but she's not. We haven't seen her for almost a cycle."

"Be…uh, Baba Yaga might not be here, but Stephen and Doc Ericson are," Kirian assured him. "The prof will have had Cerebro looking for us from the moment he realized we weren't at the arcade. They'll come for us whether or not Gralen manages to get a message out. We just have to stay calm and hold on."

That was easier said than done. The hours ticked by with excruciating slowness, made worse by the lack of any way to discern how much time had passed. Kirian drifted off with his back against the wall, exhausted by the unrelenting tension of the unknown. He napped fitfully, his dreams filled with disjointed scenes of Tor running from some unseen enemy, his mom crying as Baba Yaga told her he was dead, and tiny Shrillexians coming at him with toy weapons.

Charr'est shook him awake. Kirian came to with a start, disoriented until he remembered where he was. He sighed and groaned as he stretched the knotted ropes that had replaced his muscles while he slumped against the wall.

"You doing okay?" Charr'est asked.

"About as well as can be expected given our predicament. I wouldn't say no to three pain patches and, oh, I don't know, our rescue party showing up. Was I asleep for long?"

Charr'est shrugged. "You were out a while. You were talking in your sleep."

"I'd rather forget it," Kirian confessed. "You should get some rest. I'll wake you if anything happens."

Charr'est nodded and lay down with his back to the wall. "I don't know if I can sleep, knowing we're going to have to fight for our lives. I deserve it on some level, but you never did anything to warrant being treated this way."

Kirian was shocked into silence. "What? No! No one deserves this. Not us, and not the kids Joryan manipulates into this. I read up on Shrillexian culture. Joryan is supposed to protect those boys while he trains them for war. He's not supposed to have them killing people for kicks before sending them off before they're ready to fight for real."

"It's twisted," Charr'est agreed. "I knew Gralen was going to leave this planet to go fight, but does he?"

Kirian shook his head. "I don't know. There's an old Earth saying. 'Grow up in a house on fire, and flames seem normal.' He might know that things aren't right on some level, but he's never known any different. I wonder what the males who deployed before Joryan took control would say if they knew what was happening here. There weren't many adults in the training area."

"You think the majority know?" Charr'est wondered. "Maybe Joryan's sneaky enough to have found a way to keep the dirty details from the rest of the community."

Kirian considered that. "Maybe. Pride and honor are good ideals, but they can be used against people." He hesitated to open up and tell Charr'est the truth about the spying but decided it was better to come clean. "Look, you're not going to like this, but before we put Dex in that sim, we spent some time watching you all."

Charr'est abruptly sat up. "You did *what?*"

Kirian sighed. "We wanted to know what your weaknesses were so we could use them to teach you all a lesson. What we found…well, you know your own life. Gralen is highly thought of among his people. He might seem rough and tough, but he spends his free time taking care of others."

Charr'est's anger faded as Kirian told him about Gralen's efforts to assist the females and children in his community. "He's a brawler, but he's also a protector and role model," Kirian finished. "I wanted him for the team because I saw his loyalty and dedication."

"I still don't get why you wanted me." Charr'est's embarrassment colored his face. "You couldn't have seen anything good in my family."

"I saw you divert your father's temper away from your mother." Kirian didn't allow any pity into his voice. "I don't know much about mechanics, but I know talent when I see it. I'm sorry I spied on you."

Charr'est shook his head. "For what it's worth, I'm glad you did. No matter what happens to us, my mother is safe now. I just… I'd started to believe I had a good life ahead of me. More than being bullied by my dad while I worked for him. I wanted…"

"Go ahead," Kirian prompted.

Charr'est sighed. "I wanted to work on starships. There was going to be more than maintaining personal vehicles. My curriculum has me working toward the design and maintenance of QBS ships. Do you know what I'd give to get my hands dirty on that tech?"

Kirian grinned. "The same things I would to work with Etheric Empire communications and gaming tech? Every bit of me."

"Yeah, something like that." Charr'est lay back down and closed his eyes. "I shouldn't have gotten my hopes up."

"Hey," Kirian admonished. "Always hope. You are going to get the chance to work on those big-ass ships. I'm going to get a cool cover as a developer to conceal everything I do to find us assignments. This is our first mission, and we fucked it up. Things sometimes go sideways. Next time, we'll be ready."

Charr'est chuckled without opening his eyes. "If that's true, you'll be a great leader when you're not getting us into life-or-death situations."

His words stuck with Kirian as Charr'est went to sleep. Despite his assurance, he didn't feel like a good leader right now. While he had absolute faith that the professor would get them out of this, tearing headlong into danger without a plan or a safety net was not the action of someone who had the safety of the people he was responsible for at the forefront of his mind.

If he had one regret, it was not trusting that the professor would listen if he had explained why he'd wanted to come down. Rather than berate himself for his error, Kirian gamed the situation in his mind, considering the ways he could have done this better.

Coming to the training grounds alone had been a huge mistake. Had he considered the situation instead of rushing in, looking for Gralen at home would have been the optimal plan. He also resolved to set up an emergency alert as a backup when they got out of this. It wouldn't be much of a challenge to program their wrist-holos to alert the professor to their location if they didn't register their owners' biometric signatures for longer than five minutes.

Strangely, he was more bothered about hurting the young Shrillexians he would be pitted against than about his combat performance. Fighting multiple opponents was never an ideal situation, but he had trained extensively for it, and Joryan's minions hadn't realized he was wearing an exosuit, so they hadn't taken it from him.

Fighting for real would hurt, but he'd had months of training hard and long and could take the hits and keep going. He had come a long way from the days when he was helpless without his chair, and no pain could be worse than what his body had inflicted on him before he'd started the nanocyte treatments.

Additionally, Shrillexians became proficient in hand-to-hand combat before being allowed weapons. Young fighters wouldn't be armed, no matter what his brain had told him while he was sleeping. He might have a moral objection to hurting children, but he had a self-preservation objection to allowing the younger adolescents to use him as a punching bag like Joryan intended.

Charr'est had the harder challenge ahead. Gralen's prowess in the ring was well known, so he was often matched with the oldest and most experienced males, which was why he was so frequently badly injured. He was fighting at a professional level as he was pushed to be ready for the mercenary company that had contracted with Joryan for his services. He couldn't hold back without alerting Joryan and potentially increasing the danger to the Zhyn.

He could only think of one way to protect Charr'est, and it wouldn't be pretty. Footsteps pulled Kirian from his thoughts. He scooted over and gently shook Charr'est. "Someone's coming," he whispered.

Bright light lanced their eyes when the door opened. "Out," Joryan commanded.

Kirian raised his chin in defiance. "Make me."

Joryan stepped into the room, glowering. "You've got balls for a cripple. I'll give you...*OW!*" he yelled as Kirian drove his foot into his instep. His amusement turned to anger.

"What are you doing?" Charr'est hissed.

"Saving your ass," Kirian responded, ducking Joryan's attempt to grab him. "Run!"

They darted into the tunnel...and ran into two adult males waiting outside the door. Anger at the injustice of their situation flooded Kirian, and he fought the male who grabbed him. However, his efforts to free himself from the Shrillexian's grip on the back of his neck did little to annoy his captor, who simply held him at arm's length to avoid being kicked, punched, and bitten.

Joryan laughed at the struggling boys. "Save it for the ring." He appraised Kirian with increased interest. "I underestimated you, human. You can be Gralen's warmup."

He turned to the guard holding Kirian's chair. "Leave that. He obviously doesn't need it."

"Actually, I do," Kirian stated coldly. "Unless you want me to collapse instead of fight."

Joryan narrowed his eyes. "You stood pretty well just then."

"And now I need my chair."

Joryan lifted a shoulder. "Fine, whatever. You can have it until you get into the ring."

Kirian hid his elation at having access to the weapons hidden in his chair. He didn't like what he would have to do to protect Charr'est, but he prioritized the safety of his team member over that of the person he hoped to recruit.

Besides, he needed to prove to Gralen that he was worthy of his respect, and the only way to do that with a Shrillexian was to hand their ass to them.

They were returned to the training area with the guards' meaty hands driving them. The trainees were hard at work, sparring in pairs. Joryan clapped loudly and called for their attention.

Thirty-some pairs of eyes raked Kirian and Charr'est with interest and anticipation.

Joryan announced, "Tonight, we celebrate the blooding of Gralen. In honor of his acceptance into one of the most prestigious companies, he will take on the human and the Zhyn to prove his worthiness to us all."

A cheer went up, half-feral and totally aggressive. Gralen stepped into the circle the boys formed. Kirian glanced at Charr'est, who seemed to have gotten over his earlier nerves about fighting his friend.

"We can do this together," the Zhyn mouthed to Kirian.

"Follow my lead," Kirian murmured as they were shoved into the circle.

He caught Gralen's eye and raised an eyebrow in question. His hopes were dashed when the larger boy shook his head to indicate that he had not been able to get a message to Professor Lerr'ek.

Well, shit.

CHAPTER TWELVE

"Don't hold back," Kirian told Gralen and Charr'est as the three of them faced off across the sawdust-strewn permacrete.

Gralen frowned. "You want me to make it quick?"

Kirian got up from his chair. "Who said you're going to beat us? Things have changed since we last met."

"You're not falling over," Gralen pointed out with curiosity. "I figured."

Kirian stepped to the left, and Charr'est took the right as they'd practiced in training. Cheers and jeers echoed off the open space's vaulted ceiling, raising Kirian's adrenaline. His exosuit responded, adding the tingle of its draw on the Etheric to the buzz in his thrumming veins.

There was no easy way to win this fight. Gralen outweighed them both, and he had them on reach and experience. However, Kirian knew his weakness. As they circled, sizing each other up, Kirian saw he was favoring his left side, telegraphing that he had an injury to his ribs.

He recalled his training. An enemy who can't stand can't fight. An enemy who can't see can't fight. An enemy who can't breathe can't fight.

Gralen made his first mistake when he focused on Charr'est. Kirian got the opening he was waiting for a moment later when Gralen swung a fist to test Charr'est's reaction. Charr'est ducked and stepped back, and Kirian darted in and landed a solid punch to Gralen's ribs.

Gralen was fast, and to his credit, the only sign that Kirian's blow had landed was a slight creasing of his eyes as he caught Kirian with a leg sweep. Kirian landed hard on his ass but used his momentum to roll and regain his fighting stance. As he tired, his exosuit would give him more power. The next few minutes went by in a blur. Kirian and Charr'est took as many hits as they landed, but it became clear that all the holo-training in the world could not compare to a real fight for their lives.

The pain Kirian had expected lanced through his body, and fireworks exploded in his joints despite the support from his exosuit. However, the reprieve his nanocyte treatment had given him had not erased his lifetime of experience. If there was one thing Kirian was an expert at, it was keeping himself going when his body betrayed him.

Charr'est found his rhythm, and they worked in tandem, one dealing out hits while the other took them to keep Gralen distracted. All they had to do was hold out until Gralen was tired enough to make a mistake.

Kirian learned too late that even that wouldn't be enough. He landed a kick that should have dislocated Gralen's knee, but the Shrillexian backhanded him and continued stalking Charr'est with the red rage of battle in his eyes.

"Fight the rage." Charr'est brought his arms up to break Gralen's grip on his atmosuit and skipped back to avoid the incoming headbutt. "Fight it, not us."

Without the serum, Gralen's natural inclination toward violence was beating his desire to avoid hurting his closest friend.

Gralen shoulder-checked Kirian, then threw a vicious elbow

into his temple as he sprawled in the sawdust. Kirian's vision blurred and swam from the double impact of hitting his head as he went down. He rolled onto his stomach, his entire body reduced to one jarred nerve ending. He was certain that the elbow he'd taken to the temple would be the last hit he took.

"ENOUGH!" The command was laced with the compulsion to obey or die, and it stunned the crowd into silence.

Certain that he was unconscious and dreaming, Kirian looked around. He saw Stephen, Doc Ericson, and the professor stalking toward them from the tunnel Kirian and Charr'est had entered by hours earlier. Should he feel dizzy if he was unconscious?

Confusion battling his concussion, Kirian's vision faded to black.

***

"You are trespassing," Joryan told the two humans and the Zhyn.

"And you are a morally reprehensible excuse for a Shrillexian," Stephen retorted. He looked at Jennifer. "Please retrieve the kids while I deal with this pathetic little male."

"You will not retrieve anything." Joryan blocked Jennifer's path. He gasped when she shoved him aside and went to kneel by Kirian.

"He needs a Pod-doc." She took a quick look at Charr'est's and Gralen's injuries. "They all do."

"They are trespassers, and I am within my rights to do as I please with them," Joryan yelled. "You can't just come down here!" The tension in the atmosphere ratcheted higher as the young Shrillexian males coiled to strike at a word from their mentor.

"Can I kill him now?" Lerr'ek asked.

Stephen shook his head. "Killing him will set those males into a frenzy, and I'd rather we weren't forced to hurt children."

"Not if I challenge him," Lerr'ek pointed out. He handed his suit jacket to Stephen and rolled up his shirt sleeves. "I guess we will just have to see about that, Joryan. These kids are under my care, and I refuse to allow scum like you to endanger them a moment longer. Either you let them leave, or I will make you."

"I have a better idea," Joryan sneered. "Randro, Halmish, take this trash out."

His henchmen moved toward Lerr'ek, and Stephen's eyes flashed red as he *pushed* a wave of fear that stopped them in their tracks. "You have two choices, Joryan. Accept Lerr'ek's challenge, or allow the males who look up to you to see you for the coward you are."

The trainees looked at their leader. Joryan scoffed. "You think you can take me in a fight? Fine, but when I win, you three will join those two." He pointed at Kirian and Charr'est, who was holding Kirian's hand and whispering for him to wake up.

Stephen moved beside them, his hard expression daring anyone who lacked the instinct for self-preservation to approach. "You're sure about this?" he asked Lerr'ek.

"I'm sure. Unless you changed your mind about killing him and dealing with the Mistress' displeasure afterward."

"Not on either of our lives," Stephen replied with a wry smile.

The circle reformed as Lerr'ek and Joryan faced off, which let Jennifer carry Kirian to the side and treat his and Charr'est's injuries.

Joryan came at Lerr'ek with his arms outstretched to leverage his size and weight advantage.

Lerr'ek sidestepped the cocky attempt at bringing him down and drove a fist into the Shrillexian's jaw, then kicked him in the ankle. Joryan stumbled but recovered after a step. He pivoted and brought one leg up for a kick. Lerr'ek caught the foot aiming for his stomach and twisted it, giving his opponent no choice but to go with the twist or spend the next cycle and a half healing the damage to the joint.

Joryan threw his whole body into motion, surprising Lerr'ek

by cartwheeling into a stunning kick to his ribs with his free foot. Luckily for Lerr'ek, Baba Yaga had ensured he wouldn't break *too* badly when he sparred with her. Without his enhancements, he would have had to be careful breathing until he'd gotten medical attention.

However, he was made of stern stuff, and the fight turned back in his favor when he dropped and kicked Joryan's hands out from under him before the Shrillexian's feet touched the ground.

Joryan landed with an ungraceful thud, and Lerr'ek called to the trainees, "Fancy is for competitions and warriors who don't care if they leave the battlefield."

He followed up with a crushing stomp to Joryan's knee, then a brutal kick to the face, breaking his jaw. "If your opponent gets you on the ground, it's over."

He took a knee beside the half-conscious Joryan and delivered the knockout punch to the Shrillexian's temple. "I'll tell you males what my teacher told me. The only fair fight is the one you lose. If your enemy can't stand, *he can't fight.* He can't see, *he can't fight.* He can't breathe, *he can't fight.*"

Lerr'ek stood and dusted off his suit pants. "We're done here."

He walked over and scooped up the still-unconscious Kirian, hating how light and fragile the boy felt in his arms. Seeing the wary respect on the Shrillexian trainees' faces, he zeroed in on Gralen, who looked ready to tear someone's head off. "You need serum. Come with us. The rest of you, go home."

Gralen's home was closer than the Pod, so that was where they went. Their route took them up into the main undercity, where homes and businesses lined the wider tunnels. Gralen's struggle to contain the fighting urge became more apparent as they walked. He muttered and growled to himself, his gaze darting at the group and everyone they passed.

"Are you okay?" Kirian asked. He was still groggy.

Gralen bared his teeth and shook his head. "Need…serum. Just…keep going." Every word was an effort as he fought to prevent himself from lunging at Kirian, Charr'est, the passersby, and people pausing to stare at the odd group. Humans were a rare sight in the undercity, and the attention they attracted sent itchy shivers along his scales that could only be eased by hitting something or someone.

Stephen stopped the group and took Gralen's arm, forcing him to make eye contact. "You have control of yourself. Maintain it. That is not a request."

The quiet command in Stephen's voice triggered Gralen's submissive side. Male Shrillexians were ruled by their instinct to fight, but they would back down for someone they recognized as stronger. Few were stronger than the ancient vampire.

Gralen nodded, and some of the tension ebbed from his squared shoulders. "I… Thank you. My mother…has serum. I want to tell her… Get my things… I'm going to…the surface with you. No more fighting…for Joryan."

"No one will be fighting for Joryan after the Mistress takes him out," Lerr'ek assured him.

Gralen frowned. "Baba Yaga? Why?"

Kirian and Charr'est told him what they'd discovered about Joryan's schemes. Gralen's anger spiked again, this time aimed at the male he'd looked up to. His view of Joryan had shifted in recent days, and finding out he was getting rich off the blood of his fellow Shrillexians drove his rage to a peak again.

His control slipped.

They were close to Gralen's neighborhood, but he didn't have the mental capacity to see the sense of waiting to take action. He turned on his heel and sprinted back in the direction they'd come from.

Before he got far, Stephen stopped him in his tracks and stood in front of him.

"Get out of my way," Gralen snarled. "Joryan needs to die for what he's done."

He sidestepped, and Stephen stepped with him.

"Gralen, you are not in any state to deal with Joryan right now." Stephen's voice was soft, but there was an undercurrent of steel in his tone that dared Gralen to argue.

Unfortunately, Gralen was *not* in control of himself, so he lunged at Stephen. That was the last thing he was aware of until he woke up in his mother's house.

Stephen, Lerr'ek, Charr'est, and the human woman were nowhere to be seen. Neither was his sister, who would normally have been home at that time of day. His mother was there, and Kirian was wrapped in a blanket in what used to be Gralen's father's easy chair.

Denasi leaned over Gralen and put her hand on his forehead. "How are you feeling? Stephen had to knock you out."

"Is that what happened?" Gralen eased into a sitting position on the couch and rubbed the sore spot on his jaw, noting the empty serum vial on the table. "I feel better. Mother, do you know what Joryan has been doing?"

Sadly, she nodded. "That's how it's been since your father's cadre died in the Leath War."

Kirian put the hot drink he was holding on the side table. "My father died in that war, too. He was a Guardian Marine. That was why my family moved here."

Gralen saw the human in a different light after that revelation. He had always thought him foolish for standing up to Dex, but learning about the loss of Kirian's father in the same war that had taken his gave him insight into why he refused to give in and accept Dex's rule over the school.

"I want to go to the Institute, Mother," Gralen announced. "I'll find a way to earn the credits I would have been sending home, but no mercenary company would allow me to be home as much as I want to be. I have to take care of you and Sofi."

"If that's your decision, I'll support you," Denasi told him with a mother's pride. "I can't pretend I'm not glad you won't be in danger. As good as you are, you're too young to fight adults."

"Why didn't you say something?" Gralen asked.

The sad expression returned to Denasi's face. "Because that's how it is here. What other opportunity would you have had if I'd asked you to stay? A male who doesn't fight becomes a shell of himself."

Gralen sighed. "What about Joryan and the other males? They'll cause trouble for you if I leave."

Denasi took his hand and squeezed. "Son, things change for the better when Baba Yaga intervenes. After the blood spills, Joryan won't be a problem for anyone."

"And in the meantime?" Gralen countered.

"I'm not powerless. None of the females are. By myself, I don't have much of a voice, but I'm not alone. Many other mothers have issues with their sons being sent to war too soon. Things will change, Gralen. I believe in the humans."

Gralen nodded since he saw that she believed what she was telling him. "What else did Stephen tell you?"

"Not just Stephen." Denasi smiled. "Lerr'ek told me that he will take all the trainees at the Institute and teach them the real meaning of honor while preparing them for war. You, my love, have another path ahead of you, should you choose to accept it."

"What path?" Curiosity joined the relief he felt for the young males he'd been in competition with.

Kirian spoke up again. "My path."

Denasi smiled and caressed Gralen's head before standing. "I'll leave you boys to talk. Call if you need anything."

CHAPTER THIRTEEN

The silence between them was awkward for a moment. Kirian hoped he'd made the right decision involving himself in Gralen's life. Maybe he should have stayed out of it and found a fighter somewhere else, but their history—however checkered—was the foundation for building his team.

"We might not have been friends—" Kirian began.

"Your path?" Gralen circumvented the awkward discussion.

Kirian chuckled. "It will make us the protectors of the city. Maybe the whole planet in time."

Gralen listened without interrupting as Kirian explained the team's purpose and Baba Yaga's hopes for them.

When he was done, the Shrillexian was quiet as he processed the information. "What will this mean for my family? My community? People rely on me, and I won't let them down. If I abandon them, I might as well join a mercenary company."

"You won't let anyone down," Kirian promised. "Neither will you have to find work outside of your studies. The scholarship will replace the financial contribution you would make to your family. I need you fully focused on becoming the best version of yourself you can be."

"Charr agreed to that?"

Kirian nodded. "He's been with us for a few weeks." He didn't go into detail about what it had taken to free Charr'est from his father. That wasn't his to share.

"What's your deal? How were you able to fight me? You couldn't even stand a few months ago."

"My scholarship came with Etheric Empire medical care. I'm not dying anymore. Well, no faster than anyone else."

"You were dying?" Guilt crossed Gralen's features. "I'm sorry. I didn't know."

"Would it have made a difference? Dex had a tight grip on you and Charr."

Gralen opened his mouth, closed it again, and shook his head. "I would have done the same."

"I appreciate your honesty." Kirian winced when he shrugged and the movement sent pain coursing down his body. "Like I said to Charr, the past is the past. I want you both on my team. I'm not going to hold what you did with Dex against you as long as you do better for yourself and for everyone else."

The decision to come clean was easier than it had been with Charr'est. "There's something I need to tell you. The reason we know what Joryan is doing is that I spied on you. I didn't know enough about your people's culture to understand that what he is doing was wrong, but I've learned more since then."

"You *spied* on me?" Gralen tensed as his anger spiked, but he kept himself still.

"Yeah. I also spied on Charr and Dex. I saw that you were more than a school bully, but it was what I saw when you were at home that made me want you on my team. You're loyal, and you'll go the extra mile for your people. I'm hoping you can see what you could do for people all over Thon and for High Tortuga in the future."

"You messed Dex up."

Kirian nodded. "I'd do it again."

"You fought well. You've had training."

"The best. The same training you will get whether you join my team or decide to stay with the others who come to the Institute."

A soft knock at the door announced Doc Ericson's arrival. She poked her head around the door, gracing them with a warm smile. "Kirian, are you ready to move? We have a roamer here to take you back to the Institute."

Kirian nodded and slipped the blanket off before getting up. "You coming?" he asked Gralen.

"I'll be there," Gralen told him. "I need to make sure my mother is safe first."

High Tortuga, Northern Continent, City of Thon, Undisclosed Location, Institute of Education-Focused Extrajudicial Foundational Studies

Gralen had called for a pick up late the previous night. Kirian had left getting him settled into his dorm to the professor while he stayed in the infirmary to recover from the toll the fight had taken on his body.

"Cerebro?" Kirian called. "I'm awake."

"I'll inform Jennifer," the AI responded. "How are you feeling this morning?"

"Better, thank you for asking." Kirian stretched cautiously, careful not to disturb the cannula in his hand. "The infusion did its thing. Charr and Gralen still asleep?"

"Neither Charr'est nor Gralen has left their dorm yet," Cerebro told him.

"You raring to get out of here already?" Doc Ericson asked as she arrived.

"Call me crazy, but I've seen enough hospital beds to last *your* lifetime," Kirian quipped. "I was hoping to catch the guys at breakfast if you say I'm good to go."

Doc Ericson grinned. "Let's check you over and find out."

He bore her prodding and poking with his usual good nature, then hightailed it to the dorms to wake Charr'est and Gralen.

Kirian decided Charr'est was the safer bet to wake first. He rapped on his door and called his name until a sleepy-eyed Charr'est quit groaning for him to go away and answered.

"What time is it?" Charr'est grumbled.

Gralen's door opened, and he emerged fully dressed. "What's happening?"

Kirian grinned. "Breakfast, if Sleepyhead here gets dressed."

Charr'est rolled his eyes but closed his door.

"Breakfast sounds good," Gralen told Kirian. "I missed supper last night."

"Is your mother okay?" Kirian asked.

Gralen nodded. "When I left, she was riled up and ready to call the other mothers. Joryan isn't likely to make it to Baba Yaga's intervention now that they all know he sent their sons to war to line his pockets."

They continued chatting until Charr'est returned a few minutes later. The cafeteria was too large for the three of them, but the layout of the tables and booths gave the large space the feeling of a diner. They chose their breakfast options from the food printing units, a delightful new (to him) tech that Gralen spent fifteen minutes ordering item after item from and watching the food being assembled through the translucent door.

"Are you going to eat all that?" Charr'est asked as they made their way to a booth by the holowindow that covered an entire wall.

This morning, it featured an underwater scene with healthy corals and hundreds of brightly colored sea creatures. The dark blue pleather seating was comfortable without being too soft, and there was plenty of room for their trays on the pale green plastic table.

"Are you kidding?" Gralen laughed as he slid into the booth.

"I'm a growing male. I'll go back for seconds when I'm done with this."

Kirian eyed the mountain of flapjacks, fruit, three Shrillexian-style breakfast sandwiches, sausages, and other meats on Gralen's tray with awe. "Try the burrito when you go back. It's protein-heavy."

Gralen grinned. "That's what I'm talking about. Why'd you want to meet for breakfast? And where are all the other students?"

"It's just us three for now." Kirian told him about the upcoming open house while he ate his granola yogurt. "I wanted to talk about Tor."

Guilt made Charr'est pause with his fork halfway to his mouth. Gralen had no such reaction. "What about him?"

"He's in some kind of trouble," Kirian explained. "I'm meeting him later today. I wanted to make sure there won't be any problem if I manage to persuade him to come back with me."

"No trouble from me." Gralen tilted his head. "He's another one for your team, huh?"

"We need brains and brawn." Kirian attacked his first burrito with the enthusiasm of someone who had nanocytes running through his system. "Tor is the smartest person I know."

"That's saying something. You're pretty smart yourself."

"I don't know how to make up for what we did to him," Charr'est admitted. "It's been weighing on my mind since you told me you want him for the team."

"Easy," Gralen mumbled around a mouthful of food. "We apologize and make sure our actions going forward match our words."

"How can you say it's easy?" Charr'est asked. "We were so hard on him."

Gralen shrugged. "We did what Dex wanted. We're going to do whatever Kirian wants now. You going to feel bad about that, too?"

"Is that how all Shrillexians operate?" Kirian was genuinely curious.

Gralen nodded. "Dex had the power. Now you have it."

"You handed my ass to me," Kirian pointed out. "Everything I've read said that Shrillexians submit to a show of strength greater than their own."

"First, no Shrillexian submits. Our urge to fight ebbs when we're working for someone who shows strength, but strength doesn't just come from being able to pound someone into the sand. Tor might be the smartest, but you're the strongest person I know besides my mother. It took strength to step into that ring with me when you had no idea that the adults would come to rescue you. I could easily have killed you, yet you stood with courage."

Kirian laughed. "I was terrified. That was my first real fight."

"Courage is not the absence of fear," Gralen quoted. "It's acting despite your fear. All the times you stood up to us at the Free School gained my respect. You too, Charr. You've seen what I can do. You both earned my respect. When Tor gets here, I'll protect him just like I'll protect you two."

Kirian pointed at Gralen. "That attitude is why I wanted you for the team."

"What will this team do?" Gralen returned to his pancake demolition efforts. "The principal said you'd tell me more."

Kirian animatedly launched into his explanation. "Baba Yaga is changing this planet for the better. She told me about her plans and how we fit into them. We'll go in when corruption and crime are beyond the capacity of law enforcement but need a less permanent solution than she would provide."

"So, somewhere between prison and death?" Gralen commented.

Kirian nodded. "We'll be part of dismantling the old systems and building new ones. I've been on a few assignments already. Wealth redistribution and uncovering evidence for the police to use—whatever breaks up the gangs and cartels. Baba Yaga plans to attack the inequities on High Tortuga at every level."

"Like removing Joryan from power," Charr'est added.

Kirian grinned. "Exactly. You've seen the news holos. She's creating vacuums in the power structure and filling them with better people. People who care what happens to the people they're responsible for."

"People like you," Gralen stated. "People in the undercity aren't going to be easy to convince that the Etheric Empire is the solution to their problems. A lot of them came here to get away from that."

Kirian suppressed his urge to argue since aggravating the sense of rejection Gralen had grown up with wasn't the male's intention. "Humans might be rare on this planet, but I was born here. This is my world too, and as long as I'm alive, I have hope."

High Tortuga, Northern Continent, City of Thon, Brasak Sector

The three boys had gone their separate ways after breakfast to take care of the day's learning. Kirian had finished his lessons an hour before lunch and signed out to go visit his mom and Gramps.

Janet was in the attic. She'd set an easel up under the skylight and reclaimed that corner of the space from the myriad boxes and pieces of furniture that crowded the rest of the space.

Her music paused as Kirian ascended the pull-down stairs.

"Max, is that you?"

"It's me, Mom," Kirian called, popping his head through the access hatch. "I have some time before I meet Tor, and I wanted to see you."

Janet dropped the brush she was using to create a Torcellan sunset and came over to help Kirian through the hatch.

Kirian took the hand she offered and used the other on the rail as he hauled himself into the attic.

Janet smiled at him. "You're getting stronger."

"I'm wearing my exosuit." Kirian glanced around. "You should think about clearing this old stuff out so you can turn the attic into a real studio."

"Maybe." Janet touched a box marked Mike with a wistful expression. "There are too many memories up here to get rid of everything."

"That's my dad's stuff?"

Janet nodded. "You want to see?" They spent an hour looking at photos, awards, and letters his father had sent to Janet while he was deployed. The holopaper was dog-eared from rereads over the years.

Kirian eased off the tape holding a box together. Sitting on top of the contents was a neatly folded flag bearing Bethany Anne's emblem. Janet gasped as Kirian unfolded the item of clothing beneath the flag.

"May I?" He held the Guardian Marine jacket up.

Janet nodded wordlessly, and Kirian fed his arms into the sleeves.

"You've grown." Janet cupped Kirian's face with her hand. "It almost fits."

Kirian smoothed the jacket. "It's a little big."

"It looks good on you." Janet's eyes shone with too many emotions to name. "You should keep it. He'd want you to have it."

Kirian sat on a box marked Books, needing a moment off his feet. "Are you sure?"

Janet smiled and nodded. "I'm sure. You look a lot like him, you know. So handsome."

Kirian's face reddened. Unsure of how to respond, he shrugged the jacket off and neatly folded it. "I have his coloring, but I have your eyes and Gramps' nose."

"You have your father's posture. I never saw it before, but now you can stand straight."

"Does it make you sad to be reminded of him?"

"A little, but it's been a long time. The pain of losing him is a dull ache instead of the knife wound it was when it was fresh."

They worked together to repack everything but the jacket. "What are you painting?" Kirian asked.

"A piece I hope will secure a job I want."

"A job in art?" Kirian grinned when she allowed her hope to show in her answering nod. "Mom, that's amazing!"

Janet laughed. "Hold the celebration. I haven't gotten the job yet. It's just teaching a class at the community college."

"It doesn't matter if you get this job. The fact that you can afford to take a job you'll love instead of spending every hour rushing between jobs in healthcare makes me happier than you know."

Janet pulled him into a hug. "Not as happy as I am to see you thriving. You'll give Doctor Ericson my love when you go back to the Institute, won't you?"

Kirian held his mother close. Her light floral fragrance took him back in time. "I always do, Mom."

CHAPTER FOURTEEN

Kirian had said his goodbyes to his mother and Gramps and took the tram to the heart of the entertainment district. Tor had arranged to meet him at the juice bar attached to an arcade neither frequented.

Being in the city without his chair was an eye-opener. With the aid of his exosuit and the pain patches his mother had applied to his spine before he left, Kirian walked among the crowds for the first time, experiencing what it was like to go unnoticed.

Strangers jostled him on the crowded sidewalks, everyone in a hurry to get where they were going. He felt vulnerable without the bubble his chair provided to separate him from the masses. He also had a sense of freedom he could never have experienced in the chair.

"Your heart rate went up," Cerebro commented. "Do you need assistance?"

"I'm fine."

The professor cut in. "Are you sure? I can be there in fifteen minutes if you need me."

"I'm fine," Kirian repeated. "I have the tracker dot you gave me if things don't go the way we want."

Kirian dodged someone in a *Princess Warrior* costume who was handing out flyers and made a left turn off the main strip. Here, X-rated adult entertainment establishments vied for space with niche businesses that catered to those who couldn't find what they wanted in the larger arcades and clubs.

Many people played the *Inner Life* sim to avoid their mundane existence. Its users were both pitied and scorned for their preference for building the fantasy existence they wanted in-game. Nevertheless, dozens of places like ReImagine catered to them.

Kirian pushed the smoked glass door open and headed inside to find Tor. The juice bar's entrance was opposite the reception desk on the right. The walls were painted a garish green and decorated with neon fruits and vegetables.

He debated going to the counter to get a drink. Then he spotted Tor poking his head out of a corner booth.

"Over here," Tor called, waving Kirian to him.

Kirian eyed the other customers as he walked over. They all wore VR headsets and had the glassy-eyed stares of people lost in their games. Tor didn't look much better.

"Have you been sleeping on the streets?" Kirian asked as he slid into the booth.

Tor nodded and lifted a shoulder. "I had to avoid the gangs. I have enough trouble without them forcing me to join them." He adjusted the hood of his cloak, which had fallen back with the movement. His eyes were red from lack of sleep and wide with alertness.

Kirian noted that Tor's gaze remained on the door as if he expected someone to barge in. "What's going on with you? I've been worried since you vanished. Is someone after you?"

"It's more than that." Tor shook his head. "It doesn't matter. You said you needed my help with something?"

Kirian's chest constricted. "That can wait. I'm worried about you. Your family up and left you almost a standard cycle ago, and now you're on the run from stars knows who."

They were interrupted by the surly waitress from behind the counter. "Are you two going to buy anything? This isn't a hangout for miscreants, you know. I have a business to run."

Kirian grabbed a menu and skimmed the salads and other healthy vegetarian food. "You hungry? I could go for a veggie burger and calar root fries."

"Me too," Tor agreed. "But I need to save my credits for transport off-world."

"My treat," Kirian told him.

Tor tore into his food as though he hadn't eaten in a while, which Kirian suspected wasn't far from the truth. He tipped his fries onto Tor's plate. "Where have you been?"

"Here and there," Tor told him around a mouthful of food. He finished chewing and swallowed before speaking again. "I called in favors and crashed on couches in the undercity. The ones where I didn't care if they got caught up in my mess. Slept rough some nights. How'd you know about my family being gone?"

Kirian shrugged, but his face warmed with embarrassment. "I figured something wasn't right the first time you took me to your house. When you vanished, I asked for help finding you."

Tor was instantly on his guard again. "Help from who?"

"People who would take care of you if you'd let them." Kirian lifted his hands in a "What can I say" gesture and lowered his voice. "Doc Ericson. The principal at my school. Baba Yaga."

Tor almost choked on a fry. "You're shitting me."

Kirian shook his head. "She owns the Institute. I had the school's AI track the last time you were home. The last time your family was home. Tor, trust me, please? Tell me what's going on. Come back to the Institute with me."

"No. I know you're thinking that they abandoned me, but they didn't. They wouldn't. It's all my fault. Really. If I hadn't... If I'd just... They'd be safe, and I wouldn't be on the run."

Kirian frowned. "You're not making sense. Start at the beginning."

Tor shook his head and grabbed his backpack. "I have to go. I shouldn't have come here."

He slid out of the booth and made to leave. Thinking fast, Kirian slipped the miniscule tracker dot from his pocket and snagged his friend's backpack with his fingers. "Don't go. Let me help."

"You can't. It's too dangerous."

Before Kirian could argue, Tor slipped his backpack free of Kirian's grip and left the juice bar. Kirian pushed his half-eaten veggie burger away, his appetite absent for once.

"Tracker online," Cerebro informed him. "We can keep an eye on his location."

"Good work, Kirian," Lerr'ek added.

Kirian sighed. "Good work" would have been persuading Tor to come in off the streets. Getting him to the Institute where he'd be safe from whoever was searching for him. "Can I get a ride back, please?"

"I'm above the arcade in a Pod," the professor admitted. "Make your way to the alley behind the building, and I'll pick you up."

High Tortuga, Northern Continent, City of Thon, Undisclosed Location, Institute of Education-Focused Extrajudicial Foundational Studies

As the Pod landed in the underground hangar, Kirian spotted the *Shinigami*'s familiar outline.

"She's back." He shook his head, experiencing mental whiplash as his thoughts bounced between worry for Tor, the Shrillexian situation, and the upcoming open house. Would Bethany Anne or Baba Yaga meet them inside the Institute?

"Come on, kid." Lerr'ek patted his shoulder. "Time to face the music."

"What did you do to annoy her this time?" Kirian asked as they debarked.

"Not me. You."

Kirian swallowed the lump that had formed in his throat and followed his principal into the main building. Something told him that being confined to the Institute wasn't the option the Queen would choose for his punishment.

"The Mistress wants to see both of you in your office, Lerr'ek," Cerebro announced as they walked into the atrium.

Bethany Anne was sitting in the professor's chair with her feet up on the desk, sipping Coke from a bottle. She placed the bottle on the desk when they entered. "Oh, good. I thought you would never get back. Kirian, take a seat, please. You and I need to have a conversation. Lerr'ek, don't go anywhere just yet. You're next."

"I know what I did was wrong and stupid," Kirian blurted before Bethany Anne said anything else. "I'm sorry. It won't happen again."

Bethany Anne tilted her head with her lips pressed into a thin line. "What did you do, Kirian?"

"I endangered myself and Charr by going into the undercity without permission or protection." Kirian couldn't meet Bethany Anne's stare. "I should have trusted an adult or Cerebro with what we were doing so they could help when it went sideways. We could have been killed."

Bethany Anne sighed. "You just made my speech for me. I guess there's nothing left but the consequences of your actions."

"Punish me, but Charr just followed me. He doesn't deserve to suffer more than he did while we were down there."

"Who said anything about punishment?" Bethany Anne retorted. "I said you would have to deal with the consequences, which is not the same thing."

Kirian's brow creased. "I don't understand."

"You will," Bethany Anne assured him.

"Punishment is less effective than teaching you the lesson you need. We will be moving on Joryan in twenty-four hours. You and Charr'est will be present for the pre-op briefing, you will be in the ops center while the takedown happens, and you will work together to provide me with a detailed after-action report."

Kirian nodded. "Yes, Empress."

"Don't 'Empress' me." Bethany Anne smiled. "I just got rid of that title. Do you understand why I'm giving you this task?"

"Because I went off half-cocked and need to know how it should be done?" Kirian ventured. "So when I have my team, I won't endanger them because I don't know what I'm doing?"

"Smart cookie." Bethany Anne's eyes unfocused for a few seconds. "I'm having Cerebro add several leadership modules to your curriculum."

Kirian grinned, grateful for material that would challenge him. "Thank you for making this an opportunity to learn, Bethany Anne. I won't waste it."

The former Empress waved a hand. "You should eat. You'll need your energy. Meet us in the PT area in an hour for the next part of your lesson."

"*Us?*" Professor Lerr'ek grimaced. "This is going to hurt, isn't it?"

Bethany Anne's answering smile wouldn't melt butter. "That, Lerr'ek, is why we have Pod-docs."

Kirian found Charr'est and Gralen in the cafeteria and joined them after he got his food.

"I thought she was going to tear me a new asshole," Charr'est admitted as Kirian slid into the booth that was becoming their regular spot. "An after-action report isn't so bad, right?"

Kirian lifted a shoulder as he tucked into the chili. "I guess we'll find out. Did you get any other consequences?"

Charr'est nodded. "I have to take a course to teach me when I should follow and when I should… I don't know, something to do with exercising autonomy."

"That's already in my curriculum," Gralen told them.

Kirian pulled up the learning portal on his wrist-holo. "I got modules on leadership. Looks like the briefing is part of the course."

"I have to go too," Gralen added.

"Me three," Charr'est told them. "And we got a message from Cerebro telling us to be at the PT area in…" He checked his wrist-holo. "Thirty minutes."

Kirian grinned. "I think we're in for a treat."

Bethany Anne exchanged her heeled boots and leathers for workout clothes: a sleeveless T-shirt, cargo pants, and combat boots, and cut through the Etheric to the physical therapy area where Lerr'ek and the kids were waiting.

Her objective was twofold. First, to show the recruits the level they would reach with dedication to their training. Second, to put Lerr'ek through his paces and remind him of the cost of his failure to protect the recruits and to decide whether he was ready for the next level of enhancement.

She had tweaked his physiology to between level one and two enhancements after she'd broken him. Taking him to a solid level two and making him the best version of himself his genetics would allow was necessary if he was going to be training Shrillexian males.

However, she needed to know he was capable of teaching them, which meant finding out if he'd made the most of the advantages she'd provided to up his fighting skills.

The kids arrived on time. Bethany Anne turned as they entered the room. She pointed at the chairs on the far side of the mat. "Sit over there. Is that…popcorn?"

Kirian had the grace to blush. "Seemed appropriate for the beatdown we're about to witness."

Bethany Anne narrowed her eyes but allowed them to keep their snack. "Record this lesson, then study it and incorporate what you learn into your skill sets. We will review the session while Lerr'ek is healing."

"Why will Professor Lerr'ek need to heal?" Charr'est asked.

"Because Bethany Anne doesn't do half measures." Lerr'ek came in through the side door, his suit and dress shoes replaced by a blue atmosuit several shades darker than his skin and light boots.

He acknowledged the students with a nod before crossing the mat to stand in front of Bethany Anne. "What do you need from me, Mistress?"

"I'm testing you." Bethany Anne turned to face the kids. "You are here to observe, so I will be moving at close to human speed. Choose our weapons."

"Kubaton," Kirian called.

"Hand-to-hand," Gralen offered.

"Swords," Charr'est enthused.

Bethany Anne's mouth quirked with amusement. "You are skilled with swords, Charr'est?"

The young Zhyn shrugged. "Not yet."

"Right answer," Bethany Anne told him. "Okay. Hand-to-hand, then kubaton, then swords."

Lerr'ek groaned. "The Pod-doc is on standby, right?"

Bethany Anne took her stance. "Let's go."

Lerr'ek opened his eyes. His mind took a moment to recalibrate and inform him that he was aboard the *Shinigami* in Bethany Anne's personal Pod-doc. He felt around for the latch.

The lid swung up, and he climbed out, then checked himself. His wrists lacked the sting from deflecting Bethany Anne's blows with batons and sword. The tears in his muscles and ligaments were gone, as was the bruising that should have covered him from head to toe.

Not only had he been healed, but he had been changed. His legs and arms were longer, and his shoulders were wider. He took a deep breath and discovered that his lung capacity had increased.

Bethany Anne had beaten him soundly, but she had not broken any bones this time. Had he landed any hits on her? He couldn't recall, and she was not present to ask. A wallscreen came to life, and a face that almost looked like the Mistress' appeared.

"Hello, Shinigami."

"Clothing is in the compartment to your left," the AI informed him. "You have been in the Pod-doc for six hours. Bethany Anne is expecting you in the conference suite on Sub-level One. Cerebro sent an AEV for you to return to the Institute."

Lerr'ek retrieved the atmosuit and dressed quickly. The meeting was in the smaller of the Institute's two conference suites. He'd had this set of rooms remodeled for faculty meetings and parent-teacher conferences. The larger suite contained the Institute's auditorium and several classrooms. The smaller suite was comprised of six small meeting rooms and one room large enough to hold a full faculty meeting.

After he hired the rest of the faculty. So far, he had acquired a computing specialist and a former Armed Forces combat specialist. He still needed people to teach engineering, civics, law, politics, statecraft, and several other specialties. The Institute's learning model prioritized individual independent learning, but mentors would guide and inspire the students as they navigated their chosen fields.

His boots sank into the plush deep-green carpet that complemented the off-white and warm brown plastiwood-paneled walls and gave the corridor an air of quiet comfort. With Ms. Friday's assistance, he would find the people he needed to make this school a success.

Lerr'ek was not surprised to see his students sitting across from the Mistress, Stephen, and Jennifer at one end of the conference table. He had *not* expected Denasi to join them via holoconference.

"We have a problem," Baba Yaga stated. "Joryan took the trainees to the Southern Continent under the guise of 'survival training.' Further, he recruited a mixed bag of escapees from the mercenary companies I've taken out with him."

"The other mothers are furious," Denasi informed them. "He took our sons before I got the word out about his betrayal. Mistress, what can we do?"

"Nothing right now." Baba Yaga's voice ground on their souls, making her displeasure with the situation clear. "I will deal with the mercenaries and ensure that your sons return unharmed. What you do with Joryan is up to you, but he will face his people to answer for his crimes."

Stephen spoke up. "They'll tear him to shreds."

Baba Yaga lifted a shoulder. "So be it. Denasi, inform the mothers of my decision. I will be in touch when I have your children safe and sound."

"As you decree, Mistress." Denasi bowed her head before ending the holocall from her end.

"Plan," Baba Yaga stated. "Cerebro, I need a location for Joryan and the trainees. Something tells me he won't be in any of the cities."

"I will have the satellite network in place within the hour," Cerebro informed her.

"Co-opt the BYPS satellites as well," Baba Yaga commanded. "Lerr'ek, reach out to your associates. I want to create a perimeter around the location to ensure that not one of those fu —" She cut herself off after glancing at the three males observing in silence. "No mercy this time. They will all die for what they've done."

Kirian raised a hand. "Did you execute all the mercenaries who didn't escape?"

Baba Yaga shook her head. "No, Kirian. Just the ones who continued to support the travesty Joryan and his associates built. The majority are on their way back here to assist with rebuilding their community. Joryan has had too long to strip the Shrillexians in the undercity of their males, and the culture is unbalanced."

Gralen nodded. "Thank you, Baba Yaga. My mother was right to put her faith in you."

"It's well placed," Jennifer told him.

The stern lines of Baba Yaga's face softened a touch. "The media paints me as an indiscriminate killing machine, but the perception is just that. I do not take a life unless I judge it to be necessary, and Justice is more than the ultimate judgment. People are complex, so the consequences for their actions need to fit the circumstances."

"I will have a use for some of the returning warriors," Lerr'ek offered. "Should the young Shrillexians' training be taken up by the Institute, I will need instructors. It's the only field we will offer that cannot be taught via the learning model."

"You will be responsible for them," Baba Yaga warned.

"I expected nothing else. The question is, how long will you be here to ensure their good behavior?"

Baba Yaga tapped her nails on the table as she considered the question. "My people tell me that I will be able to return to Earth in three months."

"Around four cycles…" Lerr'ek did the math in his head. "The public part of the Institute should be running smoothly by then."

"'Should be?'" Stephen asked in a wry tone.

"Will be," Lerr'ek corrected. "Which will give the former mercenaries time to understand that while they have been given a better option, it is nevertheless their *only* option."

"What will you do if your hires decide to pursue another course?" Stephen inquired.

Lerr'ek lifted a shoulder. "I won't have to do anything. Peter will deal with any insubordination from those under his command."

The adults chuckled.

"Who is Peter?" Kirian asked.

"One of my Own," Baba Yaga told him.

Kirian's jaw dropped.

Lerr'ek couldn't suppress his smile. "The Institute will mold the best of the best. There's no one better to train those on the path to war than the former head of the Guardian Marines and an Empr—" He caught himself in time to avoid breaking Rule Number One. "Queen's Bitch."

"Stay on task," Baba Yaga stated. "We need to hammer out the plan to rescue the trainees and bring Joryan and his men to Justice."

CHAPTER FIFTEEN

<u>High Tortuga, Southern Continent, Kunacre National Park</u>

Joryan cursed the day he'd decided that humans were no threat to him. His operation was unraveling around him. Four decades in the making, and in mere cycles, the Witch had destroyed it.

He was persona non grata with the survivors of her purge who mattered. Reduced to the thirty-six mercenaries he'd trained in their youth. The ones who believed in him so strongly that they'd run rather than submit to Baba Yaga's demands. Those who had no moral quandary with using the current batch of trainees as surety for their lives should the Bitch's Witch find them deep in the jungle where they'd set up camp in well-hidden cabins.

The trainees didn't know they were hostages. Joryan did care for them, but that didn't preclude him from using them to further his agenda since that was what he'd been doing for the last three decades. That the stakes were considerably higher than they had ever been meant nothing to him.

If they threatened his life, the soft humans would back down or pay the price for killing him with the lives of the young males.

Gloren, Randro, and Halmish had each taken a team of boys out to play war games while Joryan worked from the cabin he'd taken for himself—the largest. Dracent, Yachen, Korgar, and Bralesh guarded the camp's perimeter. The rest had gone to assist with the three-way clash he'd designed to keep the trainees occupied for the next few days.

While the males fought each other to obtain the water being transported between their camps, Joryan had one last play to organize. Whatever happened, the boys would not sleep in Thon again.

Hidden by the thick foliage surrounding the campsite, Bethany Anne eavesdropped on Joryan's thoughts.

He plans to form a mercenary company from the dregs and the trainees. She spoke directly to Stephen, Jennifer, and Lerr'ek, not wishing to give away their position to the guards. *He's in there trying to arrange transport off-world for the whole group: new identities, the works.*

How is he planning on getting the boys to cooperate? Stephen asked.

By telling them I killed their families. Bethany Anne's mental voice was close to Baba Yaga's as rage boiled inside her. *Stephen, take out the guards. Lerr'ek, Jennifer, head out and track the young males down. I'm going to give that low-down lying fuck-knuckle a nightmare that will last the remainder of his very short life.*

Her hair turned white, and her skin was as black as the void as she stalked toward the cabin where Joryan was throwing money around to get himself off the hook.

It was too late. He just didn't know it yet.

Baba Yaga kicked the door off its hinges and had her hand around Joryan's throat before he had a chance to react. "Nice try, no biscuit, asshole," she snarled into his ear as she fished zip-ties out of her coat pocket.

Joryan pleaded for his life as she trussed him like the pig he was. No, that was an insult to pigs. The sorry excuse for a sentient being would not get off easy by being compared to an animal.

"I'm not going to kill you," she ground out. "You're not worth cleaning my nails afterward."

Joryan relaxed as much as someone with his arms bound to his feet could. "What *are* you going to do to me?"

Baba Yaga tilted her head, treating the quivering Shrillexian to a view of her razor-sharp teeth. "I'm going to hand you over to those you have wronged. What they do with you is entirely up to them. Last I heard, those males' mothers are pretty angry at your kidnapping, thieving ass."

She ignored his resumed pleading and left him helpless on the floor of the cabin while she walked over to his computer.

ADAM, I want every credit he stashed found and redirected into a restitution fund you're going to set up for the affected families.

>>Easier done than said. He's not very smart. Most of it is in property and shares. Transferring ownership to the... Do you like Brighter Tomorrow Foundation as a name for the trust?<<

Works for me.

She chuckled aloud, then went back to the prisoner and crouched so she could look Joryan in the eyes. He cringed, the sound of her amusement like knives running down his spine.

"I just took everything you own: every credit, every property, every share. You are destitute. That is *my* punishment for the crimes you committed against your people. All the wealth you amassed at their expense will go toward rebuilding the society you corrupted."

She rose and kicked him in the head on her way to the door, rendering him unconscious rather than carrying him through the jungle. "Stay there until I get back. I have to deal with your toadies."

Halmish rubbed the back of his neck, feeling the prickle of eyes crawling over his skin. Whatever was watching, it was dangerous enough to make him feel vulnerable, and he didn't like that one bit.

"Do you sense that?" he asked the others on the hovertruck in a low voice.

"Don't tell me you're wary of the kids." Korgar laughed. "Their scouts aren't very scary."

Halmish snorted. "I'm not talking about the youngers. This godsforsaken jungle is full of predators, and not just the enormous reptiles that we can hear from miles away."

"How long will Joryan have us playing war games with children?" Gorlen asked. "This bistok shit is getting boring."

Halmish forgot the predators and focused on the mercenary he'd known for all of five minutes. "However long he wants to. We don't get a say in the boss' plans, or haven't you figured that out yet?"

"Maybe we should," Korgar suggested. "Then we wouldn't be out in the ass end of nowhere, babysitting a bunch of youngers too green to pick up a live weapon."

"We weren't much older when we went to war the first time," Gorlen pointed out. "Some of those kids have chops."

"True," Halmish agreed. "They're good with the practice weapons. Did you see Dam'yan's squad take the tower in the last run? Those boys will be formidable in a year or two."

"If they survive that long," Korgar pointed out. "Our jobs will thin out their numbers."

"Then we'd better prepare them for what we're going to face

out there," Gorlen stated. "You heard Joryan. We're not going back to Thon."

"Dumbass!" Halmish slapped the big mouth on the skull, then glanced at a bush that had shaken, revealing the position of one of the scouts. "Joryan didn't share that with the kids yet. If they find out what's going down in the city, we'll have a mutiny on our hands. Then we'll never get them off-world when the ship gets here. Keep your mouth shut and hope whichever kid that was didn't hear you."

Gorlen rubbed his head. "Their families are just fine."

"Are you tired of living?" Halmish asked. "Joryan told us what's happening, so we'll go along with it or face the Witch. What's your choice?"

"Not the Witch," Gorlen stated with finality. "But this isn't right."

———

Dam'yan skirted the water truck and beelined for the watch tower his troop had set up in their camp. He was so caught up in what he'd heard that he missed the human concealed in the low boughs of a tree.

Joryan wouldn't lie to them. Would he? No. Gorlen and Halmish had to be wrong. They trusted Joryan. He'd been there for them through thick and thin, training them, finding them places in the mercenary companies, and protecting them from the gangs in the undercity. Even now, while the Witch ran rampant on High Tortuga, he'd protected them by bringing them out here to complete their training.

Nevertheless, a seed of doubt had been planted by what he'd heard. The seed had barely taken root when it was fed by the fear he'd had for his mother and two small brothers since Joryan had told them the Witch was searching for them. Fear and doubt fed the rage that always bubbled beneath the surface, waiting for an outlet.

He ran through the unfamiliar jungle with his rifle on his back, heedless of how much noise he was making. Branches whipped him and lacerated his tough skin. Small creatures fled in fear. Dam'yan didn't care. His weapon held seven ballistic rounds, the non-Newtonian fluid in the gel rounds enough to stun anything except persistent predators.

Were the adults included in the list of predators his fellow trainees had to be wary of? He wasn't sure. His only goal was to get back to the others to make decisions with them. Even if Joryan didn't have their best interests at heart, he had trained them well. Every trainee knew he could rely on his fellows.

He heard the fighting before he reached the camp. The scouts must have figured that the truck was headed this way. Dam'yan burst out of the thicket, his adrenaline and rage controlled, and ran for the tower.

Barely registering who he was hitting, he launched a flying kick that struck the center of Barlek's chest. He used the momentum from Barlek's fall to drop into a roll, then twisted his body in a low leg sweep to clear Frader from his path.

Leaping to his feet, he led with a solid elbow to a temple and followed through with an uppercut to the next boy in his way. Skinny in comparison to the majority of his brothers, Dam'yan's strength and natural ability to wreak carnage, combined with the explosive rage peculiar to his species, made him unstoppable.

Feet sure despite the churned mud in the clearing, he sprinted for the tower, throwing aside anyone who stood in his way until he crashed into a solid wall of muscle.

Randro.

The adult male grabbed Dam'yan's shoulder and held him at arm's length.

"What's wrong with you?" Randro asked, not unkindly.

Dam'yan uselessly swung at Randro. *"You're what's wrong!"* he yelled loud enough to be heard around the clearing. *"You lied! You all lied!"*

An awkward silence fell as Dam'yan continued struggling to free himself from Randro's grip.

Barlek came forward, face twisted in suspicion. "What do you mean, they lied?"

"Ask him!" Dam'yan screamed. "We're not going home. Not ever!"

Baba Yaga paused at the edge of the clearing and put a hand out to stop Stephen, Jennifer, and Lerr'ek from setting foot in the camp.

Hold for a moment. We might not need to intervene until this is over.

"You're going to allow the trainees to attack their captors?" Lerr'ek murmured, knowing she could hear him.

She nodded and stepped back into the shadows.

"Let him go," Barlek told Randro.

Almost fully grown, Barlek had been scheduled to ship out with Dam'yan, Gralen, and several others until Baba Yaga set her sights on Joryan's operation. The other six stepped forward when Randro didn't comply, followed by youngers who were still too green to control their rage.

Barlek raised his rifle, and the others followed. "I *said*, let him go."

"You better be serious about using that thing if you point it at me," Randro growled. He released Dam'yan with a shove that sent him toward his troop.

Dam'yan hissed at Randro and turned to the others. "I heard

Halmish's group talking. Gorlen said that everything Joryan told us about our families was a lie. The Witch didn't kill them."

"Is that true?" Barlek demanded, raising the barrel of his rifle to Randro's chest height.

Randro's split-second hesitation caused an uproar that drew the other adults from the tower. They'd been lounging around on supply crates playing a card game.

"*Stand down!*" Randro roared as the kids loosed a barrage of ballistic rounds at the adults. "Stand dow—"

A round to the face cut him off and sent him reeling. Barlek stunned him with a double tap to the temple, rendering him helpless for the few seconds it took for six of the youngers to truss him and drag him into the tower.

As the last adult was shoved inside, the water truck arrived. Halmish, Gorlen, and the others leapt to the ground with their weapons drawn.

"I *told* you!" Halmish growled at Gorlen as the troop encircled the water truck.

"I don't care," Gorlen stated. "It's not right to take the youngers from their mothers before they're ready."

"That's not for you to decide!" Halmish snarled.

Gorlen lifted a shoulder. "Alict's out of the bag now. Deal with it."

"Where are our families?" Dam'yan demanded.

A voice like cascading gravel answered for them. "Your families are safe in your homes." Baba Yaga walked into the camp, *pushing* a wave of fear strong enough to bring everyone to their knees. "You will be returned to them as soon as I've dealt with the adults."

Two humans and a Zhyn joined her from the tree line.

"You!" Halmish pointed at them.

It was the last word he ever said. Baba Yaga moved faster than any of the Shrillexians could track, and the heads of all the adults except Gorlen dropped to the mud a second or two before their bodies caught up to the fact that they were no longer connected and collapsed.

Baba Yaga tore a swatch from Halmish's clothing and cleaned her short sword before sheathing it at her hip. "Gorlen, right?"

The boys watched in stunned silence as he nodded, swallowing hard.

"Why are you here?"

Gorlen shrugged. "I heard what Joryan was planning and didn't think it was right to leave the kids without someone who cared about them for more than the credits they can generate."

"Despite knowing I would hunt the deserters down?" Baba Yaga asked.

Gorlen nodded again but said nothing until he realized she expected more from him. "I've got nothing else to say. I could have gone along with the others, but it wouldn't have been right." He took a knee and bowed his head. "Do what you have to do."

Dam'yan couldn't take his eyes off the Witch. She was ten times more terrifying than he'd imagined, and it had nothing to do with the many weapons strapped to her body or her sharp teeth. She exuded power on a scale he had never thought possible. She held herself with the ease of an apex predator, which spoke to her ability to kill anything that threatened her. She needed none of the blades and guns she carried.

Yet Gorlen still lived and breathed.

If Baba Yaga was the merciless Mistress they had been told she was, why hadn't she killed him with the others? Dam'yan was relieved that she had chosen to sate her curiosity. Gorlen was the only one besides Joryan who had taken the time to get to know them on an individual level. He had spoken out several times when the other adults pushed them beyond the point of exhaustion in training.

Baba Yaga's voice broke Dam'yan from his thoughts. "Want a teaching position?"

Gorlen's head snapped up. "A *what?*"

Baba Yaga turned to her Zhyn companion. "He's all yours. Stephen, Jennifer, get the kids ready for transport back to Thon. Their mothers are eager for their return."

She vanished as the sky above the clearing darkened with the arrival of transport vehicles. Dam'yan was confused by the vehicles, which were somewhere between ground cars and small shuttles.

With Baba Yaga gone, it was easier to recall that the other humans were also dangerous. However, they were patient and kind as they got the young males into the vehicles, which they called roamers. Dam'yan corralled five, emulating Barlek, and climbed into the roamer ahead of his group to show them there was nothing to be wary of.

Despite their power, the humans were good people. It radiated from them as surely as their ability to tear out the throat of anyone who threatened them.

The human named Stephen climbed into the roamer with them and took the empty seat at the controls. The youngers clammed up, although they had been full of questions and speculation the moment before.

"Where did Baba Yaga go?" Dam'yan asked Stephen. That was the main question on all their minds.

"She had some trash to pick up before she left for Thon," Stephen answered enigmatically.

Dam'yan was silent for the rest of the journey, resting his head against the translucent side panel. He never thought he'd be so happy to see Thon, but as the skyline came into view, his heart lightened for the first time since Joryan had told them he was taking them to safety.

His mother and brothers were safe, and he was home. Whatever the future held for him now, he would face it knowing he wasn't alone in the world.

CHAPTER SIXTEEN

<u>**High Tortuga, Northern Continent, City of Thon, Undercity**</u>

Bethany Anne struggled to maintain Baba Yaga's stoic demeanor as the boys reunited with their mothers and siblings. Her heart constricted at the thought of how close Joryan had come to destroying over sixty families.

She reached out to Stephen. *Have the parents remove the younger children. I'm about to deliver Joryan to them.*

As you wish, my Queen.

Bethany Anne stepped into the Etheric, where she'd deposited the scumbag in question. He lay where she'd left him, hands still bound behind his back and hitched to the ties around his ankles.

Unfortunately, she hadn't bothered to gag him. "I'll pay you whatever you want, bitch. Just let me go," he snarled.

She laughed at his audacity. "First, you have no wealth. I redistributed it. Second, what I took from you wouldn't cover an afternoon's shopping for me."

A cold smile replaced her amusement at his pathetic attempt to bribe her. "No, Joryan. The only thing that will satisfy me is you facing Justice for what you did to your people. You stole their sons, their fathers, their brothers. How many males died because you rushed them into war? How much did your actions reduce the ability of your people to grow and better their situation because their society had an unnatural imbalance?"

"I made them strong!" Joryan protested. "I trained them to the best of my ability and found them employment! I took care of the families of my trainees."

"You've got it twisted, fucknut. You stripped them of their strength and a portion of their income." Baba Yaga stepped closer to him. "The ability of people like you to justify their actions never ceases to amaze and disgust me. Children like Gralen took care of the families you tore asunder."

She placed a boot on his back and transferred them back to the undercity, then raised her voice to be heard by all. "Without you, your people would have the same choices Shrillexians in the Federation have: the choice to take the serum that gives them control of their rage. The choice to pursue their passions. To remain with their families instead of being sent to fight and die to increase your wealth."

Baba Yaga cut the tie that connected the restraints around his wrists and ankles. Joryan protested as she dragged him to his feet, but his words were lost in the angry shouts of the adults and their adolescent children.

"Listen up," she ground out. "Your families are back together, or what is left of them. There is now a community fund you can draw on to retrain and rebuild your lives. However, there remains the question of what to do with Joryan. I am not the one he wronged, so I leave it up to you to decide his punishment."

She kicked his legs out, forcing him to kneel before his people. Then she stepped back. As expected, the females surged forward. Their anger filled the air, thick and hot.

The mothers' and wives' voices rose as one as they surrounded Joryan, who unsuccessfully tried to shuffle away. Their fists and feet rained down upon him, each blow a testament to the pain he'd brought them. Baba Yaga stood back with

Stephen and bore witness as every female who had lost a son, husband, brother, or father released decades of suppressed grief and loss. The males watched in silence.

When they were done, all that was left was a bloody, mangled mess on the permacrete. Shattered bone protruded from the lump that was barely recognizable as a corpse, gleaming pearl-pink under the bright overhead light.

Stephen murmured, "Men usually fight, but women are as capable of wreaking total destruction as they are of creating life. That is a truth that transcends species."

"We have seen it time and time again," Baba Yaga agreed. "It takes incredible strength to be gentle. It's easy to forget that."

Several of the females stepped forward. Denasi was in front. "Thank you for allowing us to take the burden of responsibility for his punishment," Denasi told Baba Yaga. "And what you have put in place to help us rebuild."

Baba Yaga shook her head. "All I'm doing is providing the tools. The work is on you."

Denasi remained as the others returned to their children. "How is Gralen settling in at the Institute? He calls, but he just tells me he is well and learning a lot."

"He is bonding well with the others," Baba Yaga assured her.

"I speak to Lerr'ek daily," Stephen added. "He has nothing but praise for Gralen. Your son has thrown himself into making the most of the opportunities he is being given."

Denasi smiled proudly. "That's all I needed to hear. Thank you both again."

Stephen inclined his head. "I will see you at the first meeting of the board for the Brighter Tomorrow Foundation."

"The what?" Denasi asked.

Baba Yaga smiled. "Gralen gets his head for numbers from you and the effort you put into teaching him. There's no one here I would rather see head up the redistribution of the funds I recovered from Joryan. Stephen will advise and support you every step of the way, beginning with filling the rest of the seats at the table. I have jobs waiting for everyone who wants to work in construction, healthcare, or teaching, and further training and education will be available to any who wish to enter other fields."

Denasi bowed her head. "I wish my husband was alive to see this day. I won't let you down, Baba Yaga. My people will become what they were meant to be instead of being forced to fight their whole lives."

Baba Yaga chuckled. "I'm sure many will wish to continue fighting, and I will offer them something worthy of fighting for. Their home."

High Tortuga, Northern Continent, City of Thon, Undisclosed Location, Institute of Education-Focused Extrajudicial Foundational Studies

"How do I say, 'Baba Yaga decapitated twenty-four assholes in a badass move that no one saw because she was too fast' politely?"

Kirian looked up from typing his part of the after-action report. "For a start, don't call them assholes."

Gralen made a face. "I guess cursing isn't appropriate."

Kirian shook his head. "Cursing is fine. You just need to be creative about it. Hit them with something as generic as 'assholes,' and we can expect a C-minus."

"I'm definitely not about the C-minus life." Gralen sighed and tapped his stylus on the table before scribbling on his datapad. "Umm, how about this? 'Twenty traitorous twatwaffles lost their heads in a move so awesome that no one but Stephen was privileged to watch Baba Yaga make it.'"

"Twatwaffles?" Kirian raised an eyebrow. "Alliterative, but not accurate."

Gralen shrugged. "I heard Doc say it to the copier in the infirmary the other day. Maybe I should just stick to the facts, but that doesn't fit with the reports we studied to learn how to put one of these together."

"Did you choose Ranger Two's AARs?" Kirian asked. "The others were less…irreverent."

"But, *Ranger Two!*" Gralen protested. "She's a legend among legends. I thought I should learn from the best."

A chuckle from the booth behind theirs drew their attention.

The stranger interjected, "Tabitha is not the best example of how to conduct oneself appropriately in most situations."

"Who are you?" Kirian slowly twisted and pulled himself up to look over the top of the booth.

The man wearing the monk's robe was ten years older than them by appearance, but Kirian had been around Stephen enough to recognize an ancient when he met one.

"Oh," was his clever response.

The man smiled. "My name is Barnabas. You must be Kirian Larsen."

Gralen popped up beside Kirian and introduced himself. "You know Ranger Two?"

Barnabas replied, "Son, I am Ranger One, or I was. The Rangers disbanded when the Etheric Empire did. I suppose I am a free agent now."

Both boys' mouths dropped open. Gralen was first to recover.

"How do we impress Baba Yaga with this report, then?"

Barnabas finished his juice, slid out of his booth, and came around to stand by Kirian's wheelchair. "Hmm. I suggest that you focus on the outcome of the operation rather than a witty delivery. I wish you the best of luck, gentlemen. Baba Yaga is not easy to impress."

He walked away, leaving Kirian and Gralen to contemplate his advice.

Kirian returned to processing the data Cerebro had given him. "Like I said, stick to the facts. Thirty-seven hundred and seventy-four males returned from the mercenary companies

Baba Yaga shut down. Twenty of those accepted training positions at the Institute. Nineteen hundred took Baba Yaga's offer of construction work. Around a thousand joined the new planetary security force."

"What about the personal data?" Gralen asked. "The families that are back together. The hope for the future my people feel and the fear that taking a new direction as a society might fail?"

Kirian nodded. "We might need to ask for an extension."

"Or a pass to go interview some of the returnees," Gralen countered. "My mother is a great source, but she has her hands full with chairing the foundation's board."

"We need Charr," Kirian grumbled. "He just had to be stuck in exams again right when we had this report to write."

"Engineering is no joke," Gralen countered. "His curriculum is brutal."

Kirian sighed. "But he loves it. I'm not mad."

Gralen's eyes lit up as an idea hit him. "Maybe we can get Barlek and Dam'yan to help us. Would that break any rules?"

Kirian grinned and shifted himself from the booth to his chair. "Only one way to find out. Let's go ask."

<u>High Tortuga, Northern Continent, City of Thon, Undisclosed Location</u>

Stephen rubbed his eyes and sighed. "Bethany Anne, I know you normally say what you want done and wave your hand, and we come back six months later, and it's done."

"Well, yes. I don't see the issue."

Stephen wearily pointed out, "The issue is that this planet has finite resources, both material and physical, and you are using most of those to construct the BYPS."

"I just hired two thousand workers," Bethany Anne countered.

"What about the material resources? Steel and other refined alloys and rare metals for wiring? The Etheric engineers to install comms and other specialized equipment? The short timeframe? I could go on..."

Bethany Anne waved her hand. "Please don't. I need a secure base here on High Tortuga, and I need it by the time I get back from retrieving my man from Earth. Don't tell me what I can't have. Tell me what we *can* make happen. Logistics, Stephen."

"You could open the planet to trade," Lerr'ek suggested.

"That would be, 'Fuck, no!' Not until I have full control of who comes and goes. There's no point spending billions to hide the planet and put the BYPS in place if I advertise its location."

"You could divert resources from the Federation," Stephen suggested.

"Same issue, different direction. Besides, everything I have there is going into the Annex Gate project. Barnabas, you haven't said anything."

"There is a solution you are not considering," Barnabas offered.

"Are you waiting for me to read your mind?" Bethany Anne asked when he didn't elaborate. She glanced at Lerr'ek, who shifted uncomfortably in his seat. "A location I already own. Like the Institute."

"You want to put a military base on the site of my school?" Lerr'ek shook his head. "I'm barely up and running, and you're going to pull the plug."

"Who said anything about pulling the plug on the Institute? The building has sublevels you haven't explored yet, and the surrounding area is undeveloped. It wouldn't be difficult to expand what's already there to meet my needs without impinging on yours."

Lerr'ek grumped, "A secret military base on the site of the school I'm about to open to the public would not remain secret very long."

Bethany Anne waved him off. "We keep them separate for everyone coming in from outside. Easily achieved. I'll be bringing in personnel who will cart their families along. Their children will need an education equivalent to what they are already receiving."

"I don't even have a full faculty yet, and you're flinging more students at me." Lerr'ek groaned. "Okay, but keep me in the loop. No surprises."

"That's why you have Cerebro. Stephen, does this solve the shortfall in time and resources?"

"No, but retrofitting the existing building rather than building from scratch takes us from the realm of impossible to merely impractical."

"When have I ever cared about impractical?" Bethany Anne pressed her lips together. "Make it work. I don't care about cost at this stage. My need is greater than any budgetary concerns."

CHAPTER SEVENTEEN

<u>**High Tortuga, Northern Continent, City of Thon, Brasak Sector**</u>

Kirian said goodbye to Charr'est, and they went to their respective homes. Gralen, Dam'yan, and Barlek had remained in the undercity, wanting time with their families before they all returned to the Institute.

As he made his way to his house, it occurred to Kirian that not long ago, he would have had to rely on his chair's motor instead of choosing to use it to save his energy for being on his feet at home.

So much had changed in a short time. He was determined never to forget the struggles he had endured before Doc Ericson had changed his life and given him the ability to choose his battles instead of being at the mercy of his body's limits.

He wasn't the only one who had been given a new lease on life by the nanocyte treatment. Leaving his chair outside the kitchen door, Kirian walked into the house and was greeted by framed canvases leaning against the walls by the door. He brushed his fingers over the thick layers of bubble wrap. The memory of how good it felt to pop the bubbles made him smile.

"You've been busy, Mom," he called.

"Kirian?" Janet came into the kitchen, wrestling an overly large canvas. Her headscarf and paint-spattered overalls were covered in bits of fluff and tape. She gently placed the wrapped canvas against the island and hurried over to embrace her son. "What are you doing home, sweetheart?"

"I had some free time after a field project." Kirian returned the hug with feeling. "Thought I'd come visit the soon-to-be-famous artist."

"It's just a gallery show." Janet brushed Kirian's hair off his forehead and planted a kiss there. "But you're good to your mother for saying so. How are you?"

"Good, Mom. I have a couple of hours if you want some help getting all this loaded up. Where's Gramps?"

"He's at the senior center with the reprobates he hangs out with." Janet waved at the large canvas. "If you're up to it, I could use your help with the bigger pieces."

Kirian flexed his arms and grinned. "I feel great. I've been in my chair all day. I wanted to save my energy for you."

They loaded his chair into the rental truck last and headed to the arts center on the edge of the theater district where Janet was holding her show. Kirian wheeled in beside her, and they located the gallery's director.

"Are we going to stay while they hang all those?" Kirian asked after the woman greeted them and excused herself to take care of business.

Janet grinned. "I have to dress the space. These fine gentlemen are here to do the heavy lifting. You get to help me decide where everything goes."

The two burly humans introduced themselves as Tobey and Francis before heading out to empty the truck. Janet walked around the room, taking notes as she explored the alcoves and partitioned spaces.

"I'm so proud of you, Mom," Kirian commented after Janet

instructed Tobey and Francis. "You took the chance to be an artist and ran with it."

Janet ruffled his hair. "Anything worth doing is worth overdoing. You know that."

Kirian chuckled. "I get that from you."

"Tell me about the fieldwork you've been doing. I thought your studies would be mostly computer-related."

"There's plenty of computer work involved. We had to write a report on a Shrillexian community that's going through significant changes."

"Shrillexians? Isn't that dangerous?"

Kirian shook his head. "They're also getting access to the serum from the Empire...I mean, the Federation."

"It seems like there are big changes happening everywhere." Janet sighed as she looked around the gallery. "As long as you're safe and you enjoy the direction your life is taking, I'm happy for you."

"I'm safe, Mom. If anything, the work I'm doing on the census is boring. I enjoy data processing, especially when I'm in control of the data I use. A lot of the people I interviewed today are former mercenaries. They told stories that helped me understand what their lives have been like and what they'll need to adjust to being back home with their families."

"What does that have to do with game developing?" Janet's confusion came through in her tone.

While Kirian couldn't tell her about the team, he was happy to talk about his post-graduation plans. "You know that our curriculum is set according to our talents and interests, and I've been developing sims for Dreamland?"

Janet nodded. "You're giving me more credits every month than I know what to do with."

"We're not having the conversation where you say I don't need to give you anything, you're fine." Kirian smiled. "Well, it turns out I'm suited for leadership, so my curriculum is teaching me how to be a good leader. When I graduate, I'll be ready to launch my own company. When I'm old enough to file the paperwork, I'll transfer everything I did as a freelance developer to the company and have my best sims ready to launch."

Janet flushed with pride. "You're learning business as well?"

Kirian nodded. "There's a reason I'm so busy, Mom. I don't intend to waste a second of this opportunity. I had some help setting up the freelance stuff, but the rest is on me to deal with. If you think I'm making a lot of money now, just wait a couple of years. My sims are only licensed to Dreamland now because I need to focus on my studies. When I graduate, I'll open them up to other arcades and companies that provide in-home gaming systems."

"That's a big dream you're making come true." Her eyes shone with tears. "It's the future I always wanted for you, whatever miracle brought it to you."

"The one you thought I'd never have," Kirian finished for her when her words trailed off.

Janet wiped her eyes with the heel of her hand. "I'm sorry. I can't help thinking of how boisterous you were as a toddler, and how hard it was when your mobility issues became apparent. Now, you get better with every week that passes. It's more than I could ever have hoped for. You're living a full life!"

"I know, Mom. I feel the same about you getting to teach and paint now that your whole life doesn't revolve around taking care of me." Kirian blinked away tears of his own, wishing he could tell his mother everything. "Can I talk to you about something on the drive home? Just between us. I don't think Gramps needs to know."

"You can talk to me about anything. We're just about done here."

Kirian waited until Janet pulled out of the gallery parking lot to start, using the time to decide where to begin and how much to tell her.

"What's on your mind, sweetheart?" she asked.

"My therapy. You don't know everything."

"What else is there to know?" Janet turned onto the expressway. "Whatever vector the doctors used to circumvent your immune system is working. I never thought I'd see the day you walked without needing pain management."

"There's no vector, Mom. The treatment isn't gene therapy. It's something called nanocytes. The same ones that give enhanced humans superpowers. For me, they repair my muscles and maintain them by producing the dystrophin my body can't. It's way more complicated than that, but that's the basic explanation."

Janet's hands tightened on the wheel. "Nanocytes? Then why aren't you cured?"

"You know about them?" Kirian was surprised.

"I worked in healthcare before we left the Empire, and I saw what the Empress' gift did for some people. I should have known, even if I don't understand how they work."

"Right now, I'm getting regular infusions of level one nanocytes. Level two alters genes to express the best combination of recessive traits. It makes people taller, stronger, faster, and smarter. That won't work for me since my issue is the faulty gene that causes Duchenne's. There's no good gene to select."

Janet sighed. "You've really studied this, huh?"

Kirian nodded. "Level three would cure me, but it comes with...all the extras, and I don't want that life. Maybe one day, if I'm offered the chance, but not now. Not when I've just gotten the chance to be normal."

"You know..." Janet paused. "Gramps guessed what was really going on. He said you'd tell me in your own time. Is this really why you're doing fieldwork? Because you're caught up in the Empire's affairs?"

"Not the Empire-slash-Federation," Kirian told her. "My report will go to Baba Yaga, and she will use it to decide how best to help the Shrillexians. I'm making a real difference, Mom. My friend Gralen is from that community."

He spent the next few minutes explaining the situation with Joryan, leaving out the parts he had been personally involved in.

"Gralen?" Janet didn't hide her surprise. "Wasn't he involved in the trouble you were in with that video game? He was bullying you."

Kirian lifted a shoulder. "He didn't know any better. It turns out he and Charr'est are pretty cool."

"'Pretty cool?'" Janet glanced at him. "I hope those pretty cool guys aren't getting you into more trouble."

Kirian laughed. "With Professor Lerr'ek watching me? Not likely. Besides, they're both smart and really hard workers, just like me. I enjoy having friends on my level academically, even though we're on different study paths."

"What about your other friends?" Janet asked. "The triplets, Ari, Fern, and Xander?"

Kirian sighed. His mind went straight to Tianel's impending departure. "I'm still spending time with them. Not as much, but a lifetime of friendship doesn't go away because we're growing up, and things are changing for us all."

"That's good to hear." Janet chuckled. "You boys were always close. It's been quiet without you all yelling in the basement."

Kirian shook his head, unable to suppress a smile. "I was worried that going to different schools would cause a rift, but it hasn't turned out that way. We planned a farewell party for Tianel next week."

"The pretty one?" Janet flashed a knowing look at him. "You like her, don't you?"

It wasn't a question. She knew him better than anyone. Kirian nodded. "Yeah, but it's…complicated."

"It's not too late to tell her how you feel."

"What's the point? She's going back to Torcellan, and we'll probably never see each other again. You know, she was the only girl apart from Fern who saw beyond my illness. She's kind and smart and—"

"And you should tell her," Janet insisted. "What happened to not wasting a moment? It's okay to be scared. What's not okay is living with regrets, and now you'll have a long time to live with the regrets you accumulate, baby boy."

She laughed at Kirian when he made a face. "Too much? Well, you're my baby boy, and you always will be."

Kirian relented. "Love you too, Mom. Thanks for the advice."

"Will you take it?"

Kirian sighed. "I don't know. I'll think about it."

High Tortuga, Northern Continent, City of Thon, Undisclosed Location, Institute of Education-Focused Extrajudicial Foundational Studies

Kirian had plenty to think about, and adding whether to confess his feelings to Tianel before she left for Torcellan left him exhausted in a way he hadn't felt for a while.

His body complained as he stripped the exosuit off and took a quick shower before gratefully collapsing onto the bed to scroll through his messages.

There was still nothing from Tor despite his efforts to connect. He approved Charr'est's last-minute edits to the after-action report and uploaded it to the group chat. They were presenting it first thing in the morning, so he was glad one of them was on point and dropped a quick message to say so before messaging Doc Ericson to ask for an extra therapy session if she could fit him in.

He got a call from the doc a minute after sending the message. He answered by apologizing for reaching out so late.

"It's not a problem, Kirian. Are you okay?"

"Yeah, but I might have overdone it today. I helped my mom after we were done with the census research. Her gallery show is opening this weekend. I ran out of pain patches yesterday and forgot to pick any up before I left."

"Sounds like you had a good day if you got through without pain management. Did you remember to eat enough for your nanocytes to be at their most effective?"

Kirian was glad she couldn't see his blush. "Um, no. That was why I asked for the extra session."

"I'll be there in a few minutes." She ended the call.

When she arrived with sandwiches, an IV stand with the bag of nanocyte infusion, and her med kit, Kirian was sitting up. "Thank you," Kirian told her as she inserted the cannula. "I hope I didn't wake you."

"I was going over the medical reports for the Shrillexian trainees. You were out with Dam'yan and Barlek today, right? How did you do?"

Kirian grinned, then groaned as he reached for half a sandwich. "Dam'yan is hilarious. I kind of thought they'd all be serious like Gralen, but he has a wicked sense of humor. Barlek makes Gralen look like the class clown, though. He's going to be a tough nut to crack."

The nanocyte infusion was well underway, and the food and pain patches started doing their job. Kirian's pain faded.

"It's not like you to be so absentminded about your care," the doc commented without judgment.

Kirian finished the last bite of thick-cut bistok and rye bread. "I just forgot. I felt pretty good until I didn't."

Jennifer chuckled. "Then you felt like you were hit by a transport Pod."

Kirian nodded. "That's good though, right? A whole day where I was as normal as everyone else?"

"I bet it felt good, but you need to remember that the infusion only works as long as you don't overdo it."

"I talked to my mom about this today. If she was in charge of my treatment, I would be in the Pod-doc getting level three enhancement, like, yesterday."

The doc chuckled, then got serious. "Do you want level three?"

Kirian shook his head. "Not yet. I know I'll have to have it at some point, but not now. I have enough on my plate without having to come to terms with extra abilities. I just want to be a teenager, you know? Study and spend time with my family and friends. Ordinary stuff."

Jennnifer smiled. "You have plenty of time for you to do those things now. You know Bethany Anne won't allow you to take on any serious assignments until you have that enhancement, right?"

Kirian nodded. "I'm not ready for serious assignments. Getting kidnapped by Joryan showed me that I have a long way to go before I take on the big leagues."

CHAPTER EIGHTEEN

Kirian clicked over to the last slide in the presentation. "In conclusion, the actions taken during and after the operation ensured that the ring of mercenary groups is no longer exploiting the Shrillexian community. Additionally, handing Joryan over to the community for Justice fostered a sense of trust in Baba Yaga and returned the empowerment his actions had stolen."

He clicked the projector app off and sat between Charr'est and Gralen across from Baba Yaga. The last ninety minutes had gone well, with Charr'est's breakdown of the preliminary investigation leading smoothly into Gralen's coverage of the events on the Southern Continent, including the work the three had done to assist with the transport of the Shrillexians back to Thon.

Kirian's data breakdown had rounded out the report. Despite his confidence in their report, he waited nervously for Baba Yaga's response.

She smiled, although it wasn't comforting, given those serrated teeth. "Well done, students. I expected a lot from you, and you delivered."

Kirian heaved a sigh of relief, echoed by Gralen and Charr'est. All three made to leave.

"Not so fast." Baba Yaga waved to indicate that they should stay where they were. "What did you learn from this?"

This was the inquisition Kirian had expected. He sat back down. "That planning is key to success. Even if the plan doesn't pan out, making sure we're prepared for anything that can go wrong and having failsafes and backup in place minimizes the risk of failure."

"Failure meaning your death," Baba Yaga pointed out. "Every action has consequences. Going into the undercity without anyone knowing where you were or what you were doing could have ended with Lerr'ek having to inform your mothers that you had died. It was sheer luck that was not the outcome, and rescuing you led directly to Joryan kidnapping the rest of the trainees."

Kirian lowered his head. "I know, and I won't make the same mistake again. I swear."

Baba Yaga's stern expression softened. "Kirian, you *are* going to make mistakes. It's part of growing up, but being a good leader means acknowledging where you went wrong, working to put it right, and learning from your errors so you can choose more wisely in the future."

"It's not about growing up," Kirian responded. "I am responsible for everyone on my team. I didn't take that seriously enough, and it led to us having to chase Joryan halfway across the planet."

"Is that going to stop you from doing what you know is right in the future?" Baba Yaga asked.

Kirian thought about it, then shook his head. "I'm still going to do it, but in the future, I'll go about it the right way. What we did in the jungle operation had value, and it was more suited to our skill sets. Fighting onsite would have put us in danger and distracted you and the other adults from what you were there to do. We work best as part of the whole team."

"Then you learned the lesson I intended. Charr'est, what did you learn?"

Charr'est squirmed, uncomfortable with the attention. "The same as Kirian. That success comes from working as part of a whole."

"Would you blindly follow Kirian into another dangerous situation?"

Charr'est paused. "I can't say no. He's our leader, and there will be dangerous situations as we get older and take on more serious assignments. But I won't be afraid to ask questions. Kirian isn't Dex. I trust him to hear me."

Baba Yaga inclined her head. "Right answer. Gralen. You were not required to take part in this exercise, yet you did. Why?"

"Because they're my team," Gralen told her confidently. "Where they go, so do I. Besides, this wasn't a punishment. I'm here to learn."

Baba Yaga's smile returned. "You are functioning as a unit. That's promising. Okay, you're free to go. I believe you are all wanted in Lerr'ek's office."

They made their way to the atrium, where they discovered Lerr'ek waiting for them.

"Good, you're done with the report." He waved them into his office. "The Shrillexian students have their official intake tomorrow. I hope I can count on you three to help them settle in."

"What do you need from us?" Kirian asked.

"I'll be onboarding the new faculty over the next forty-eight hours. I want you three to show the new students around and help them find their dorms and tour the facilities. The transports arrive in two hours."

Kirian grinned. "We could test the virtual learning environment I've been working on."

"Virtual, *what* now?"

"A virtual space modeled on the Institute."

Lerr'ek tilted his head. "Why do we need a virtual space when we have, you know, a real space? One that cost a considerable amount to build so the students of the Institute could get the best education this side of the Federation?"

"That is why offering a virtual experience is necessary," Kirian countered. "Classroom time for academic subjects is limited, which reduces the amount of time students spend together and with their mentors."

"What about friends on different study paths?" Gralen pointed out. "Or those who need to take a module from another course to supplement their curriculum? It would help to be able to download previous lectures."

"I have a math class that clashes with others," Charr'est told the prof. "And a whole day where I have nothing scheduled. I could have more control over my schedule with the option to move my practical engineering class to that day."

"The advanced math class you have the Yollin tutor for?" Lerr'ek asked.

Charr'est nodded. "Right now, I have fourteen straight hours of class twice a week because Dr. P'alimar is only available for video conferences on those days, and I'm not qualified to be in the shop by myself yet. I can't get hurt in a virtual shop."

Kirian waved as he'd seen Bethany Anne do. "See? There's a need for it."

"Don't get ahead of yourselves," Lerr'ek told them. "Kirian, the sim needs to go through all the safety checks the sims you write for Dreamland pass. That means no testing it on the student body.

"Gralen, your job today is to explain the points system for the fighters. Kirian and Charr'est, yours is to work with Cerebro to identify the students we should be looking at pushing academically. Everyone will be tested by the learning program, but it's about more than aptitude. We need to identify those who want to do something other than military service."

Gralen grinned. "Like me?"

Kirian threw an elbow into his friend's side. "There's only one of you."

Professor Lerr'ek shook his head and smiled. "Check in with Ms. Friday before the transports arrive and ask if she wants help. She took it upon herself to prepare for their arrival."

"Yes, sir," all three chorused.

Tel'ah Friday was bustling around the second sub-level electronics store, putting together tech bundles for the incoming students, when she heard the unmistakable sounds of trouble headed her way.

"Ms. Friday, you in here?" Kirian called.

"Back here." Tel'ah placed the wrist-holos she'd selected on the cart as they came around the stacks and into sight. She smiled, happy to see the trio. "What can I help you with? I'm short on time today."

"It's more what we can do for you," Charr'est told her.

"Professor Lerr'ek sent us," Gralen confirmed.

Kirian grinned. "How can we help?"

"You can cut my prep time in half." Tel'ah's smile got wider. "Let's see." She waved a hand at the cart. "Kirian, you could set up the new students' IDs." She grabbed a datapad. This one was covered with iridescent film to mark it as hers. "I'll send you two the rest of my list for picking if you don't mind?"

She led Kirian to a metal table by the entrance to the storage area, and they all got to work personalizing the new students' tech bundles.

Kirian made conversation as they worked. "How are you finding High Tortuga compared to the *Meredith Reynolds*, Ms. Friday?"

Tel'ah chuckled. "It's definitely a change of pace. I'm used to being busy 'round the clock. The Institute is so quiet."

"Not for long. The Shrillexians are only the start. When the rest of the faculty arrives from the *Meredith Reynolds* and the Institute opens its doors to the flight school and the rest of the academic students, it will get pretty busy. Probably not around the clock. What did you do there?"

"I was the administration coordinator for all the high schools on the station. The administrators for each district answered to me."

Kirian's eyes widened. "Wow, you really *were* busy. Isn't this, I don't know, a step down for you?"

"For the moment." Tel'ah lowered her voice. "Bethany Anne recruited me for this post, and I would never refuse my Queen. Besides, there's more to the Institute than the outward-facing parts."

Kirian nodded. "You're going to run the secret base."

Tel'ah looked shocked. "You know about that?"

"I didn't, but I do now." Kirian held up his hands. "Sorry. I figured that with the Empire folding and the terms of the Federation's founding, including Bethany Anne stepping down, there was a reason she showed an interest in this planet. Three-quarters of this building is unused, so it makes sense for the new base to be here."

Tel'ah shook her head. "You're too smart for your own good, Kirian. We should be including you in meetings."

Kirian grimaced. "I'm good, thanks. There will be plenty of time for that when I'm older and farther along in my education. Right now, I'm happy figuring things out for myself and seeing how it turns out."

An hour later, all that was left was inputting the new students' biometric data into their student accounts to lock their devices to their personal use. Kirian had been sitting too long and needed to get his chair before meeting everyone at the Sub-level One hangars half a mile from the center of the Institute.

Getting there was easy. It was a straight run from corridor

2B1 near the cafeteria along corridor 2X9.1 to the hangars. The trouble began at the end of 2X9.1, which branched in several directions where it met the hangar access corridors.

Kirian could have sworn they were meeting at the hangar designated 2X9.16. When he went in, he found not Professor Lerr'ek, Doc Ericson, and Ms. Friday ushering the new students off plain but serviceable transport Pods but a vaster space than he'd thought it possible to have underground and three ships large enough to fit most of the sector he called home inside their battle-scarred hulls.

"I…should not be in here." He stopped his chair, turned around, and made a beeline for the main corridor. "I saw nothing. Definitely not any Leviathan-class battleships. Nope. Nuh-uh. None of my business."

There was interest and investment. Then there was moving your most valuable assets somewhere very few people knew existed. If Bethany Anne was hiding ships here, was she planning on bringing her whole outfit to High Tortuga? What did that mean for the Federation?

He filed the thought away for later consideration. He was late and lost. "Cerebro?"

"Yes, Kirian?"

"Where am I supposed to be?"

"Definitely not in hangar 2X9.16." The AI chuckled.

Dammit. Kirian grimaced. "I figured that. Which hangar?"

"Hangar 2X9.19."

Kirian thanked Cerebro and made his way to the appropriate corridor. He arrived just as the transport Pods arrived. They landed in a neat row spanning half the hangar as Kirian made his way to the long folding table that had been set up to deal with intake.

Lerr'ek took one look at him. "We don't see your chair much these days. Are you sure you're okay to be here?"

"I'm good. Just tired." Kirian wheeled into the open spot

between his friends and Jennifer. "I wouldn't miss this." He gestured at the young males debarking from the Pods alongside the former mercenaries who were going to teach. "Our first real intake. I can't tell if you're nervous or excited."

"Yes." Lerr'ek left the table and headed toward the new arrivals, calling for them to form a line in alphabetical order along with, "Welcome to the Institute."

As the new students shuffled into line and the head of the Institute gave his welcoming speech, Kirian noticed two of the males glancing at him with a mixture of disgust and predatory assessment.

"What's their deal?" he asked Gralen quietly.

"Who, Corek and Flu'uth? They need to unlearn the habit of preying on the weak to increase their status." Gralen grimaced. "Not that you're weak, but they don't know that."

Kirian sighed. "Let me guess. All they see is the chair and that I'm human and half their size."

"They need to remember you held your own against me." Gralen glared at the offenders, and they found somewhere else to look. "The only one who could maybe take me in a fair fight is Barlek."

"What about an unfair fight?" Charr'est asked.

Gralen laughed. "It would take more than any five of them could bring. Besides, look who's giving you the stares. None were ever top twenty in the rankings when Joryan ran things."

There was no time to discuss it further. Kirian had to help get everyone's biometric data into their tech bundles, which included their datapads, wrist-holos, and student or faculty ID badges. He scanned the new arrivals' faces and handprints while Ms. Friday took voice prints and Doctor Ericson took DNA samples. They uploaded the information to Cerebro, who synced the data to the tech bundles. Professor Lerr'ek, Gralen, and Charr'est issued the bundles to the new students.

The whole process took an hour, after which Lerr'ek led the

way to the atrium. Kirian allowed everyone to get ahead of him, preferring to observe from the back of the group heading down corridor 2X9.1. Gralen and Charr'est were conversing with Barlek and Dam'yan and didn't see Corek drop back.

Kirian did, and he didn't think the younger Shrillexian wanted to introduce himself. However, he wasn't sure how to handle the situation without making an enemy. The Institute was supposed to be a fresh start for the Shrillexians, and none of them could help that they'd been taught to mistrust and reject outsiders.

Conversely, he hadn't had any issues with the rest. They were secure enough to embrace the change that had come with Joryan's downfall.

Thankfully, Gralen chose that moment to look back in search of Kirian. "Come meet the guys," he called.

Kirian wheeled over, glad for a distraction that gave him time to decide how he would handle Corek's dislike before it grew into hatred. Gralen introduced him to a few people he hadn't met yet, and he easily fell into the banter.

Lerr'ek pointed out the cafeteria as they passed it. "Our food preparation is automated, so the cafeteria is open around the clock. The menus are all nutritionally balanced for the different species we have here, so you can choose from sub-menus that align with your specific dietary needs. For example, those who will constantly be training can choose protein-heavy meals."

He answered everyone's food-related questions as they continued to the atrium. When they arrived, he directed the adult Shrillexians to proceed to the faculty meeting room with Ms. Friday.

"Orientation will be in the auditorium in three hours," Professor Lerr'ek informed them. "You have until then to unpack and settle into your dorm rooms. Please follow Doctor Ericson, Kirian, Gralen, and Charr'est. They will help you find your assigned rooms and answer any questions you have."

When they were done, Kirian was beyond exhausted, but the situation with Corek still weighed on his mind. He pulled Gralen aside as they left. "I don't know what to do about him. He has no reason to dislike me."

"There's always one," Gralen commiserated.

"Super helpful, Gray," Kirian complained.

Gralen bumped his shoulder gently, seeing that his friend was in pain. "Well, if you wanted my advice, all you had to do was ask. Kick his ass. That's what I'd do in your shoes."

"I'm not you." Kirian indicated his chair. "In case you didn't notice, I've overdone it enough that I needed to take a step back."

Gralen lifted his hands. "I'd kick his ass for you, but it would undermine you. You know I've got your back, but you need to take care of this yourself if you want him to leave you alone."

A beep from Kirian's wrist-holo cut his reply short. "Dammit. What I've got to do is get to therapy before I get my ass handed to me by Doc Ericson."

CHAPTER NINETEEN

Kirian wobbled on the lunge but caught himself before he lost his balance. "Sorry, Doc. My mind is everywhere but here today. How do you do it? You work here, see patients at the clinic, and then there's everything you do for Bethany Anne. I'm finding it hard to stay focused."

"The first thing you do is complete your set. Come on. Three more, and we can move on to cardio."

Kirian nodded and pushed the last three lunges out of his aching muscles. He racked his weights, grateful for the burn in his arms and shoulders. He knew pain. He was intimate with it from a lifetime of his body consuming itself. This was different. It was a good ache that came from the strength he was building.

Stretching his arms one at a time, he walked to the treadmill and climbed on, ready for the final part of his workout. "I'm plateauing."

"That's okay. There's only so far you can go without enhancement, and you're around that point."

Kirian concentrated on his rhythm. "There's going to be trouble with some of the Shrillexian kids, especially Corek. He has some kind of problem with me."

"Huh." The doc circled the treadmill, keeping her eye on Kirian's form. "He's Shrillexian. Kick his ass, and your problem will disappear."

"You're advocating fighting? Why am I not surprised? I guess I'd feel bad. Gralen said he's one of the lowest ranked in the group."

"So he's going to pick on the one human student to make himself feel better?" Jennifer snorted. "Sounds like he needs to be taught a lesson. The smallest of those boys is twice your size. Not one of them has half your heart, though."

"It's not their fault they were taught their only value was in how well they could hold their own. I could take him, no question. I'm holding my ground against Gralen in training, and Gralen is a beast on the mat."

"You're hoping time will break the hold Joryan's abusive training methods have on Corek?"

Kirian grunted, and she sighed. "It's going to take a while for that to happen. If you try to wait it out, it will make you a target for others with low status. You need to beat him publicly at the first opportunity to make sure no one else views you as an easy target."

A thought hit Kirian. "Corek wasn't there when I faced Gralen in the undercity, so he has no idea how bad I could mess him up. I don't like the idea that the only way to get his respect is to hurt him, though."

"Channel your inner Bethany Anne. She doesn't enjoy handing people's asses to them either, but it's the only way with too many species."

Kirian thought about Lerr'ek telling him that the Queen had broken him to earn his respect and realized he was looking at the situation from a human perspective.

The only diplomacy that would work was the kind that ended with his opponent bleeding.

The next few days passed without incident. Kirian's schedule kept him busy with studies and the latest sim he was developing for Dreamland. His circadian rhythm tended to flip when he was deep into writing since, unlike Charr'est and Gralen, he had no classes to attend.

He was often in the cafeteria at three AM, eating what passed for dinner while he worked out the bugs in his murder mystery sim. The only in-person obligation he couldn't miss was therapy with the doc, but she was happy to fit him in at the beginning of her day.

At last, the weekend arrived and, with it, the pass for the camping trip with his friends. This wouldn't be a normal trip, however. It was Tianel's last week on High Tortuga and the last opportunity Kirian would have to tell her how he felt. He was still conflicted. Did he risk ruining their last few hours together, or should he keep his feelings to himself and allow them to part as friends?

As he loaded the roamer, he couldn't stop thinking about Tianel's smile and how her silver-gray eyes lit up when he made a joke only she was smart enough to get. He couldn't stand the thought of being the reason that light went out. It was better to be her friend and not be like all the other boys who hung around her, hoping for her attention. He cared too much for her and respected what they had built over the last year.

Kirian settled into the front seat of the roamer and gave Cerebro the rundown on the day's activities. "We're picking up the triplets before we head to Ocie. Everyone else is meeting us at the falls later today."

When he got to the triplets' house, they were ready and waiting with their camping gear and enough food to feed everyone for a week.

"Let's go!" Nerril whooped as the roamer landed.

Kirian lowered his window, and Meddox and Lutian fist-bumped him. "I take it you guys are keyed up for the trip."

"You're kidding, right?" Meddox laughed. "It's not the same without you. Everyone misses you while you're at school."

"The gang is back together," Lutian sang as he dumped his gear in the back of the roamer.

For the next hour, they chatted and laughed and sang along with the radio as Cerebro drove the roamer to the national park. Kirian let everything on his mind go. They had two nights of freedom from responsibility, and he intended to make the most of it.

"We should hike the falls trail," he suggested between songs.

"If you're sure you can do it," Meddox agreed.

"I'm wearing my exosuit, and I had an infusion this morning. It's doable if we take it easy on the ascent."

"We can turn back if it's too much for you," Nerril pointed out.

Kirian grinned. "We won't know if we don't try."

The triplets persuaded Kirian to save his strength for the hike while they set up camp. He started the fire while they pitched the tents, collected firewood and water, and swept the clearing free of debris and bugs.

Fern's driver dropped her, Tianel, Xander, and Ari off as Kirian was getting the blaze going.

"Just in time for lunch!" Meddox called as they piled onto the logs around the campfire. "Our dad fixed kabobs. They just need to cook."

Kirian and Meddox took care of that while the Torcellans pitched their tents. Soon, everyone was back around the fire with Cokes and kabobs.

"What do you all think about hiking the falls trail this afternoon?" Kirian asked. "I checked the trail guide. If we add an hour to the expected time, we should make it to there." He pointed at a jutting outcrop of rock halfway up the falls where the water split into a shimmering cataract that ended in the deep, clear lake across from their campsite.

"That looks like a good place to dive from." Ari's enthusiasm faded. "It wouldn't be cool to leave you out, though. Maybe we should just go for a swim."

"You'll be swimming on your own." Kirian wiped a trickle of meat juice off his chin and flashed Ari a grin. "While I appreciate the concern, I'm hiking that trail."

The weather was perfect. Warm light bathed the trail, but a soft breeze prevented them from getting too hot. Kirian had preemptively slapped pain patches on the base of his spine, and his heart soared as he went with the others.

He'd wanted normal, and there was nothing more normal than this. Everyone slowed after their rapid excited ascent of the gradual incline at the head of the trail. The sun warmed Kirian's skin as he followed Tianel and Fern, who had taken the lead on the second switchback.

"I heard there's going to be another tournament at Dreamland," Xander called from the back of the group.

"Maybe we'll win this one," Meddox retorted.

Kirian winced. "I hate to break it to you, but I'm not allowed to compete in tournaments that use the sims I made."

"It's one you made?" Lutian asked. "Which one?"

"Yeah, we've got to get an in." Ari tapped Meddox on the arm. "What will you guys do without Kirian to make up a full team?"

"All I know is it's one of mine," Kirian told them with regret.

"So, there *is* a tournament coming up." Nerril punched the air.

"Give me a second." Everyone stopped when Kirian paused to catch his breath. "Isn't Teri looking for a new team? Jax and Gamor went south to study, right?"

"They should have waited for your Institute," Tianel

commented. "I'm hearing good things about it. I wish I wasn't going back to Torcellan so I could study politics there."

"Would your mother allow that?" Kirian's heart skipped a beat, and it had nothing to do with pushing to keep pace with the others.

"Not in a million years," Fern cut in, dashing his hope. "Not from lack of her trying, either. You two got into it pretty loudly last night, Tee."

Tianel flushed a pretty pink, glancing back at the boys. "Life is good here. I don't want to leave, but my mother isn't giving me a choice. She wants me to take the traditional path she took."

Kirian caught up with her and wrapped an arm around her shoulders. "We just have to make the most of the time we have left." He squeezed and let go. "No being sad, okay?"

"Yeah," Ari and Xander chorused.

"We're here to have fun!" Lutian exclaimed. "Save the tears for guilting your mom into letting you stay."

Tianel laughed. "Like she ever falls for that. Come on. We're wasting the day, and it's almost hot enough to swim."

"We're only a mile from the falls," Ari told them, looking at his wrist-holo.

Fern whooped and picked up her pace. "Let's do this!"

Kirian was ready for the relief of the cool water when they reached the turnoff to the outcrop. The path left the trees and changed from dirt to smooth stones that were slick with moss and spray from the falls.

The water rushed past the outer edge of the path, its thunder making conversation almost impossible. Kirian kept one hand on the crumbling rock wall as he stepped from one stone to the next, being careful not to lose his footing. His heart hammered, and adrenaline rushed through his body at the thrill of the risk they were taking to get to the diving spot.

Meddox looked back to ensure he was okay, and Kirian gave

him a thumbs-up. It was his first time up here, although everyone else came up here every summer to dive. He didn't think about what the adults would say about him shinnying along the narrow path. His entire world came down to the spray on his exposed skin and the next step.

CHAPTER TWENTY

Meddox jumped first, followed by Xander and Fern. Then it was Kirian's turn. He stepped onto the slick finger of rock and looked over the edge. Apprehension and adrenaline clouded his mind.

"I'm not sure…"

"Do it! Do it! Do it!" the three chorused from below.

Kirian still hesitated. The water sparkled far below, inviting and calm. "What if I injure myself? The impact on my spine."

Nerril stepped onto the rock. "You're on speaking terms with the boogey-Witch. You can make a twenty-foot jump."

"It's more than twenty feet," Kirian retorted.

Tianel's fingers interlaced with his.

"We'll jump together. It's my first time, too."

Her touch gave him courage, shoving his reticence to the back of his mind. He looked into her eyes and nodded. "Together."

The moment of fear was gone, and his sense of adventure returned with a vengeance. Kirian grinned as they took the final two steps to the edge. Then he was flying…falling…*free.*

He managed to gulp air. Then he was underwater, and Tianel was in front of him with her hair floating around her. She looked like a mermaid, the sunlight filtering through the water making her into an ethereal creature.

Kirian forgot his resolve to be her friend and stared at her through the water like he was seeing an angel. His lungs burned with the need for air, but he didn't care.

Tianel grinned and kicked her legs up to the surface. The moment passed. Kirian broke the surface to cheers from the others. Blood rushed to his face, and he scooped water in his hands and flung it at his friends.

"Oh, no, you didn't!" Fern squealed as the splashes hit her.

She swooped an arm along the surface, sending up a huge splash, and chaos descended as everyone joined the free-for-all. The battle took them away from the falls and over to where they could clamber onto the rocks and dive-bomb each other. Kirian took a soaking the first time Meddox cannonballed beside him but soon learned to duck beneath the water when anyone jumped.

Despite his earlier misgivings, he felt no pain while they played. His muscles withstood the exertion, supported by the water. Finally, they swam to the shore by the campsite and lay on the sand in the late afternoon sun.

Kirian dozed off, exhausted in a good way. When he awoke, the sun was going down. He smelled meat cooking and heard the gentle music of a Torcellan finger harp. He eased up to a sitting position and did a full check on his body before standing.

"Look who's finally awake!" Meddox called from the campfire. He and Lutian were preparing dinner. "You good?"

Kirian stretched his arms over his head. "Yeah, I think so. Let me switch out my pain patches, and I'll be right with you."

Fern and Tianel were playing an acoustic version of *Love for Me Tonight*, which was popular in their age group at the moment.

Kirian wished Tor was there to share the memories they were creating. He would remember this weekend for the rest of his life, and not only because Tianel looked beautiful playing her finger harp.

Friends, Kirian reminded himself as he walked to his tent. *We are just friends. Nothing more. No spoiling it.*

He had left his wrist-holo in his tent while they were hiking and swimming, not wanting to risk damaging it. He checked his messages after changing his pain patches for fresh ones and found he had a message from Tor, as if thinking about him had encouraged the universe to get him to respond at last.

Kirian followed the breadcrumb trail to get to the real message, and his heart sank as he read long paragraphs filled with fear and regret.

Tor was sorry for running that day in the juice bar. He hadn't stayed in one place longer than a night since then, afraid that whoever had taken his family was coming for him. He thanked Kirian for being his friend and told him they wouldn't see each other again. He planned to leave High Tortuga and disappear into the Federation so those hunting him could never find him.

The final two lines cut like a knife.

Stop trying to find me. You can't help me.

Kirian wouldn't and couldn't leave Tor to flee. He sat for a few minutes, thinking about what he should do. Even Cerebro's net hadn't been able to locate the runaway Noel-ni. He hated to consider what it meant that Tor was hiding in places so dark and dingy that no one cared to look.

All thoughts of relaxation with his friends gone, Kirian left the tent and made for the roamer. He almost ran into Nerril and Xander coming back from the tree line with arms full of deadwood.

"Dude, you look like you've seen a ghost," Xander told him.

Kirian paused. The urge to get in touch with Lerr'ek caused

him to shift from one foot to the other. "I heard from Tor. He's in trouble. Big trouble."

Nerril cursed. "You going to call Baba Yaga?"

Kirian shook his head. "She's not on High Tortuga right now. Tell everyone I'll be there as soon as I've spoken to my principal."

Both males looked at him in confusion.

"Trust me. He's the one I need to talk to right now, but I don't know if it's already too late."

"Go," Xander urged. "We'll tell the others."

Kirian nodded and dashed to the spot where he'd landed the roamer. He climbed in and switched on the comm. "Cerebro, please put me through to the prof. It's urgent."

"Of course, Kirian."

A moment later, Lerr'ek calmly greeted him, which took the edge off Kirian's panic. "What's the emergency?"

"I heard back from Tor." Kirian explained the message and his fears for his friend's safety. "I don't know what to do. Maybe I should come back and help search for him."

"Stay where you are. That is actually good news. If young Tor is searching for a way off-planet, that makes him trackable, given that he immediately ditched the one you put on him. It's more than we've had to go on since he met you at the juice bar."

Kirian hadn't considered that. "Won't that mean he's at more risk?"

"Unless they can match us resource for resource, we'll find him first. We'll find the bad guys, too." Lerr'ek chuckled. "Believe me when I say that anyone who tried to capture Tor is letting themselves in for a world of hurt. Enjoy your time with your friends. I'll keep you updated."

Only slightly mollified, Kirian thanked the professor and returned to the campsite. Fern and Tianel fussed over him while he told everyone what he'd learned.

"What does your principal have to do with this?" Fern asked.

Kirian swallowed hard. The guys knew almost everything

since Baba Yaga had busted them and fixed the Dex situation. "Baba Yaga owns the Institute. My principal, the whole faculty... They're all her people."

Those who hadn't known asked questions.

"I have nothing to be afraid of," Kirian assured them. "The only people who need to be afraid of Baba Yaga are people who hurt others to get what they want."

"Then why did Charr'est and Gralen disappear?" Tianel asked. "They're bullies, but they're kids like us."

Kirian winced. "They, um, didn't disappear. They came to the Institute. On my recommendation."

"I can understand that," Xander told him while the triplets complained in triplicate. "Wait, guys. We saw their lives and what they were going through."

"They met the criteria for enrollment," Kirian added.

"And we don't?" Nerril retorted.

Kirian shook his head. "I'm not sorry you don't. Every student had no hope for whatever reason, but they're not my stories to share. Just trust me when I say the Institute is all about giving a future to kids who didn't have one. You're all going to do well. You have families who love you, and you're all healthy. You have access to a good education."

Tianel laid a hand on his arm. "I understand. Seeing what the Institute has done for you is enough for me."

Meddox sniffed and turned back to the sausages cooking over the campfire. "I guess I was jealous. It's been hard adjusting to life without you being part of every day."

Ari lifted a shoulder. "I'm happy where I am. I just missed you, is all."

"What about Tor?" Fern asked. "Surely he qualifies?"

Kirian nodded. "He got an offer, but he freaked and ran. I wish I could do something to help him get out of this situation with whoever took his family."

"What more can you do?" Lutian consoled Kirian with a pat on the shoulder as he passed him to get his hotdog. "Let the adults take care of Tor. They'll find him before anyone else can hurt him."

The conversation moved on as they ate. However, Kirian continued to worry about Tor. He barely tasted the food and only took a couple of bites before abandoning the hotdog for the ants.

The girls retrieved their finger harps as the sun went down and provided the group with music. Eventually, they switched from harps to Ari's portable speaker and a playlist Xander had curated for the trip.

Kirian set his brooding aside and threw more wood on the fire. The flames jumped and flickered, bathing the campsite in warm light and moving shadows that invited dancing.

"Wait!" Nerril vanished into his tent and emerged with a medium-sized blue crate that had a wrapped box and a bottle balanced on top.

"What have you got there?" Xander asked.

"Pepseh," Nerril told them in a stage whisper. "Also, chocolate and some kind of human alcohol. I figured since this was a special occasion, we'd see Tianel off in style."

"Why are you whispering?" Kirian laughed.

"In case Cerebro hears us and tells the adults," Nerril retorted. "If our parents find out we had chocolate, we'd be grounded until adulthood and probably longer."

Meddox and Lutian looked at their brother with newfound respect.

"How did you get all that stuff?" Meddox asked.

Nerril winked. "I know a guy."

"I don't know." Fern glanced at the contraband with curiosity. "Isn't Pepseh the outlaw drink?"

Kirian made a face. "It's the inferior drink. I've tasted Pepseh, and I'll stick with Coke. What's in the bottle?"

"That's for you." Nerril held out the bottle. "Chocolate doesn't have the same effect on humans. Maybe rum will do."

Normally, Kirian would have rejected the idea of drinking. However, between the news about Tor and his heartbreak over Tianel leaving, good sense did not prevail. Just once, he was going to do the dumb thing.

He took the bottle, twisted off the cap, and took a large swig. The rum burned down his throat, and he coughed as fire filled his stomach. The heat went to his face, then dissipated.

"Wait, *what?*" Kirian took another long pull from the bottle, and the same thing happened a minute after drinking.

So much for doing the dumb thing. Once again, he felt left out of the experience his friends were having. He figured the nanocytes in his blood were to blame. Everyone else was too occupied with sharing the box of chocolates to notice his disappointment.

Maybe the nanocytes were using the alcohol as fuel? If so, would drinking until they'd reached saturation allow him to get the experience he wanted?

Kirian sat on a log and put the theory to the test. As he choked the rum down, he watched the others with amusement.

Tianel giggled and twirled with Fern to the beat of the dance song playing on the speaker. Ari, Xander, and Meddox joined them. Lutian suddenly sat down, staring into space. Nerril ran for the trees and fertilized the undergrowth with his half-digested dinner.

Everyone stopped what they were doing when he retched. He half-turned and waved.

"I'm okay. I'm good," he called before retching again. "I shouldn't have eaten that third hotdog."

Kirian got to his feet, pleased to find that his head rushed at the sudden movement, and picked up the half-empty box of chocolates. "Seventy percent cacao? Are you guys crazy?"

"Shaysh Mishter half a bottle of rum in twenty minutsh," Meddox slurred with a grin and glazed eyes.

"It's not hitting me anything like that chocolate is hitting you guys," Kirian protested.

"Let's play a game!" Fern insisted. "Nerril, are you done puking?"

Nerril came back to the group, swaying as he walked. Kirian pulled Lutian to his feet and guided him to the logs around the fire while Ari passed around bottles of Pepseh. Kirian passed on the Pepseh, waving his rum bottle.

"What's the game?" Xander asked.

"Truth or Dare," Fern decided.

Kirian saw a thousand ways that could go wrong and smoothly interjected, "How about Never Have I Ever? Everyone has a drink, right?"

"I'll go first," Ari offered. "Never have I ever gotten into a fight."

Kirian took a drink, as did the triplets.

Surprisingly, Fern sipped her Pepseh. "What? I don't like bullies."

Kirian raised his bottle. "I'll drink to that."

"Me next." Fern closed her eyes and thought for a moment. "Never have I ever...lied to my mom."

Kirian cursed and drank again.

"You lied to Janet!" Lutian exclaimed.

"Would you tell my truth?" Kirian asked. "I didn't want her to freak out about...well, everything. I told her in the end, though."

Xander, Ari, and Tianel drank.

Tianel went next. "Never have I ever been kissed."

She looked at Kirian, who didn't lift his bottle. Fern, Ari, and Nerril drank from theirs.

"Names," Kirian demanded with a laugh. Fern and Ari blushed.

"You kissed each other?" Xander squealed.

"Wait. I thought you two were cousins?" Meddox asked.

"Distant cousins," Ari clarified.

"Very distant," Fern confirmed. "Our moms are always trying to push us together, so we tried it."

"It was weird," Ari told them.

"Like kissing my brother," Fern agreed. "Won't be happening again."

"Definitely not!" Ari agreed. "Everyone knows about Nerril and Tola Mae."

"*I* didn't know," Kirian pointed out.

"Your turn, Kirian," Nerril hurriedly cut in.

"Hmm, okay." Kirian pressed his lips together. "Never have I ever...backed down from a challenge."

"Not even when it was good for you," Meddox teased.

"Drink up," Kirian retorted with a laugh.

Much later, when everyone else had crawled into their tents to sleep off the effects of the chocolate, Kirian was still awake and filled with a restless energy he couldn't put a name to.

He had wandered down to the lake shore and was skipping stones over the moonlit water while he turned over the thoughts crowding his mind when he heard a noise behind him.

He turned and saw Tianel emerging from the tent she shared with Fern.

"Hey," he called softly, not wanting to wake anyone else. "Did I disturb you?"

Tianel shook her head. "I couldn't sleep either. Want some company?"

Kirian gestured at a rock, and she joined him there. They sat in companionable silence for a while, the only sounds coming from the nocturnal forest creatures and the occasional splash when a fish jumped.

Eventually, Tianel broke the silence. "You're still worried about Tor?"

Kirian nodded. "Yeah. He's all alone somewhere. And you're leaving. And things are changing at the Institute."

"Changing? How?"

"Maybe not changing," Kirian admitted. "More like falling back into old patterns. This Shrillexian kid is being an ass to me to make himself feel better."

"Won't the faculty do anything about it?" Tianel asked.

Kirian shrugged. "They would if I asked them to, but it wouldn't help. I'll have to fight him."

Tianel wrinkled her nose. "That's awful."

"It is, but you know how Shrillexians are. The only way to earn their respect is to take it. Except this won't be like when I fought Gralen. This time, I'll have to win."

Tianel's mouth formed an O. "You fought *Gralen*?"

"Charr'est and I were kidnapped by the former training master. He was a piece of work." Kirian glanced at the water. "Tee, can we keep in touch after you leave? I know you're going to be—"

She cut him off by leaning in for a kiss.

Kirian pulled back before their lips met. "Wait, no. Not… You're…"

Hurt clouded her silver-gray eyes. "I thought you felt the same."

"I do," Kirian insisted. "But you're leaving. It's not fair to you."

"Don't I get to decide what's fair for me?" Anger replaced her hurt expression. "You know, for a smart boy, you're as dumb as a box of rocks at times."

Before Kirian could say anything else, she stormed back to her tent.

CHAPTER TWENTY-ONE

Kirian didn't sleep much that night, and when he woke, his body was so stiff that his exosuit wasn't much help. He was the first to wake. After applying pain patches to his aching joints, he left his tent to start breakfast.

There were no new messages on his wrist-holo, so he paused at the roamer to check in with Cerebro.

"I have no news for you," the AI apologized. "Lerr'ek has me monitoring all off-world traffic for passengers even roughly fitting Tor's description. You will be the first to know when we find him."

Kirian thanked the AI and headed around the back of the roamer to rummage in the supplies for breakfast items. He came up with a carton of eggs and two packages of bacon.

The fire had burned down to glowing coals covered in ashes during the night. Kirian nursed it back to health, raking the ashes off with a stick to give the coals oxygen. When he had a small fire going, he placed the tripod cooking plate that came with the campsite over the heat and dumped both packages of bacon on the heating metal.

Soon, the scent of the cooking meat permeated the campsite, drawing the sleepers out of their tents.

Meddox was first to emerge, stomach rumbling. "Good call."

"There will be eggs as well. How are you feeling this morning?"

"A little queasy," Meddox admitted. "Nothing a solid breakfast won't fix."

"Speak for yourself," Fern groused as she joined them. "Can you make that smell somewhere else?" She looked around and spotted the bottles of juice Kirian had chilling in a bucket of lake water. "Oh, thank the stars."

"You good?" Kirian asked.

Fern glared. "I'm fine. *You're* an ass."

"What did I do?" Kirian protested.

"You made Tianel cry," Fern snapped. "Anyone can see how much you two like each other, but *noooo*! You decided to be all noble and broke her heart. *Ass.*"

She stalked to the lake shore without another word.

Meddox looked at Kirian with wide eyes. "Dude, what did you do?"

"I don't know. Everyone was wasted last night. It wasn't right." Kirian stabbed the bacon with the tongs. "I might have messed up."

"You think?"

They whirled. Tianel was standing behind them.

"Tee, please!" Kirian had no idea where he was going. "I didn't mean…"

"Mean what?" She grabbed a bottle of juice and followed Fern to the water, calling back over her shoulder, "To reject me when I was being vulnerable with you? Fern is right. You *are* an ass, Kirian."

"Tianel!" Kirian called after her. "I'm sorry!"

She ignored him.

Meddox cracked an egg onto the cooking plate. "Sucks to be you today, buddy."

Kirian resisted the urge to throw the bacon at him. "Gotta love the support from my best friend."

"Hey, you're the one who messed it up." Meddox scooped the egg and a few strips of bacon onto his plate. "I'm sorry for you, but I'm sorrier for Tee."

Sighing in frustration, he left Meddox at the fire and went back to his tent to think. Or sulk. Either worked right now.

Would everyone be on Tianel's side? Why did it have to come down to sides, anyway? He'd done the right thing, so why did he feel like shit?

Kirian made a face. He felt like crawling back into his sleeping bag and scrolling the morning away, but that wasn't him. He wouldn't waste his day on a pity party. He needed to work the stiffness out of his muscles before they seized up, and he had to go home early.

He changed into swim trunks and went down to the lake, avoiding the spot where Fern and Tianel were deep in conversation. He didn't need to be a genius to know he was the subject of their animated discussion. Well, if they could ignore him, he could do the same.

The lake was warm, even this early in the day. That was one of the reasons they always came here to camp. Kirian waded up to his waist before striking out in a gentle breaststroke. The soothing water took the pressure off his body.

Slowly but surely, the stiffness binding his muscles eased, and his joint pain receded to a manageable level. Focusing on his body allowed his mind to take a back seat. His self-pity had also ebbed when he returned to shore.

There was no sign of Fern and Tianel, but he had resolved to apologize for his reaction to her attempt to kiss him last night. First, he had to get dressed.

He made his way back to the campsite in time to hear his wrist-holo beeping in his tent.

Kirian ran past everyone around the campfire and all but dove into his tent to answer the call.

"I'm here," he managed breathlessly.

"Kirian?" Lerr'ek sounded concerned. "Are you okay?"

"I was swimming. Did you find Tor?"

"Tor found us. He took the bait we set. He thinks he's shipping out on the *Infinite*, one of the cargo ships whose captain we made an arrangement with. Our young friend is resourceful, it seems. He's somewhere in Matraxes."

Kirian's jaw dropped. "The city?"

"We were surprised he made it that far, too. Despite that, I'm glad Cerebro suggested we cast the net so wide. We still don't have a firm location for him. He vanished from the holonet as soon as he made his travel arrangements. We'll get him tomorrow night before the *Infinite* departs."

"I'd like to be there when you pick him up."

"I don't see why not. It might help him adjust to the idea of coming with us if he sees you."

"You know you have to grab him on sight, right?" Kirian didn't like the idea, but Tor was likely to slip away when he realized their intentions.

"He's not going to like that, but that's the plan."

They said their goodbyes, and Kirian dressed, very relieved.

"You planning on coming out any time today?" Ari called.

"Only if you're that anxious to see me without pants on," Kirian retorted.

"Yeah, we'll wait. Just hurry up. We want to know what your principal said about Tor."

Kirian threw on a clean pair of shorts and a T-shirt and scrambled out of the tent. The girls and Xander were nowhere to be seen. He grabbed a Coke from the cooler and sat on one of the logs around the campfire before giving the others the rundown of what Professor Lerr'ek had told him.

"They're going to snatch him?" Ari looked shocked.

"For his own safety," Kirian clarified. "He's very good at disappearing, and this might be our only chance to save him from whoever is hunting him."

"I can't believe he's trying to leave the planet." Meddox sounded awed. "Can you imagine how he must feel right now?"

"He's brave," Kirian agreed. "But running to the Federation is a stupid idea. We can keep him safe. When Baba Yaga gets back, she'll deal with the bad guys."

"At least you're not talking about dealing with them by yourself," Lutian conceded.

Kirian shook his head. "I learned my lesson. This is a job for adults. I'll stick to taking care of Tor after we have him safe and sound." He hesitated before asking, "Where did the others go?"

"Fishing." Nerril hooked a thumb in the direction the three had taken while Kirian was swimming. "We weren't feeling it today. The girls were trashing you pretty hard."

Kirian grimaced. "Yeah. I need to set things right with Tianel. I can't let her leave the planet mad at me."

"Who's brave now?" Lutian teased.

"Fern is mad-mad." Meddox patted Kirian's shoulder. "Better you than me, buddy."

Ari lifted a shoulder and Kirian nodded, meeting his sympathetic gaze as he got to his feet. "If I don't come back, you'll know they made fish bait from me," Kirian joked.

He made his way to the path that encircled the lake. The packed dirt and sand led beneath the trees. He figured they were at the jetty fifteen minutes' walk from the campsite and wasn't let down when the sun-bleached wooden structure came into sight.

They turned away from the water when they heard him approach, and their laughter died. Kirian sighed and kept walking. "Hey. Tee, can we talk?"

"You can talk," Fern snapped. "She doesn't have to listen."

"It's okay," Tianel told Fern, placing a hand on her friend's forearm. "I'll hear him out."

They walked a short distance from the jetty and sat on the rocks that crowded the shoreline. Tianel sighed. "Talk."

Kirian rubbed a hand over his hair. "I'm not sorry I didn't kiss you back. I am sorry I didn't handle it well. I was surprised."

"How could you be surprised?"

Kirian lifted a shoulder. "I don't know. I guess I didn't think you liked me like that. I'd been telling myself to be decent and reminding myself we were just friends for so long. So, yeah. You caught me by surprise, and my brain kinda exploded."

"But you're not sorry you didn't kiss me back?" Tianel narrowed her eyes in confusion. "That doesn't make sense. You know I'm leaving in two days. We don't have time to waste arguing."

"I swear, I don't want to argue with you," Kirian promised. "But last night, we were both under the influence. You more than me. I didn't want that for my first kiss or yours."

Tianel frowned. "You don't get to say what I want. Do you know how much courage it took to make that move?"

"More than I had," Kirian admitted. "But it still wouldn't have been right. I felt like I would have been taking advantage of you, and I'm not that kind of person. The first kiss…it's special. It only happens once."

Tianel sighed. "I guess you're right, but I was hurt, Kirian."

"And for that, I am *truly* sorry," Kirian swore. He took her hand and was relieved when she didn't pull away. "Let me make it up to you?"

"How are you going to do that?"

Kirian grinned as the perfect plan came to mind. "Trust me. Give me a couple of hours to get everything ready."

Tianel looked at him, then nodded. "Okay, but this better be good."

Kirian held her hand to his lips. "I promise. It will be everything a first date should be."

"First and last," Tianel wistfully pointed out.

Kirian ignored the pang in his heart. "All the more reason to make sure it's perfect."

Almost exactly an hour later, Kirian had everything loaded in the roamer and set off to find the perfect spot. With the roamer in flight mode, he circled the peaks, searching for the view he wanted for their date.

When he found the spot, it took him another forty minutes to set up, leaving him twenty minutes to get back to camp and wash up.

Tianel looked as beautiful as always in a floaty top and shorts. She'd gone with her hiking boots for footwear.

Kirian held out his hand. "Ready for a magical experience?"

Tianel blushed and grinned. "You bet."

The sun was setting when they landed on a plateau high above the valley.

Tianel took in the seating area made up with cushions and blankets, the strategically placed lanterns, and the music coming from Ari's speaker and hugged Kirian. "It's perfect!"

Kirian took her hand. "Come on. The show's about to begin."

"Show?"

Kirian pointed at the peaks across from the plateau. "Sunset."

They settled on the cushions beneath the groundsheet Kirian had strung up to keep the wind off them. Tianel took Kirian's hand as the setting sun washed the plateau in golden light. The sky blazed orange and pink, and the land darkened as shadows wreathed the ground where the light no longer touched.

"You're forgiven," she told him with a soft smile. "This is gorgeous."

"Nowhere near as beautiful as you." Kirian put his arm around her shoulders to pull her into him, and she rested her head on his chest. "I wish we'd done this sooner."

"Now is better than never." Tianel sighed in contentment and wrapped her arm around Kirian's waist. "I could stay like this forever."

Kirian couldn't find the words to reply so he kissed her hair and held her tighter. They stayed like that until the last rays of the sun speared the sky. Then Tianel tilted her head up to look him in the eyes. "Now?"

Kirian nodded. "Now."

CHAPTER TWENTY-TWO

<u>**High Tortuga, Northern Continent, City of Thon, Undisclosed Location, Institute of Education-Focused Extrajudicial Foundational Studies**</u>

Kirian returned to the Institute on Cloud Nine. His elation only lasted as long as it took him to answer the summons to the ops center.

Lerr'ek greeted him with, "Tor booked transport on eighteen ships spanning three cities and seven spaceports."

The central wallscreen showed a map of the Northern Continent with red dots marking the spaceports. Kirian sighed. "My guess is that he's still here in Thon. Did he book them all on the holonet?"

Lerr'ek nodded. "You could be right, and I don't have the resources to send teams to every spaceport. We'll have to narrow it down from the most to least likely and go from there."

"I can take a team to the port in Matraxes," Kirian offered. "It's not the most likely, but it will free up your people to concentrate on the ports here in Thon."

"I have another use for your team. I want you here to work

surveillance with Cerebro. You know the kid better than anyone, and he's likely to use disguises to avoid AI identification."

Kirian conceded that the professor was right. "Okay, sir. I'll see if I can figure out an algorithm Cerebro can use to identify him."

Professor Lerr'ek nodded. "Good idea. Go get something to eat and see Jennifer before you start. She wants you to check in after your camping trip."

Kirian went to the infirmary. The doc was going over paperwork in her office. He knocked on the doorframe. "You wanted to see me?"

Doc Ericson smiled and closed her holoscreen. "Hey, Kirian. Thanks for stopping by and saving me from admin hell. Come in and take a seat."

Kirian grinned. "Happy to help."

"How are you feeling after your trip? Any pain or other issues? I know you were planning on hiking with your friends."

Kirian shook his head. "Swimming helped a lot, actually." He hesitated. "There was one strange thing, but I don't want to get in trouble."

Doc Ericson frowned lightly. "Why would you get in trouble?"

Kirian grimaced. "Because I was drinking."

Doc Ericson laughed. "Let me guess: the effect was different than you expected?"

Kirian nodded. "I never touched alcohol before. I was feeling sorry for myself and tried to get drunk, but it didn't work out that way."

"The nanocytes in the infusion you had before you left converted the alcohol into fuel. I'm going to need blood samples before I administer your infusion if you don't mind a bit of poking and prodding."

Kirian nodded and rolled up his sleeve. "Poke away."

Her smile shifted to sympathy as she drew the blood from his arm. "Want to talk about why you were feeling sorry for yourself?"

Kirian's face warmed. "It's nothing."

"'Nothing' seems to have had you acting out of character." She placed the vials in one of the machines at the back of her office. "It's not like you not to share your troubles, either. You know you can talk to me, right?"

Her kindness and lack of judgment had been a guiding light for him for as long as he'd known her. Kirian realized he felt ashamed.

"I haven't been making great choices recently," he admitted. "Avoiding things instead of facing them. I don't want to fight Corek. My friend is gone, and I'll probably never see her again. I almost messed that up because I hesitated. Tor...I'm scared for him. I don't know. Everything keeps changing, and I want it to stop so I can get my feet under me again."

He sighed and put his head in his hands. "I don't feel like I'm as strong as I need to be."

A hand on his shoulder made him look up. Jennifer smiled at him.

"You're doing fine, Kirian. It's okay not to want to meet Corek on his terms. It doesn't change that you need to find a way to gain the respect for you he lacks. Could you be hesitating to act because of everything else you have going on?"

Kirian considered that, then nodded. "I'm sad about Tianel leaving, and I'm worried about Tor. Fighting Corek feels like an unnecessary complication."

"We're all worried about Tor, but he's been smart enough to keep himself safe this long." A beep came from the machine analyzing Kirian's blood. She opened her holoscreen and checked the results. "Everything looks fine here. Let's go to Treatment Room One and get your infusion hooked up."

Kirian followed Doc Ericson to the treatment room across from her office and sat for the cannula to be inserted. "Call me if you need anything," she told him after she attached the infusion bag to the IV stand.

"Will do." Kirian had plenty to occupy himself with for the hour it took the infusion to empty into his system. However, his conversation with the doc had unlocked the thoughts he'd been avoiding. He had to deal with Corek sooner rather than later. The longer he left it to fester, the more likely it was that more of the Shrillexians would think the same way.

He would not get into a situation where he had to fight everyone but his friends, though. Many of them had seen him fight Gralen, but he had only held his own with Charr'est's help. He had to take care of this himself. Only then could he devote his full attention to rescuing Tor.

When his hour was up, he thanked Jennifer for listening and made his way to the cafeteria. At this time of day, the space was what counted for busy. The cafeteria was large enough to serve a couple of hundred people at once, so several dozen students spread out among the tables and booths, eating and studying, didn't feel like a crowd.

Kirian scanned the occupied spaces and spotted Charr'est, Gralen, and Dam'yan in their usual booth. He returned Gralen's nod and made his way to the food printers. He didn't see Corek or Flu'uth at any of the tables.

The infusion always left him hungry enough to eat a bistok whole. He ordered two high-protein burritos, a chicken salad, and a slice of apple pie and made his way to the booth, balancing the tray on one of his crutches.

"How was the trip?" Charr'est asked as Kirian slid into the booth and leaned his crutches against the outside.

The memory of Tianel's soft lips against his surged to the front of Kirian's mind. He unwrapped his first burrito to hide the heat that rose to his face. "Pretty good. Did I miss anything here?"

"We all went home for the weekend," Gralen told him. "My

mother needed me to take care of my sisters while she was at meetings."

"It was good to watch the little ones running riot," Dam'yan added. "We should get together with them more often."

Gralen nodded. "It helps our parents, and it's good to stay in their lives while we're here. Maybe Barlek will bring his brother and sister next time."

"We can help too," Kirian offered. "Well, maybe not you, Charr. We know you have commitments on the weekends."

"I think we found a full-time mechanic for the shop," Charr'est announced.

"That's great!" Kirian enthused. "It took a while."

"Right?" Charr'est grinned. "Now I can have my weekends back instead of keeping the shop running."

"Weekends for babysitting the little terrors," Gralen joked.

Kirian laughed. "I was thinking we should arrange something for the five of us. I managed the camping trip pretty well. If you guys don't mind some wilderness time, I'd like to start hiking to keep building my strength. Could be fun. What do you think?"

Before anyone had a chance to answer, an unwelcome voice cut in. "Aww, the cripple wants to try walking by himself."

"Maybe he should do everyone a favor and walk into oncoming traffic," was the sneering reply.

Kirian looked up and saw Corek and Flu'uth coming toward their booth. Charr'est and Dam'yan started to get up, but Gralen waved them down. "Kirian has this."

Kirian placed the last burrito on the table beside his tray. "Thanks, guys, but I need to deal with them by myself."

With a passing regret about the meal he'd been enjoying, Kirian picked up the tray and hit Corek in the face with all his strength. The chicken salad and the half-eaten burrito covered and then slid off the Shrillexian, making the floor slippery.

Kirian didn't waste the advantage of surprise. He dropped the tray, which had a faint outline of Corek's face in it, then grabbed his crutches and used one to jab Flu'uth in the throat, which put him out of commission for a few minutes.

While Flu'uth was clutching his throat and gasping, Kirian locked his crutches to his exosuit and used them to swing his body into a double-footed kick to Corek's chest.

The Shrillexian slipped on the dropped food. He windmilled his arms in an attempt to remain upright, but Kirian was too fast. He dropped his crutches and leapt knees-first into Corek's chest, sending him sprawling on his back on the nearest table.

By this point, everyone in the cafeteria had gathered around. As they yelled, "Fight! Fight! Fight!" Kirian repeatedly punched Corek in the face, aiming for his eyes and nose.

Corek tried to hit back, but Kirian had his knees on the Shrillexian's shoulders, pinning the nerves so he couldn't move his arms. He moved with the bucking, refusing to be thrown off and lose his advantage.

"That's enough!"

The professor's command was absolute. The yelling immediately ceased, and everyone found somewhere else to look. Kirian scrambled off Corek and got to his feet, his hands still shaking with adrenaline and anger.

"Sir, he started it," Corek whined.

"I don't care who started it," the professor thundered. "Both of you. My office. Now." He turned on his heel and stalked out of the cafeteria.

Kirian grabbed his burrito from the table before following.

Lerr'ek eyed the two students. One was defiant, the other sullen. He'd be sullen too if he'd had his ass handed to him by someone half his size. Still, it wasn't like Kirian to start a brawl, and he wanted to get to the bottom of what led to the fight. "Well?"

"He attacked me!" Corek complained.

Kirian rolled his eyes. "You have spent every moment since you got here giving me crap for the crime of being human and disabled. You're a bully, and you got what you deserved."

"A bully?" Corek's spikes rose in anger. "I was establishing dominance over someone weaker than me."

"How'd that work out for you?" Kirian laughed. "I didn't want to fight you, but you left me no choice."

"You wouldn't have won if I'd been ready," Corek spat.

"You want to go again?" Kirian asked. "I'm happy to kick your sorry behind up and down this school until you accept that I'm not weak or a target."

Corek dropped his gaze. "No."

"Gentlemen," Lerr'ek cut in. "It seems to me the matter has been resolved. Corek, bullying is not tolerated at the Institute. Kirian, while I appreciate that standing up for yourself was the right thing to do, the cafeteria is not the appropriate place to settle these types of disputes. Should either of you feel this is not over, you will meet on the mats in the training facility and fight it out under supervision. In the meantime, you both have detention."

"What is detention?" Corek asked.

"How does detention work when we have individual schedules?" Kirian added.

Lerr'ek hadn't considered that. Dammit. Start with the easy question.

"Detention is a loss of free time as a consequence of your actions," he explained to Corek. "As for when it will be given, consider your weekend passes revoked. Additionally, you will clean up the mess you made in the cafeteria."

"What about the orphans?" Kirian pleaded. "They're expecting me to be there to read for them. They shouldn't be punished because of me."

"You should have thought about that before you made your

stand in the cafeteria," Lerr'ek told him firmly. "Corek, you can leave. Kirian, stay a moment."

"Take a seat, Kirian," Lerr'ek directed after the young Shrillexian had vacated the office. He waited for Kirian to get comfortable. "You can eat. You had an infusion this morning?"

"Right before I went to the cafeteria," Kirian confirmed, retrieving the slightly squashed burrito from his pants pocket and unwrapping one end. "Why did you ask me to stay? Is there news about Tor?"

Lerr'ek shook his head. "Everything is in hand. Jennifer told me you were having trouble with some of the Shrillexian students. I take it Corek and Flu'uth are the ones she was talking about?"

Kirian nodded, his mouth full of burrito.

"While I don't condone the way you dealt with the problem, I'm glad you did it before the issue spread to the others." Lerr'ek pressed his lips together. "You are only cycles away from becoming an adult, so it won't be long before the Mistress decides you're ready for real assignments."

Kirian hadn't given his upcoming birthday any more thought than he had given what would be expected of him once he was not legally a minor anymore. He swallowed the mouthful. "I know, and I'm ready. I'm sorry I didn't address the issue immediately or in the right way. I know enough about Shrillexian culture to know it wouldn't go away. I guess I was feeling overwhelmed with everything that's been going on lately. I'm on top of everything again now. I promise."

Lerr'ek suppressed a smile. "That's good to hear. I'm going to make some adjustments to your training sessions. I want you and Charr'est to train with the rest of the students. You will still take advanced combat with me. However, I want to make sure that nothing like this arises again. You will prove yourself on the mat and nowhere else."

"Works for me. I don't think Corek accepts that I'm a better fighter than him yet."

"I think you're right. Your detention this weekend should fix that. You will be spending it in the training area with me."

Kirian grinned. "I thought detention was a punishment."

Lerr'ek laughed. "Only you would see extra training as a reward. Check in with Jennifer before we begin. She might decide you need an extra infusion to counter the workout I intend to put you and Corek through. When I'm done with you, Corek will know who the better fighter is. Now, finish eating and go clean up the cafeteria before you go to the ops center. Cerebro is waiting for you."

CHAPTER TWENTY-THREE

<u>High Tortuga, Northern Continent, City of Thon, Thon Intergalactic Spaceport</u>

The spaceport was full of people, personal transport vehicles, and commercial transport vehicles of all sizes. Tor's disguise allowed him to mix with the people waiting for their ships to depart. His fur was gray and slick with colored wax, and he looked old, tired, and frail.

He was only one-third acting. Tired and hungry had become a way of life since he'd fled his home. Hopefully, he would not have to run much longer. He had spent too many nights in the under-city, barely able to sleep in some sheltered spot without someone trying to rob him or press-gang him.

This was his fault, and he deserved every hardship he'd suffered since his family was killed. He thought back to the night before they had been taken, an ordinary evening. His parents had been watching a movie, and he and his sisters had been in their rooms. He'd been annoyed by the noise his sisters were making as they played games.

He'd do anything to hear them squealing with laughter again. But no, he'd been too into his latest obsession. Tor cringed at the memory of how he'd yelled for his sisters to be quiet so he could concentrate like he was some hotshot vigilante, his identity hidden by digital means instead of a mask.

It had begun around the time the rumors of Baba Yaga taking out the gangs in the undercity had started circulating. He'd found hacking their accounts to be child's play.

What he hadn't counted on were the side effects. The loss of their funds had driven the gangs into the open, making it easier for Baba Yaga to cut them off at the knees...or, more accurately, the necks.

The rush of knowing he was partly responsible for weeding out the worst of the worst criminals in the city had been incredible. His computer skills came from a life of being shunned by the rest of the kids his age. He supposed he had Dex to thank for that. No one wanted the attention the bullies paid Tor to be redirected their way, so he'd learned to live on the holonet, then the dark net. He'd run in the same circles as Kirian, although he'd never let Kirian know who he was. The beauty of anonymity was reinventing himself.

By the time he'd gotten involved with Kirian in real life, the rush of outing the gangs had worn off, and he'd begun seeking out bigger fish. Targets who were operating from a place of true wealth and power. Baba Yaga seemed unable to resist a money trail, and he'd been unable to resist providing them for her.

Until he'd missed, and the fish had bitten back.

Now here he was, sitting hunched over in a first-class departure lounge with no clue how he would get revenge for his family when he couldn't figure out who was after him. All he could do was flee to the Federation and hope his pursuers lacked the boldness to act inside its borders.

He had debated traveling third-class and hiding among the poorer travelers but decided that he could blend better with older, wealthier passengers. No one would think to look for him on a senior citizens' pleasure cruise.

Kirian settled into the comfy chair at the central desk and pulled up multiple holoscreens that displayed the potential ports for Tor's departure.

"What are we looking for besides Tor?" he asked Cerebro.

"The concern is that our people won't look much different from those pursuing Tor," Cerebro explained. "Lerr'ek's sources are his former criminal associates, who are now employed to keep tabs on gang activity in the undercity."

"Are they trustworthy?" Kirian asked. "What if they find him, and the bad guys offer them a ton of credits to hand him over?"

"Every one was vetted by Baba Yaga," Cerebro assured him.

Kirian was satisfied by that. "Okay. We have seven spaceports and seven identities, so we have seven chances to catch Tor before he's outside our ability to protect him. When does the first ship start boarding?"

"In twenty-four minutes. Screen three, the *Flotsam Treasure*."

"And the next?" Kirian inquired.

"The *Golden Phoenix* in thirty-three minutes. Then the *Splendor of Taraxan* in thirty-nine minutes, the *Y'nwa H'gat* in forty-two minutes, the *Staria's Beauty* in fifty minutes, the *Alict's Claw* in fifty-two minutes, and the *Starplough* in fifty-nine minutes."

Kirian considered the information. Seven ships departing within minutes of each other from three cities spread across the continent, and none stood out.

"Let me see the identities he's booked passage under," Kirian requested.

Cerebro pulled them up on the main wallscreen. Kirian frowned as he perused the names, ages, and personal details of each identity. Something felt off. "Tor is smarter than this," he murmured.

"What are you thinking?"

"None of these are particularly clever. They're all what you'd expect from a sixteen-year-old, but Tor is no ordinary sixteen-year-old. Are you sure these are all the passengers that were flagged in your search?"

"If there were any others, they would be onscreen. Lerr'ek's parameters were clear."

"Bring them up for me, please."

Cerebro did as he was asked, and Kirian read what Lerr'ek had given the AI. One point stood out for him.

"Why did the prof limit the search to third-class travelers?"

"You would have to ask him."

Kirian shook his head. "No time. Expand the search to second- and first-class passengers leaving today, and increase the age range. Include all Noel-ni passengers leaving from Thon. I think the other cities are red herrings designed to spread his pursuers' resources."

"You can't be sure."

"I know, but my gut tells me that Tor's resources are based in this city, and he wouldn't operate from a position of weakness. He's a programmer like me. He knows how to use what he has to get the result he wants. He's not on any of those ships. I'd stake his life on it."

"You are staking his life on it. I have the updated passenger list. Would you like to see it?"

Kirian sighed when he saw the huge list of names. "I need to speak to the prof. He's working on incomplete information."

"I will connect you," Cerebro informed him.

"Kirian, what's up?" Lerr'ek's calm voice came from the overhead speakers.

"I don't think Tor is on any of the ships you're tracking."

"What do you mean? We marked all the passengers traveling under fake identities and narrowed it down to those seven. One of them has to be Tor."

"That's just it, sir. It was too easy. I think he is using another ID. Maybe a real one that belongs to someone else."

The professor sighed. "It's a little late to come in with this, but perform your due diligence. If you come up with actionable information, reach out immediately."

"Yes, sir. I'll work with Cerebro to check the other Noel-ni passengers."

Time was short, and Kirian was not immune to the pressure. However, he wasn't alone in the monumental task.

"Cerebro, I need real-time locations for every passenger on the updated list. Use every resource available to you to find out what they're doing right now. I want to know if any of them are missing travel documents in their names."

"As you wish."

Cerebro put the list up on the main wallscreen. Every few seconds, one of the hundreds of names turned green as Cerebro cleared them as being genuine travelers.

Kirian couldn't tear his eyes from the screen. His heart raced as he waited for a name to turn red. Everything rode on finding the name that didn't fit. He was almost certain the seven original names were a diversion set up by Tor to make good his escape from High Tortuga.

"I have a name," Cerebro announced as one of the names on the screen turned red.

"Put me through to the prof," Kirian requested. "And get us eyes on the ship's departure lounge."

"Bad news," Cerebro informed them as Lerr'ek came online. "The Starset Liners ship boarded almost an hour ago and has already departed."

"Starset Liners?" Lerr'ek echoed with confusion. "That's a pleasure cruise company for senior citizens."

"Pulling video footage from the departure lounge," Cerebro told them. "This was shortly before the ship left Thon Intergalactic Spaceport."

Kirian pulled himself to his feet and searched the faces of the passengers as they milled around, waiting to be called. "Well, the good news is that he got off-planet without being taken."

"The bad news is that we didn't catch him either," Lerr'ek countered. "Where is the ship headed?"

"The Ebinaxi Nebula," Cerebro answered. "It's four-point-six light-years from Ixtali space and is considered one of the sights everyone should see."

"Why would Tor go there?" Kirian asked.

"The cruise includes a three-day stop on Ixtali Prime," Cerebro told him. "It is no reach to assume that Tor intends to vanish into the Federation from there."

"Ixtalis are known for spycraft and subterfuge," Lerr'ek explained. "For the right price, Tor can purchase the documentation he requires to disappear for good."

Kirian's heart sank. "He can't! We have to stop him."

"I will contact the Mistress and have him intercepted on Ixtali," the professor assured him.

"It might be too late by then!" Kirian exclaimed. "We have to do something now. Catch the ship and rescue him before we lose him forever."

"Tor is safe as long as he is aboard that ship," Lerr'ek stated.

"But, sir!" Kirian pleaded.

"No buts." The professor's tone left no room for argument. "I will ask the Mistress to meet the ship personally. Nothing will go wrong."

Kirian's heart sank to his stomach. He had a bad feeling about this that even the promise of Bethany Anne dealing with it personally couldn't shift. Nevertheless, he wouldn't get anything else from the professor, and he knew it. "Yes, sir. Keep me informed, please?"

"Of course, kid. I know he's your friend and you're worried about him, but he's going to be fine. I will return to the Institute in a few hours. I have to recall my people and pay them for their time. You may return to your studies."

"Yes, sir."

Kirian left the operations center with his mind racing. He'd learned his lesson about going off on his own to resolve issues the adults said they had handled. However, he didn't believe this was being handled correctly. Tor had already outwitted them and escaped the planet. Who was to say their assumption about him planning to make his next move on Ixtali Prime was correct?

He realized he was panicking, and he couldn't do Tor any good if he didn't maintain control of himself. There was no question that he was going to act. The decision was whether to involve Charr'est and Gralen, and for that, he needed information.

Diverting to his dorm to pick up his chair took precious minutes. However, he made the time up as he raced down corridor 2B1. While he was capable of the walk, it would have taken him too long on foot.

As he approached 2X9.16, Cerebro asked, "What are you doing, Kirian?"

Kirian stopped at the door to the hangar and got to his feet. "I'm taking a walk to clear my head. Do I still have access to the hangar?"

"Bethany Anne did not revoke your access after you discovered the ships within."

Kirian nodded and pulled the door open. "Can I access one of the superdreadnoughts?"

"That depends on what your intentions are."

Kirian laughed. "I wasn't planning on taking it for a joyride if that's what you mean." He gazed at one behemoth, craning his neck to see *Aeternitatem* emblazoned on the side in fifty-foot letters. "I've never seen anything so big."

"You may enter," Cerebro informed him.

CHAPTER TWENTY-FOUR

<u>High Tortuga, Northern Continent, City of Thon, Undisclosed Location, Institute of Education-Focused Extrajudicial Foundational Studies</u>

A ramp extended as Kirian approached the *Aeternitatem*. He went aboard and jumped as a voice that wasn't Cerebro's addressed him seemingly out of nowhere.

"Welcome aboard, Kirian. How may I help you?

"Oh! Um, I'd like to look around, if I may. I've never been on a superdreadnought before. Or any big ship, really." He glanced around. "I assume some places are off-limits, but I'd love to see everything else."

He hoped to gain enough information about the auxiliary ships to make "borrowing" one to rescue Tor feasible. He would have to devise a compelling reason for a ship's EI to assist him, and that didn't factor in whether there was a skeleton crew. If there was, the difficulty increased.

A thought struck him. *What if these ships have AIs, not EIs?* He shivered and hoped it didn't show. If that were the case, his idea was already shot.

His manners nudged him, and he blushed. "I'm sorry, I'm being rude. How should I address you?"

"You may call me Aeternitatem. I am the ship's EI. As for looking around, I can guide you on a tour of the non-restricted areas if you like. Cerebro indicated that a shorter version might be better than crisscrossing this ship multiple times. Is that your preference?"

"That would be great. Thank you. I would love the full tour sometime, though."

"That is up to the Queen."

"You mean Bethany Anne?"

"Yes."

Kirian's thoughts churned as the EI directed him to a starboard passage, then instructed him to take an elevator up two levels. He exited and turned right as Aeternitatem provided a running commentary about the hatches he passed. Most were personnel quarters, but some were offices.

The next one he approached irised open, and the EI invited him to step inside. Kirian's eyes widened as he gazed around a room set up as a training area. The space dwarfed anything he might have expected from shipboard accommodations.

"This is the training area for those with enhancements, particularly the Guardians and Guardian Marines. I'm not sure how familiar you are with what can happen when they spar?"

Kirian chuckled. "Enough to know that speed and distance are factors."

"Exactly. This is why every surface in this room is reinforced to withstand flying bodies moving at high velocities."

"Makes sense. Otherwise, you'd have people damaging your interior structures and possibly flying out into busy passageways."

A hint of humor entered the EI's voice. "Something like that might or might not have happened in the early days. I wasn't around then, nor did I see old footage."

"It makes you wonder, doesn't it? If I had to guess, that's one of several reasons why it's an interior room and not next to the hull." He exited, and the hatch closed. "Where to next, Aeternitatem?"

"If you continue in the direction you were heading, a cross-corridor ahead will take you to the port side."

"Looping me back toward where I started?"

"Eventually. You're a couple of levels up from where you came aboard."

"I appreciate the tour and your time."

"My pleasure, Kirian."

Kirian was tired when his abbreviated tour ended. However, it had given him time to think. His good sense and hard-learned lessons finally overrode his intense desire to rescue Tor by himself.

He needed his team and support from the adults.

He said goodbye to the EI, went down the ramp, and exited the hangar. His wheelchair was where he'd left it.

Being aboard the *Aeternitatem* had made him realize that getting access to a ship and going after Tor would be nowhere near as simple as asking Cerebro for a roamer or using public transport around the city. Then there was the matter of having a plan and backup. Right now, he had neither. *Time to fix that.*

He wheeled back to the Institute's main areas. "Cerebro, please check Gralen's and Charr'est's schedules and see if they're free. If they are, ask if the three of us can meet. I need their help."

"Is this about Tor?"

"It is. I can't shake my gut instinct that says waiting for him to reach Ixtali Prime is the wrong call, but I promise I won't go off half-cocked. The three of us will come up with a workable plan, and we'll bring it to one of the adults. But it needs to happen right away. I don't think we have any time to waste."

"Gralen will be free in half an hour. Charr'est says he can meet an hour from now. Both would like to know where."

"Any suggestions? We could use my room, but I'd like a place with a wallscreen and work surfaces for all three of us." Kirian hastily added, "I'd prefer not to use the ops center. That might be a step too far right now. The classrooms might not be the best idea either."

"Planning is one reason the ops center exists. However, you have a point. Might I suggest one of the small meeting rooms? Those have the requested features and are away from the other students to ensure privacy."

"Good point. Thanks. Yes, that would work. Which one? I'm going to grab a snack and get started. If nothing else, I need to get my thoughts in order to lay everything out for Gralen and Charr."

"The information is on your tablet. Gralen and Charr'est have it as well. Both will meet you there." Cerebro hesitated and kept his next words to himself. Kirian didn't notice.

"Thanks again, Cerebro. I appreciate your help."

Kirian wheeled into the cafeteria and ordered a snack. As he ate, he laid out the facts as he knew them and jotted them down on his tablet, then put it away after checking to see which room Cerebro had chosen. It was near the conference room where he and the adults had met when Denasi joined them via holoconference call.

When he reached the room, he pulled out the tablet and brought up his notes. A few moments later, he had them on a large screen and added more things he needed to do and account for as they occurred to him. He was hard at work when Gralen arrived and jumped when the Shrillexian entered unannounced. "Stars! Has it been a half-hour already?"

Gralen laughed. "A little longer. It took me a bit to find this room." He indicated the screens. "Planning?"

"Mostly notes at the moment, but yeah. I'll lay out everything when Charr gets here, but the short version is that Tor made it off-planet, and we need to bring him back before whoever's after him finds him."

"That's a tall order."

"Yes and no." Kirian indicated his notes and the screens he'd pulled up about the ship Tor was on and its route. "Take a look at these. I already have a lot of the data we need. We'll take it from the top when Charr arrives so we all have the full story to work with. Then we'll see what holes we need to fill and pull together an action plan."

Kirian consulted his wrist-holo. "He shouldn't be much longer."

"What are you planning to do once we figure everything out?"

"Go to one of the adults and persuade them to help. This isn't something we can do on our own. There are too many risks to go off half-assed."

Gralen nodded. "Good answer."

Kirian cracked a smile. "I *did* promise Bethany Anne I wouldn't make the same mistake twice."

The Shrillexian laughed and sat on a nearby chair. "Not a promise I'd want to break either." He reviewed Kirian's notes and the available data, then pulled up a screen and added his notes as he studied the information.

The two worked quietly until the door opened and Charr'est entered. This time, Kirian didn't jump.

"Charr! Good, you're here. Thanks for making the time."

"Cerebro said you asked for help and it was about Tor. What's going on?"

"Grab a seat, and I'll go over everything. Tor made it off-planet, and we need to bring him back before whoever's after him finds him. That means coming up with a plan and getting additional support. That's what all this relates to." He gestured at the screens.

"You might want to set up a screen for notes," Gralen added. "I suggest we all make our own, then see where they fit in the ops plan as we develop it."

"Good idea." Kirian nodded. "You two might think of something I didn't. Jotting it down while I give you the overview means I can keep going and we won't lose key points or questions."

He met Charr's gaze. "I already told Gralen and Cerebro, and I'll tell you too. We're not doing this alone. It's too risky for the three of us. We'll come up with a plan, then convince one or more adults to help us."

"What if they won't?" Charr asked.

Kirian's jaw tightened. "We'll deal with that if it happens. I'd rather not borrow trouble before we start."

"Agreed." Charr brought up a screen and waited for Kirian to begin.

CHAPTER TWENTY-FIVE

Kirian, Charr, and Gralen were exhausted by the time they had a plan they thought would work. All three had labored to identify and fill the holes the others found. Kirian had enlisted Cerebro's help to plot the Starset Liners cruise ship's timing and course. They knew where it should be and when. They also had the data for an overtake vector.

"It's time to approach an adult for help," Charr'est stated.

"Which one?" Gralen asked.

Kirian sighed. "Lerr'ek said he wants to have the Mistress intercept Tor when he reaches Ixtali. We all know I think that's too late. The prof knows too, but..." He shrugged.

"Who else do we know who could help and would listen to us?" Gralen asked.

No one spoke for a minute. Kirian tapped his fingers on his armrest as he thought.

"Doctor Ericson is approachable, and I think she'd listen. We'll have to convince her, which might be a tough sell, but I believe she's our best bet. If she doesn't agree with us being the ones to go after Tor, she'll raise the issue with the other adults."

He looked at the other two. "Thoughts? Objections?"

Charr'est shrugged. "You know her better than I do, but I liked her that day I hung out during your treatment and PT. I'm good with going to her for this."

"Gralen?" Kirian prompted.

"I'll go with whoever you two suggest. You trust her, Kirian, and she was your first choice, which counts in her favor."

"Good point," Charr'est agreed.

"All right." Kirian ensured he had their plan and supporting data on his tablet and rose. "Cerebro, would you please ask Doc Ericson if she has time to meet with us? Tell her it's time-sensitive about Tor."

"She says she can meet with the three of you now," Cerebro responded. "I took the liberty of letting her know you were in this room. She'll be there in a couple of minutes."

"Thanks, Cerebro." Kirian sat and brought everything up on the wallscreen again.

Jennifer walked in soon after. "What's going on, Kirian? Cerebro said it's about Tor. Hi, Gralen. Hi, Charr'est. I take it you two are now involved?"

They nodded. Charr'est added, "We're a team and work best together."

"They were a big help in pulling this together, Doc." Kirian gestured at the wallscreen.

She sat and gave him her full attention. "Okay. Start from the beginning."

Kirian drew a deep breath. "Tor escaped the planet. We know which ship he's on and where it's headed." He indicated the relevant information on the screen. "Professor Lerr'ek said he would let the Mistress know, and she would intercept him when it arrived.

"The problem is, my gut says that will be too late. We need to intercept him in transit and get him back here so we can protect him before whoever's after him catches up. I raised that with the prof, but he didn't agree.

"I know I can't go after Tor alone. Hell, the three of us can't do it by ourselves. It's too dangerous, and the resources and support we'll need require an adult or adults with us for it to work. With that in mind, we put together a plan and decided to approach you first. Here's what we've worked out."

Kirian walked her through what he, Gralen, and Charr'est had put together, including the speed and vector they would need to intercept the Star Liners cruise ship.

Jennifer raised potential sticking points. "Assuming you intercept the cruise ship, how do you plan to convince the captain to let you approach? Then, if he or she allows it, how will you get Tor off the liner and on your ship? I doubt he'll be willing if he's refused all your entreaties so far."

"As I see it, we have two options for approaching the cruise ship," Kirian replied. "One, we ask permission from the ship's captain, explaining that one of the passengers is at risk and we're there to take him into protective custody. If that works, we'll transfer him in a small craft."

"And if it fails?"

Gralen spoke up. "Then we force the issue. Nothing lethal, and nothing that will bring lasting harm to either ship, the passengers, or the crew. We board, get Tor off, and get out of there."

"Hmm." Jennifer studied them. "How do you plan to convince Tor?"

Kirian shrugged with an unhappy look. "I'm not sure we *can* convince him, to be honest. I'll try, but he has it in his head that no one can help. If I don't succeed, we're looking at a snatch-and-go situation. I'd prefer to have him leave willingly, but restraining or sedating him might be necessary. We'll have to be prepared for all three."

"The last two might not go over well with the cruise ship's captain," Jennifer pointed out.

"True, but none of us can pull a Baba Yaga." Kirian raised an eyebrow. "It would be a whole lot easier if we could. That's the one part of the prof's plan I'm in favor of, but like I said, I don't believe we have that much time. No, I'm *certain* we don't."

He leaned forward. "I've learned from my mistakes. I'm not going off half-cocked. I'm asking for help, but I'm not going to ignore my gut instinct. If we don't get to Tor before whoever's after him does, the chances are good that he'll be dead or wish he was."

Jennifer sat back and studied them in silence. All three met her gaze without wavering despite their tension.

"All right. I'll help you." She raised a hand to prevent them from speaking. "We'll need to refine a few things in your plan, and I want to add some provisions. They're for everyone's safety and are non-negotiable.

"You three did a good job putting this together despite having limited experience. I expect you to learn from our next steps. Clear?"

All three nodded.

"Good. Now, here's what we're going to do."

CHAPTER TWENTY-SIX

<u>High Tortuga, Northern Continent, City of Thon, Undisclosed Location, Institute of Education-Focused Extrajudicial Foundational Studies</u>

Thirty minutes later, Kirian, Gralen, Charr'est, and Jennifer wrapped up their revisions to the plan. Jennifer had secured a ship for them, and the quartet had conferred with Lerr'ek. He wasn't happy about letting them go after Tor but agreed that discounting Kirian's gut instinct went against what Bethany Anne was training him for.

The professor was part of the safety provisions Jennifer had mentioned. He wouldn't be back in time to go with them, but he would follow in a second ship. The plan called for him to stay stealthed and intervene if anything went wrong.

"*Always* plan for things to go wrong," Jennifer had emphasized as they worked out how to approach the cruise liner and gain access to Tor. "That way, you'll know how to react when the bistok shit hits the high-speed mass dispersal device."

The team had cringed at the imagery, which made her laugh.

They also refined how to get Tor off the cruise ship if he

chose not to go. Sedation would be their first alternative. Jennifer had chosen a safe, fast-acting drug that would leave him conscious enough to move under his own power but not fight them. Restraining him by physical means was their third and least desirable option.

"All right." Jennifer stood. "Grab whatever you need and meet me at the front entrance in ten minutes. We'll take an AEV up to the ship. Any questions?"

Kirian spoke up. "Should I bring my combat chair, Doc?"

She regarded him with a level gaze. "What do you think?"

He swallowed hard. "Yes. Contingency planning."

"Correct answer. Now, get to it."

Ten minutes later, Kirian, Gralen, and Charr'est climbed into the AEV. Jennifer was at the controls. She drove away from the building, picking up speed, and mashed three buttons on the dash. The vehicle took off and sped up with its nose pointed at the sky. Kirian whooped. Charr'est paled, and Gralen looked out the windows as they shot through the planet's atmosphere.

High Tortuga Orbit, over the Northern Continent

Not long after, they approached a dark object. Jennifer brought them into a landing bay and shut down the AEV after a green light flashed on the dash. "Let's go."

She led the students to the bridge. "Grab seats. They're all set up as shock couches. You can deploy the screens, but no messing with any controls except the ones to adjust your seats unless I give you permission." She suited actions to words as a central screen showing their flight path and target lit up, and a woman's voice emanated from hidden speakers.

"Greetings, Jennifer. I have the vector Cerebro sent and the ID of the cruise ship you wish to intercept. It should not take long."

"Thank you, Isis. Let me introduce Kirian, Charr'est, and Gralen." She indicated each as she spoke. "They're an integral part of this mission. Kirian is their team leader. Kids, Isis is the ship's EI."

A chorus of "Hi, Isis," followed.

"I'm pleased to meet you," Isis responded. "Do any of you need special accommodations?"

Kirian glanced at the others, who shook their heads. "We're good, Isis. Thank you. Unless you need me to lock my combat chair down?"

"That should not be necessary. I will let you know if or when it is."

"Sounds good."

Gralen and Charr'est looked around. The former appeared to be taking things in stride. The latter goggled at the arrays of screens by their chairs.

"This is unbelievable," Charr'est muttered. "I didn't expect to be on a starship anytime soon." He glanced at Kirian. "Is this what you meant when you said I'd get to work on big-ass starships?"

Isis chuckled, startling him. "I'm not a big-ass starship. More like a small one. Yes, my hull and components meet current technology standards. Cerebro informs me that you're doing well in your classes, Charr'est. I encourage you to keep it up."

Kirian snickered at his friend's flummoxed reaction. "Alict got your tongue, Charr?"

"Kind of," he admitted. "Not the response I expected. I didn't realize Cerebro had mentioned that to anyone outside the Institute." He cleared his throat. "Thank you, Isis. I appreciate the information and the encouragement."

"My pleasure, young sir."

Jennifer interjected, "The ship is a newish acquisition, meaning it's built to current standards and has readily available technology. It was not built for Isis from the keel up, but she graciously made it her temporary home as part of a pilot program."

She pinned the others with a sharp look. "One thing you need to understand now rather than later. If you're on a ship with an EI or AI and get into an unsalvageable situation, do everything possible to ensure the intelligence's survival.

"I expect you to read up on that when we return to the Institute. Have Cerebro provide you with the material. For this trip, I'm responsible for that aspect."

"Understood, Doc." Kirian's stomach churned as he met her gaze. He hadn't considered what would happen if an EI or AI was involved in a catastrophic incident.

You should have before now. Things happen on land, too. What would happen to Weston and Saima if Dreamland became a target? Or Cerebro if someone or something leveled the Institute?

He resolved to start thinking bigger. *A leader needs to consider all aspects. That includes potential risks to EIs and AIs in high-threat situations.*

Charr'est and Gralen gazed at him. Their expressions and subtle nods indicated that they had drawn similar conclusions.

Silence settled over the bridge as the illuminated line connected to the dot representing the cruise ship shortened. Kirian reviewed the plan and gamed "What if?" scenarios in his head. He started simple and cascaded out to increasingly unlikely possibilities. By the time he reached truly outlandish events that were so far from believable they were laughable, it was time to contact the other ship.

"Isis, please contact the Star Liners cruise ship and request a direct connection with the captain. Inform them that Dr. Jennifer Ericson needs to speak to him or her on urgent business before they transit the Gate nexus into Federation space."

"Of course."

Soon after, a screen near Jennifer's seat changed to indicate a holocall, and she tapped to accept the connection. An older man with prominent jowls and brown eyes under bushy eyebrows appeared. His uniform shirt was dark blue, and a multi-colored starburst showed on his left shoulder when he twisted to look at something offscreen. He looked concerned.

"Dr. Ericson, this is unexpected. Would you please elaborate on this urgent business and how it involves me or my ship?"

"It's a simple matter, Captain…" She waited for him to supply his name.

"Captain Shallor."

"Thank you, Captain Shallor. I'll be brief. One of your passengers is running from a serious threat. I and the young gentlemen with me wish to bring him to the Institute of Education-Focused Extrajudicial Foundational Studies. I am the resident doctor and physical therapist there. He has a scholarship placement awaiting him, and we can protect him. To that end, we need to board and speak to this passenger."

"Under whose authority?"

Her eyes flashed yellow. "Mine. And if that's not enough for you, I'll call in the Mistress of the Planet. I'm sure Baba Yaga would be delighted to take time away from her work for a chat."

Charr'est wasn't the only one who gulped at the not-so-veiled implications.

Captain Shallor blanched. "No need to involve Baba Yaga. You said one passenger? Do you have their name?"

Kirian relayed it to Jennifer, who read it aloud.

The captain glanced offscreen and muted his voice as he spoke to someone. His gaze went to a different screen. Then he faced Jennifer and unmuted his connection. "We have a record of this person boarding. Please alter your vector to these coordinates. I presume you have a ship-to-ship transfer craft aboard?"

"We do."

"Very well. Enter Hangar Seventeen near the ship's aft end. A crew member will meet you there and guide you to the appropriate cabin. They will remain in the passageway while you converse with my passenger and escort you back to your craft afterward."

"That is acceptable. Thank you, Captain. Altering vector now. We'll be with you shortly."

The holocall ended, and Jennifer stood. "Let's get into the AEV. We have to try to convince a stubborn Noel-ni to accept what we're offering."

CHAPTER TWENTY-SEVEN

<u>Aboard the Star Liners Cruise Ship, in Space</u>

Kirian's stomach clenched as Jennifer landed the AEV between two of several small ships in Bay Seventeen. They waited for the green light, then exited to meet their guide, a female Noel-ni wearing the same style uniform shirt as the captain.

"Greetings, gentle beings. I am your escort." She gestured for them to follow and set off at a quick pace across the hangar toward an interior hatch. She punched in a command on a touchscreen beside it and stepped through when the hatch opened. It automatically closed behind them.

Kirian followed Jennifer, with Charr'est behind him. Gralen brought up the rear.

A glance back showed that the Shrillexian was alert but not tense. *He's acting as rear guard.* Kirian wondered if it was necessary, then mentally shook himself. *We're on a strange ship as unplanned boarders, trying to rescue someone who's fleeing an enemy who wants him captured or dead. That's plenty of reason to watch our six—and everywhere else.*

They traversed several more passageways. The farther they

went, the wider and better decorated their surroundings became. There was also more space between the passengers' cabin entrances.

Finally, the Noel-ni stopped. "These are his quarters. The panel on the wall allows communication with the cabin's occupants. I will remain here until you are ready to leave."

Jennifer nodded. "Thank you. We hope this won't take long."

Kirian echoed her sentiments, then moved closer to use the communicator. He considered what to say after identifying himself and convincing him to open the hatch. Several options came to mind, and he settled on one that had personal meaning to them but wouldn't tip off the crewmember that Tor was anyone other than who his documents claimed.

"Hey, it's your werewolf sim partner. We need to talk. Urgently. Please let me in. Uh, I have other friends with me, so don't be surprised when you see them."

Kirian's tension ramped up as he waited for a response. Charr'est shifted his feet. Gralen and Jennifer stayed still, betraying no outer signs of worry.

A voice emanated from the communicator. It held hints of Tor's but was different enough to be almost unrecognizable. "Name the way to beat that sim in one word."

"Empathy."

The hatch opened partway, and an old, clearly exhausted Noel-ni peered out. He glanced at Kirian and the others, spotted the crew member, and motioned for Kirian's group to enter. He opened the hatch enough to accommodate them and closed it when they were through.

"What the hell, Kirian?" Tor hissed when they were in private. "I told you to stop trying to find me. You can't help me. I need to disappear."

"We *can* help you. All of us, including Professor Lerr'ek and others at the Institute. And Baba Yaga if needed." He gestured at

Gralen and Charr'est. "We want you to join us and be part of our team. Please, Tor."

Tor glanced at the other males skeptically. "No more bullying?"

They both shook their heads. Gralen spoke up. "Nah. Kirian straightened us out. Our families, too. Like he said, we're a team now. We have his back, and he has ours. He's been trying to get you to join us for a while."

Jennifer nodded. "I can confirm that. I'm Dr. Ericson, Kirian's doctor and physical therapist. I also work for the Institute and its Mistress. I'm here because these three convinced me that we need to get you off this ship and into our protection immediately.

"Kirian didn't take 'no' for an answer when the headmaster proposed an alternate plan. He insisted that waiting until you reached Federation space would not work for you."

Tor stared at her. When she stayed silent, he looked at Kirian. "What did you do?"

Kirian shrugged. "Got together with these two and came up with a plan. Convinced Doc to help us, and here we are. I meant it when I said there's a spot reserved for you, and we want you to join us."

"You know I have trouble on my tail."

"We know."

"Thing is, I don't know *who* it is. I haven't been able to figure it out."

"Then let us help you."

"I already told you—"

"Cut the bistok shit, Tor. We have resources you don't know about. We also have Baba Yaga on our side. Stuff like this is why I got recruited. It's also why I nominated you, Gralen, and Charr for scholarships. Figuring out who these guys are and taking them down is exactly what we're training to do."

Jennifer's eyes flashed yellow as Kirian gestured at the others. "We tracked you down, intercepted your ship, and boarded with the captain's permission. Are you still gonna tell me we can't help?"

Tor was silent, but his expression said he was thinking hard. Kirian watched the slight nuances in his body language, trying to predict what Tor would decide. He hoped for the best but feared the male would force a less-optimal outcome.

Several minutes passed before anyone spoke. Then Tor broke the silence. "Okay. I'll go back to High Tortuga with you and accept the scholarship."

Kirian relaxed into his chair and refrained from cheering. "Thanks, Tor. Now, how about you grab your things and we get out of here? We have a ship and transport back to it waiting."

CHAPTER TWENTY-EIGHT

<u>Aboard the Team's Unnamed Spaceship, in Space</u>

It hadn't taken long for Tor to gather his possessions. Most were still in his small travel bag. The walk to the AEV and subsequent transfer to their ship went smoothly. Isis had complied with Jennifer's request to get underway and started heading toward High Tortuga. Everyone was in seats with their screens deployed.

Kirian tensed when he spotted an anomaly. Jennifer stiffened at the same time.

"Uh…" Kirian began.

Isis cut him off. "Unknown ship approaching. No hails and no identification available. They're headed toward us, not the Star Liners vessel."

"Weapons free, Isis. Maneuver at will. Swing toward the Gate and see if you can shake them," Jennifer calmly ordered. "Let's find out if they want to chance entering Federation space."

"Kirian, lock your chair down, then get on your couch and web in. Gralen and Charr'est, get into your shock webbing. There's a control on the right-hand screen and a backup manual control on each couch to deploy it. Tor, same goes for you. I don't want you four to lose your feet if Isis has to use extreme evasion tactics."

They all complied.

Kirian studied the screens after he was webbed in. "Looks like whoever's approaching has a much bigger ship than we do. And —" He interrupted himself. "Permission to use the screens for information searches?"

"Granted," Jennifer replied.

He swiped through the available data and set the search parameters to compare it against known ship profiles, trying to identify the intruder's class and potential armament. He came up with a ninety percent match, double-checked his parameters, and reviewed the results again.

"Shit."

"Explain," Jennifer ordered.

"That ship is much larger than ours and has a lot more firepower. That's if it's still to spec and the profile match is correct. If it's been modified…"

Jennifer shook her head. "Don't borrow trouble. What are we looking at for weapons?"

"Energy weapons. Railguns. Possibly missiles, depending on how old their hull is. Decent shielding, too. A tough nut to crack for anything smaller than they are."

"Kirian is correct," Isis interjected. "Also, they're letting us run for now, but I suspect it's only to get clear of the cruise ship. Odds are they'll strike when collateral damage isn't an issue."

Jennifer sighed. "I concur. Isis, keep trying to evade. Fire only if fired upon or under threat of deliberate collision. Kirian, find creative ways for us to go up against these guys if they don't back off. In fact, all four of you should work on that."

She pinned Kirian and Tor with a stern gaze. "Do *not* try to hack into the other ship's systems. That's an order."

"No hacking the enemy. Got it, Doc. Although it would sure help if we could figure out who those folks are."

Tor snorted. "We know they're after me. I'm not sure names would help right now. That's assuming we could get into their system without triggering worse traps."

"You have a point."

Charr'est mumbled unintelligibly, then cleared his throat. "I think I found something. Isis, can you sharpen the scan of their port side? The one you got before they swung in behind us?"

"Is this better?"

"Yes. Thank you. Uh, is there a larger screen we can all view at the same time?"

"There is. Would you like the enhanced scan on it?"

"Please mirror my display."

An image appeared on the wallscreen beside the one tracking their vector toward the Gate and the ship pursuing them. The new image showed multiple openings for weapons arrays. Charr'est circled several of them.

"Unless I miss my guess, these are all energy weapons." He switched colors and circled several more. "These are railguns. Notice anything odd?"

Kirian reviewed the presumed ship class' base specs, then studied the scan. "More weapons than spec, and it looks like they skew toward more energy weapons than normal. That what you see, Charr?"

"That's part of it. I'm looking at the openings I didn't circle."

Everyone looked closer. Kirian shook his head when no one spoke up. "I have no idea. If it was an old hull, I'd say they were missile ports. With this ship, I don't think that's the case. I have no idea what they're for, though."

Charr'est looked up. "I think they converted them to launch single-person assault craft."

Jennifer frowned. "As fighters? That would be the next thing to suicide."

Charr'est shook his head. "Not as fighters, or rather, not as additional combatants outside the ship. I could be wrong, but I think that's how they deploy boarding teams."

Gralen broke the silence after that unwelcome news. "I think he has the right idea. Not many people did it and fewer would try with modern ships, but there have been instances of crews launching their boarding parties at high speed to get them through the engagement zone. It was also a sneak-boarding tactic. They used personal craft with augmented inertial dampeners, and the people wore specially designed shock suits. It's risky as fuck, but a good crew can make it work."

Jennifer looked incredulous. "You're telling me it's happened before?"

Charr'est and Gralen nodded as Isis interjected, "Yes, and it's documented. It's not a common practice, as Gralen said, but it's been successfully used multiple times with older ships."

The main screen changed as Isis warned, "We've hit whatever distance they had in mind before they engaged with us. I detect energy weapons coming online." A few seconds later, she added, "Their railguns are operational."

"Shields up, Isis. Look for optimal firing solutions. Let's be smart and stay alive." Jennifer glanced at Kirian and his team. "Any other ideas to contribute?"

"Not right now, but we'll yell if we come up with any," Kirian replied. "There is one thing, though. Is it possible to do a real-time data dump to my tablet? I'm talking the raw scans and our conversations, not filtered."

Jennifer frowned. "Why?"

"Call it a combination of a hunch and a contingency plan. Can it be done? If not, can you feed it to Professor Lerr'ek's ship?"

"Isis?" Jennifer asked.

"You're talking about massive amounts of data, Kirian. I doubt your tablet could handle that much. I can give you compressed files of your conversations if I package them in shorter segments.

Everything else will have to go through Cerebro when we return or the professor's ship's EI."

"Okay, let's do that. I'll take the compressed audio files now. We can handle the rest later. Thanks, Isis."

Jennifer covertly studied Kirian. His initial request and answer to "Why?" had triggered the sense there was more behind the question than he let on. Given that he had called it part hunch, part contingency, she ordered Isis to begin the emergency download.

She murmured so the others wouldn't hear, "Isis, initiate full disaster recovery plan, effective immediately. Add new interactions and raw data in real-time. Maintain that until we escape our attacker, or it's no longer possible for you to continue. Authorization Doctor Jennifer Ericson. *Ad Aeternitatem*."

"Authorization authenticated. Full disaster recovery plan in effect under the specified parameters. *Ad Aeternitatem*, Doctor Ericson."

CHAPTER TWENTY-NINE

Energy beams lanced out on the screen, and virtual lines indicated railgun fire. They multiplied faster than unenhanced eyes could keep up with.

Indicator bars showed their ship's shield strength, which dropped fast under the barrage. Isis returned fire, and their craft shuddered as the shields weakened further and it took more hits. Evasive maneuvers were all but useless in the maelstrom that engulfed them. Isis kept trying to forge toward the Gate despite it.

Jennifer shifted in her shock webbing and hoped to hell they could pull off a miracle.

Kirian and Charr'est called out suggestions, and Isis implemented them, but their success was short-lived. Tor monitored everything and warned the others when he spotted an opportunity to try something. Their ideas were sound, but the deck was stacked against them since they were outgunned and couldn't outrun their adversary.

The battle raged until their failing shields died. Railgun fire shook the ship, and energy beams lanced through the hull. Gralen shouted, "They launched single-person assault craft! Multiple incoming! I count fifteen, but there might be more."

Jennifer snarled as her eyes flashed yellow. "Time for combat, gentlemen. I'll take point. Gralen, Charr'est, Kirian, protect Tor. Those misbegotten, putrid-bistok-cock-sucking wastes of space want to destroy and board my ship? They can fucking well pay the price and receive Justice."

The boys' eyes widened as they unstrapped and gathered around Tor.

Kirian muttered, "I guess the prof was right when he told me creative cussing was preferred. I don't think she'll have to do push-ups for that one."

Muffled snickers emerged from his teammates as he got into his combat chair, locked in his exoskeleton, cross-drew his batons, and took a position ahead and to one side of Tor. Gralen stood opposite him, leaving some distance between. The two angled so they could observe the hatch and the area immediately behind Tor. They were the second line of defense.

Charr'est was the third line. He would function as a spotter until or unless he needed to join the fight.

The four muttered snippets as they identified and prioritized places Tor could go if they needed to yield their current spot. There weren't as many on the bridge as they would like, but they would take any advantage.

Kirian suddenly remembered Jennifer's earlier remarks about protecting EIs and AIs in untenable situations. *Shit. Did she do whatever we needed to do for Isis?* The EI spoke before he could ask.

"Disaster recovery plan complete. Adding ongoing details as long as possible per your instructions, Doctor Ericson. By my estimation, I have sixty seconds before I can no longer continue."

"Has Lerr'ek contacted you?"

"He is en route but not close enough to affect this fight's outcome."

"Goddamned slowpoke. What the hell did he do, take the

scenic route? He should have been here by now," Jennifer grumbled.

"He didn't say," Isis replied.

Kirian could have sworn he heard amusement in the EI's reply.

Metal screeched on metal as the first attackers forced the hatch open.

"Here we go," Gralen muttered as Jennifer snarled and charged.

The hatch had functioned as a chokepoint long enough for Jennifer to whittle down the number of attackers. Unfortunately, there were more than the fifteen Gralen had counted, and they didn't go down easily.

No one could identify their race, thanks to clever clothing and masks. All the defenders could tell was that most were big, strong, bipedal, knew how to fight, and probably didn't have snouts or other flagrant distinguishing characteristics.

The remaining invaders had gained access to the bridge some time ago, forcing Kirian and Gralen to join the fight. They had kept Tor safe thus far, but both were tiring since they each fought multiple opponents.

Kirian's combat chair had surprised a few, especially when he deployed the energy beams on its wheels and sliced through limbs. His batons had also delivered nasty surprises in the form of electrocution. Mostly, the current only stunned his opponents, but a few times, it did serious damage.

He had no qualms about backing up the electrical attacks with physical blows. This was a fight for survival. If his strikes ended lives, so be it. He could think about it later.

"Kirian!"

The cry from behind him made his blood run cold. He took

down the two hulking brutes who had forced him to focus on them and spun his chair on one wheel. Charr'est was fighting three attackers who had gotten around the first two lines of defense. Tor cowered in one of the alternate spots they'd chosen before the fight began. A fourth assailant stalked toward him.

"Oh, no, you don't," Kirian ground out and sent the chair forward at full speed.

Before he could engage, Charr'est's opponents broke away and charged Kirian. They blocked and counterattacked, keeping him boxed and leaving Tor undefended. Charr'est tackled one but was flung into a bulkhead several feet away. He slid down and shook his head, looking dazed.

Kirian caught vignettes of the fighting. Jennifer was a snarling, whirling fiend in Were form as she dealt with multiple attackers. Blood sprayed as she fought with a level of ferocity Kirian had never seen. He wouldn't have been able to keep track of her if it weren't for her opponents dropping.

Gralen was holding his own but couldn't break free to assist. There were several bodies nearby.

Charr'est rose but wobbled when he got to his feet. His jaw tightened as he staggered two steps forward, then lurched sideways and almost fell.

Tor fought with all his might, but he was no match for his assailant. A blow to the head rendered him senseless. His captor scooped him up, flung him over one shoulder, and sprang past his cohorts. His boots hit the deck with dull *thuds* as he sprinted through the hatch and down the passageway.

The remaining attackers allowed the defenders to push them toward the hatch, controlling their retreat to buy the kidnapper time to escape. Finally, they all left in a rush. Their rearguard prevented Jennifer from getting past them since she had proven she was the fastest and thus had the best chance of catching up.

Jennifer stopped. Her sides heaved as she panted.

Gralen and Kirian gasped for breath as they caught up with

her. They glanced at her, then at each other. The blood spray covering her looked like a patchy mural.

Kirian managed to ask, "What now?"

Gralen answered. "Emergency suits. We all need to get into them. Then we go to the AEV."

Jennifer shook herself and headed toward the bridge. Shortly after that, she reappeared in human form, supporting Charr'est as he stumbled along.

"Next hatch down on the left," she called to Gralen and Kirian. "It's a locker with emergency suits and supplies."

They were selecting appropriate suits when she and their teammate entered. Charr'est still looked dazed.

Kirian grimaced. *Probably a concussion. Hopefully, it's not worse. No telling how much longer we'll have to wait for the prof.* He concentrated on getting into his emergency suit and sealing it properly.

Jennifer beat everyone. She suited up and got her oxygen flowing, then helped the Zhyn into his suit before Gralen or Kirian were ready.

Kirian would have been last if his teammate hadn't been contending with a head injury. *Another thing to work on. I've never even done practice drills in one of these, let alone needed to use one in hazardous conditions.*

Jennifer checked Charr'est's suit and verified that he had oxygen, then checked Gralen's and Kirian's. She moved to another locker, grabbed a coil of a light but strong line with attached anchor spikes, and slung it over her shoulder. Then she motioned for everyone to head out.

She supported Charr'est, keeping him moving as Gralen slipped ahead to take point. Kirian waited and brought up the rear.

They encountered no ambushes as they moved toward the hangar and the AEV. The closer to the hull they got, the more damage they discovered. At the last cross-passage, Jennifer stopped them.

"Wait here." She cautiously moved ahead after anchoring one end of the line to the bulkhead. Each time she reached a spike, she drove it into the nearest surface.

About every third spike from the halfway point on, there was nothing to anchor it to. The initial barrage had taken its toll. Kirian reflected that if this part of the ship hadn't already depressurized, her journey would have been even more fraught with peril.

Finally, she secured the line at the other end and returned. "Gralen, you go first. Kirian, you go next. Wait until he's across. I'll bring Charr'est after the two of you are at the other end."

Kirian opened his mouth to protest.

"Not negotiable, Kirian. Gralen, get moving."

The Shrillexian pushed off without protest and crossed without incident. He turned to face them, keeping a hand on the final spike. "Come over, Kirian. Focus on keeping your chair below you and move slow enough to go hand-over-hand on the line. Gravity's not a thing in this section. The energy weapons must have taken out the local field."

Kirian kept his grumbles behind his teeth as he crossed. He didn't relax until he was beside Gralen. "All yours, Doc."

Jennifer guided Charr'est and kept one arm banded around him as they moved. Partway across, Gralen warned, "I feel some extra vibration in the line that wasn't there when you started."

"Noted." She didn't speed up or look worried.

Kirian wondered how she could be so calm. His nerves were reacting like hotshot pilots doing barrel rolls and other stunts in a sim. He moved out of the way as the pair arrived. Gralen headed for the nearby hatch.

"Kirian, follow him. I'll take the rear until we're safely in the hangar. Gralen, check the telltales for pressure on the other side of the hatch. If the hangar is pressurized, vent it to space before you try to go in."

"Got it." He checked as instructed. "No pressure. Brace yourselves anyway."

He waited until everyone complied, then opened the hatch and stepped through. "AEV intact. No visible intruders or other threats. Proceeding to craft."

Kirian heaved a sigh of relief when they all reached the vehicle and climbed in without incident. Jennifer sealed the hatch and started the AEV. Its built-in communicator came to life as she ran the pre-flight checks.

"Jennifer, is that you? Are the kids with you?"

"Yes, it's us, Lerr'ek. We just reached the AEV. Do you have eyes on the ship that took us out and the ass-munching wankers who grabbed Tor?"

"Grabbed Tor? Shit. Yes, I have— *Oh, you pox-rotted sons of dockside whores. You did NOT JUST GO THERE!*" His volume increased with each word, and he roared the last part.

Kirian's stomach sank as Lerr'ek continued to curse. "Go *where?*" he interrupted. "Prof, what happened?"

Lerr'ek's voice was heavy when he finally answered. "They went through the Gate into Federation space."

AUTHOR NOTES: MICHAEL ANDERLE

NOVEMBER 21, 2024

First, thank you for not only reading this story but also for taking the time to delve into these author notes at the very end! I truly appreciate you hanging around to let me chat with you for a bit.

Patience is a Virtue (or so They Tell Me)

So, there's that old saying, "All good things come to those who wait." Lately, I've been holding onto that one like a lifeline—especially since some of you might be contemplating sending a horde of angry werewolves my way for the time it took to get this book into your hands.

But before you fans start crafting voodoo effigies of me down in New Orleans (please don't, those pins hurt!), allow me to share ten more timeless nuggets about patience to soothe any lingering frustrations:

1. "Patience is a virtue."
2. "Better late than never."
3. "Good things come to those who wait."
4. "Rome wasn't built in a day."
5. "Slow and steady wins the race."

6. "Haste makes waste."

7. "The best things in life are worth waiting for."

8. "All in good time."

9. "Patience is bitter, but its fruit is sweet."

10. "Great things take time."

I bring these to your attention, so you don't wish ugly things upon me because this book is fashionably late.

No Promises, But Plenty of Hope

Now, I'd LOVE to say that Book 03 in the series will burst onto the scene faster than you can say "vampire queen," but experience has taught me to be cautious with such promises. The last thing I need is fans turning me into a human pincushion (my knees already creak enough as it is!).

I'm old enough to have my own aches and pains, thank you very much.

Gratitude and a Dash of Real Talk

On a more serious note, I can't express how much your support means to me. Writing can be a wild ride—full of unexpected plot twists, character rebellions, and the occasional Coke spill on the keyboard. (No s#it, just got Sprite on my keyboard last Saturday, fortunately, didn't affect it. Would have been an EXPENSIVE fix if it screwed it up.)

But knowing that you're out there, eagerly awaiting the next installment, makes all the late nights and rewrites worthwhile.

Once again, THANK YOU for supporting LMBPN, me, and all of the incredible people who work tirelessly to bring you the books you love to read!

Looking Forward

Rest assured, the adventure is far from over. The characters are itching to leap back onto the page, and I'm just as eager to share their next escapades with you. While I can't promise lightning-fast releases, I can promise that I'm pouring my heart (and perhaps a bit too much caffeine) into crafting stories that are worth the wait.

Until then, here's to patience, shared adventures, and avoiding any need for voodoo dolls.

Ad Aeternitatem,
     Michael Anderle

P.S. Please hold off on those effigies—I swear I'm working diligently on the next book!

P.P.S. For updates, sneak peeks, and the occasional ramble about the perils of aging (did I mention my knees?), don't forget to subscribe to the MORE STORIES with Michael newsletter HERE: https://michael.beehiiv.com/

CONNECT WITH MICHAEL

Michael Anderle Social

Website: http://lmbpn.com

Email List: https://michael.beehiiv.com/

https://www.facebook.com/LMBPNPublishing

https://twitter.com/MichaelAnderle

https://www.instagram.com/lmbpn_publishing/

https://www.bookbub.com/authors/michael-anderle